A CRUST TO DIE FOR

Also by T.C. LoTempio

Tiffany Austin Food Blogger mysteries

EAT, DRINK AND DROP DEAD *
A CRUST TO DIE FOR *

Nick and Nora mysteries

MEOW IF IT'S MURDER
CLAWS FOR ALARM
CRIME AND CATNIP
HISS H FOR HOMICIDE
MURDER FAUX PAWS
A PURR BEFORE DYING

Cat Rescue Mystery

PURR M FOR MURDER
DEATH BY A WHISKER

Urban Tails Pet Shop Mystery

THE TIME FOR MURDER IS MEOW
KILLERS OF A FEATHER

* available from Severn House

A CRUST TO DIE FOR

T.C. LoTempio

**SEVERN
HOUSE**

First world edition published in Great Britain and the USA in 2023
by Severn House, an imprint of Canongate Books Ltd,
14 High Street, Edinburgh EH1 1TE.

severnhouse.com

British Library Cataloguing-in-Publication Data
A CIP catalogue record for this title is available from the British Library.

ISBN-13: 978-1-4483-1003-6 (cased)
ISBN-13: 978-1-4483-1004-3 (e-book)

All Severn House titles are printed on acid-free paper.

Typeset by Palimpsest Book Production Ltd.,
Falkirk, Stirlingshire, Scotland.
Printed and bound in Great Britain by
TJ Books, Padstow, Cornwall.

Praise for *Eat, Drink and Drop Dead*

"Captivating characters and plenty of intrigue . . . Delightful"
Publisher Weekly on *Eat, Drink and Drop Dead*

"This light-hearted series debut has oodles of charm,
mouth-watering descriptions of southern cuisine,
and a sassy, savvy heroine"
Booklist on *Eat, Drink and Drop Dead*

"It's sure to satisfy fans of Lucy Burdette's 'Key West Food
Critic' mysteries"
Library Journal on *Eat, Drink and Drop Dead*

"Easy enough to appeal to a variety of cozy palates"
Kirkus Reviews on *Eat, Drink and Drop Dead*

"An exciting mystery – Tiffany and Hilary are a hoot! I was
hooked from start to finish!"
Laura Childs, *New York Times* bestselling author of the Tea
Shop Mysteries on *Eat, Drink and Drop Dead*

About the author

T.C. LoTempio is the award-winning, nationally bestselling author of the Nick and Nora Mysteries, the Urban Tails Pet Shop Mysteries, the Cat Rescue Mysteries and the brand-new Tiffany Austin Food Blogger Mysteries. Born in New York City, she now resides in Phoenix, Arizona with her two cats, Maxx and Rocco. Rocco prides himself on being the inspiration for her Nick and Nora series.

www.tclotempio.net

For my buddy Cathy Collette in Florida who always knew
I could do it. And I did!

ACKNOWLEDGEMENTS

Thanks to my agent, Josh Getzler and his assistant Jon Cobb, and to my lovely editor, Rachel Slatter, whose insights and comments helped to make this book better! Also to the entire team at Severn House, whose dedication and professionalism are unparalleled! Thanks also to all the foodies and fans who embraced the character of Tiffany and wanted more!

And a special thank you to the late Carole Nelson Douglas, my friend and mentor. You and Midnight Louie will never be forgotten.

ONE

Lily woke me from a sound sleep, first with her rumbling purr and then with a gentle but insistent tapping of paw to cheek. I blinked my eyes open – reluctantly – and glanced at my bedside clock. Seven thirty. I threw back the down comforter, jostling Her Royal Highness out of her supine position on my chest. 'Of all days to oversleep,' I grumbled. I ran one hand through my hair, tousling my auburn curls even more, and ran the other along Lily's glossy fur. 'Thanks, Lil. Although you could have tried that an hour ago.'

Lily shot me a look that clearly said, *Humans. Never Satisfied*, and trotted out of the room, tail held high. No sooner had she departed than I heard a familiar *woof* and Cooper, my black and tan King Charles Cavalier spaniel, bounded in. He screeched to a stop next to my bed, limpid brown eyes fastened firmly on me as I swung my feet to the floor. I looked at him and waggled a finger. 'And you,' I said to the dog. 'I'm surprised *you* didn't get me up. Or did you decide you could do without your morning walk today?'

Cooper cocked his head, then let out a sharp yip. Apparently my two furry children had decided I'd been working too hard and deserved a break today. Cooper gave me two more short yips, and I laughed. 'Yes, I know. Normally we sleep in on Sunday, but today's special, remember? It's the Bon-Appetempting Pizza Bake-Off!'

A few weeks ago I'd been bumped up from contract status to full time on *Southern Style* magazine. No one had been more surprised than me when the powers that be there decided to implement my first brainstorm, a pizza contest for home cooks. The semi-finals had been held last week at Branson High Auditorium, and today the three finalists would compete for the title of 'Best Home Pizza Cook' – and a ten-thousand-dollar prize.

I pulled on my robe and went downstairs to the kitchen, Cooper padding along right beside me. Lily was already sprawled comfortably across the counter. She watched me with her wide blue eyes as I spooned food into their bowls: yellowfin tuna for Lily, chicken with broccoli florets for Cooper. They hunkered down to eat while I went over to my Keurig. Usually I preferred to grind my own beans and make my morning coffee in my French Press, but since I was running more than a tad late a pod of Newman's Special Blend would have to suffice.

While the coffee dripped into my mug, I saw my cell start to twirl madly on the kitchen counter where I'd left it the night before. I snatched it up before it could fall on to the floor and looked at the screen. The incoming text was from Dale Swenson, editor-in-chief of *Southern Style* magazine and my boss. *Can you get to pre-contest gathering at ten? Something's come up. We need to talk.* My curiosity sufficiently aroused, I shot a quick text back: *I'll be there.* As I pondered what crisis might possibly have arisen, I got a second text, this one from my BFF and fellow co-worker, Hilary Hanson. *Arleen's in a panic. Nerves! C U at the contest.*

I sent a quick text back: *Don't worry. All will B Fine.* And then went to grab my mug of coffee. Hilary's sister, Arleen, was one of the finalists. There were five different categories of pizza: Traditional, Non-Traditional, Pan, Specialty, and Gluten-Free. Arleen's Eggplant Pizza had won the Gluten-Free category, and she'd been selected as a semi-finalist last week. The other two semi-finalists were Colleen Collins and Kurt Howell, the winners in the traditional and the specialty categories, respectively. Colleen's Margherita pizza had looked like a work of art, and Kurt's pie, a decadent blend of smoked mozzarella, pancetta and butternut squash puree, had received the highest marks of any category. Advance buzz had it he was the one to beat, but Arleen was also determined to take home that ten-thousand-dollar payday.

I felt something furry brush my ankle and I looked down to find Cooper looking at me with his big brown eyes. I glanced over toward his food bowl, which looked spotless, and waggled my finger at him. 'No seconds for you, little man. The vet said you put on a few pounds last time.'

Cooper gave his head a shake, then angled it in the direction of the far wall, where his leash hung suspended from a peg. 'Oh, ho. So you changed your mind? Want to take that morning exercise after all, huh?' I asked the pup.

Cooper let out a short yip of assent and I bent down to give him a quick scratch behind one floppy ear. I cast a quick glance at the clock on the wall. I'd planned on taking the spaniel for an extra-long walk later, but if I got my rear in gear I could take him now, before I had to leave. I gulped down the rest of my coffee and started for my bedroom. As I replaced my PJs with running shorts, pink sneakers and an old Atlanta U T-shirt, I couldn't help but puzzle over Dale's summons. He wasn't one to panic, and I hoped there wasn't some sort of complication with the contest. I went back out to the kitchen, where Cooper was dancing around his leash, which dangled from a peg near the back door. 'I know, I know,' I told my eager pup as I grabbed my phone and slid it into my shorts pocket. 'We're leaving right now.' I'd just snapped the leash on his collar when my phone pinged with another incoming text. It was from Hilary. *PUT ON CHANNEL 21 NEWS. NOW.*

I looked at Cooper, who didn't hesitate to give another impatient yip. 'Just another minute, OK? Then I promise we'll take that walk.' I had a small TV on the table in the kitchen. I went over and switched it on. Darla Gravesend, a local reporter, was in the middle of a news bulletin. 'We repeat, esteemed food critic Pierre Dumont was rushed to Branson General late last night after collapsing in his home. So far the nature of his illness is undisclosed . . .'

My stomach did a flip. Pierre Dumont was one of our judges! No doubt this was the 'something that's come up' Dale had referred to. I shut the TV off and looked down at Cooper, who let out an impatient bark. 'Oh boy,' I said. I dragged a hand through my auburn hair. 'With Dumont sidelined, now what?'

Cooper let out another bark, then rubbed his head against my legs. I bent down to give him a reassuring pat. 'Don't worry, we're leaving now,' I said soothingly. 'But then Mommie has to get moving. The sooner I meet with Dale, the sooner I'll find out just what's going to happen to my contest.'

I took Cooper for a quick walk. The spaniel wasted no time doing his business, not even stopping for sniffs along the way like he usually did. I figured he sensed my unease. We returned to the house. I unclipped Cooper's leash and he ambled over to his doggie bed, stretched and lay down. I went upstairs for a speedy shower and dressed in khaki pants, a crisp white shirt, beige striped cardigan and beige Mary Janes. I sent Dale a quick text: *On my way!* Jumped into my trusty convertible and I was off.

Ten minutes later I slid my convertible into a prime parking spot right near the side entrance of the high school. We'd originally planned to hold the contest at City Hall, but a broken heating system had put the kibosh on that venue. Fortunately, the teachers' convention was this week, so the school was in recess. I hurried up the back steps and into the auditorium. Two maintenance men were just leaving the stage, and I paused for a moment to look at it. Two of the five identical pizza-making stations of last week had been removed, leaving three complete with individual ovens, refrigerators and prep tables. Mazzo's, a local restaurant supply outlet, had generously supplied all of the prep tools we'd need. I glanced around. It was nine forty-five. No one was scheduled to arrive before ten thirty, but Dale had to be around here somewhere. No sooner had the thought crossed my mind than the man himself hurried through a side door. He bustled over, took one look at my face and said, 'You heard.'

'I got a text from Hilary. It was all over Channel Twelve news. What made him collapse, do you know?' *Please, don't let it be a heart attack.*

'Gallstones. Not as bad as it could be, but bad enough. Last I heard he was out of surgery and doing fine, but he'll be bedridden for a few weeks.'

I let out a sigh and pushed a hand through my hair. 'Swell. I'm glad he's going to be all right, but it sure puts a big hole in our premier panel of judges.'

I'd been extremely proud of our judging panel. We'd gotten them thanks to *Southern Style*'s newest board member, Frederick Longo. Longo was a former New York City chef with whom I had a brief acquaintance and who had already expressed an interest in judging the contest. Due to some other commitments, Longo himself wasn't available to judge, but he'd been instrumental in bringing aboard some big names: Anastasia Ricci, a well-known chef who'd written several cookbooks on Italian cuisine and hosted a cable cooking show; Giovanni Ferrante, a chef who owned a string of pizza parlors and had written several cookbooks on the subject; and last but not least, Pierre Dumont, one of Georgia's leading food critics, whose specialty was Italian cuisine.

Three jewels in a culinary crown. And then there were two.

'Yes it does, but there might be a solution.' He paused. 'I got a call from Leon Santangelo.'

'Santangelo? What did he want?' My radar pinged instantly. Leon Santangelo was the owner of Santangelo Pizza Dough. No one had been more surprised than me when the man had offered to pony up the entire ten-thousand-dollar grand prize, in exchange for our using his pizza dough in the contest. I'd never met the man in person, but I knew he had a reputation for being somewhat of a letch. Anything he might have to say couldn't possibly be good, and I paled as a sudden thought struck me. 'Don't tell me he wants to take Dumont's place?'

'Relax, Tiff. He couldn't even if we wanted him to. As a sponsor, he's ineligible.' Dale paused. 'He did, however, have a recommendation.'

My antennae rose again, stronger than ever. 'He did? Who?'

Dale shifted his weight from one foot to the other and didn't look me straight in the eye. 'Bartholomew Driscoll.'

I felt sweat start to break out on my forehead. This was worse than even I'd imagined. 'Bar-Bartholomew Driscoll? You're kidding?'

Dale sighed. 'I wish I were. Unfortunately, I'm not.'

I frowned. 'Why on earth did he recommend Driscoll? I didn't think the two of them even knew each other.'

'Apparently they've known each other for some time,' answered Dale. 'Santangelo said the minute he heard about Dumont, he thought of Driscoll.'

I took a deep, calming breath. 'Well, just because Santangelo recommended him doesn't mean he's available. Driscoll always had a busy schedule.'

'Guess again,' Dale replied. 'Since Driscoll gave up reviewing restaurants on a full-time basis to concentrate more on restaurant management, he has more free time. According to Leon, he was very amenable to judging the contest.'

I balled my hands into fists at my sides. 'Surely there must be someone else who's available. What about some local chefs? Bob or Nita Gillette from Po'Boys, or maybe Henri from Bella Pasta?'

'I thought of them too,' Dale admitted, 'But the board wants blockbuster names, ones that they feel will ensure this undertaking's success.' He reached out to cover my hand with his. 'You know as well as I that if we want to keep this as a regular feature on your blog, not to mention the oh-so-generous winner's prize, the first showing has to be nothing less than spectacular.'

'We could postpone it until another big name is available,' I suggested.

'True, but who knows when that will be? I know the board would like it to continue uninterrupted.'

I let out a breath. 'Sounds like there isn't too much of a choice, right? We have to use Driscoll.'

Dale gave my arm a quick squeeze. 'It'll all work out, Tiff. You'll see.' He whipped out his cell and moved away. I figured he was contacting the board and letting them know Driscoll would be taking Dumont's place. I eased myself into one of the aluminum chairs and just sat there, resting my chin in my hands. I knew this was what was best for the contest, but I felt like I was about to face a firing squad. I leaned back in the chair, closed my eyes, and let my mind drift . . .

I'd only been working for *Southern Style* a few weeks when it had happened. For the first time in my short career as a food blogger slash critic, I'd had to write a negative review. I'd always prided myself on being able to spin some positive out of every negative, but this time I'd been unable to work any magic. I'd figured it was bound to happen sooner or later – unfortunately, in this case, it had been sooner. Branson had a ton of restaurants, which was why *Travel* magazine had once referred to it as a 'foodie paradise'. But just like anywhere else in the good old US of A, along with the good meals came the bad. In culinary school and during my career as an assistant chef, I'd heard plenty of horror stories about critics suffering through horrendous meals. Reading about them, though, and actually writing one were two different animals. And, as a former chef, I couldn't imagine ripping apart a horrible meal. I had visions of the chef sweating bullets over a stove, painstakingly plating the meal, and praying that his special dish was impressive. Oh, no, I'd told myself. I'd never diss some poor chef's food. Not in a million years.

Until that fateful night.

It had started out well enough. Hilary had accompanied me to the site of my second review, a restaurant over on Thirty-Third Street. Ambrosia's ads had promised a unique dining experience, and I was fully prepared to be delighted, especially in light of the fact I'd heard that the restaurant owner was a food critic. Just what food critic I had no idea, because the owner was keeping his or her identity very low-key, probably so as not to have opinions about the food pre-formed. Hilary and I had ordered glasses of Riesling and settled down on the pleasant outdoor patio to enjoy our dinners. The night was cool enough for a sweater, and the tantalizing aroma of roasting meat that wafted to our nostrils from the kitchen had my stomach growling in anticipation. Our waiter was pleasant enough, but the half-loaf of stale Italian bread and the rancid pool of olive oil he delivered to our table with a smile were the first harbingers of disaster.

'Hey, it's only been open two months,' Hilary said as she spit out a mouthful of bread into her cloth napkin. 'Any restaurant should be allowed one mistake, right?'

I'd agreed even as I jotted notes into my smartphone. One basket of stale bread did not a bad restaurant make.

But then came the other courses.

The salads were delivered next: a small pile of soggy lettuce in thick blue-cheese dressing that had a definite overtone of the plastic bottle it had no doubt been squeezed from. On top of the lettuce were large chunks of pale pink tomatoes. Still I was optimistic, not giving up hope until the main course was served. My thirty-nine-dollar sea bass smelled fishy and Hilary's filet mignon, pricey at forty-two fifty, was stringy. When our waiter came around with the dessert cart, we both politely passed on both that and coffee and asked for the check. I felt guilty signing the chit with the *Southern Style* account number, because I knew

I could never give a three-star review to this place, let alone a four or a five. While neither of us had gotten ill from the meal, my stomach had kept me up all night in spite of the gallon of antacid I'd downed upon returning home. And according to a text I'd gotten from Hilary the next morning, her gut still didn't feel quite right (although she'd finished her steak, I'd pushed my sea bass away after five bites).

To my credit, I suppose, I hadn't tried to wriggle out of writing it up. Of course, there was no time before my deadline to substitute another restaurant, either, so the die had proverbially been cast:

> *It's said all kitchens have an off-night. Unfortunately, this was especially true at the trendy new restaurant, Ambrosia. I was willing to forgive the stale basket of bread and the soggy chef's salad, but when the sea bass smelled like three-day-old fish and my companion's filet mignon started mooing back at her, the evening just seemed hopeless. One can only hope the quality control in the kitchen had an off-night, and this isn't a daily occurrence. And considering the owner of the restaurant is reputed to be a food critic himself, one can only hope for improvement. Unfortunately, this food blogger has to give this restaurant one and a half stars. At least the water was cold.*

Dale called me into his office the next day. 'That was some review,' he said as I settled myself into one of his comfy leather chairs. 'I just got off the phone with the owner. He wasn't exactly thrilled with your piece.'

I shifted in my seat. 'To be honest, I was disappointed myself. I was expecting more.'

Dale perched himself on the edge of his desk and looked down at me. 'The owner said he wasn't aware they were being reviewed. He said you should have said something.'

'My presence shouldn't have mattered,' I protested. 'Even Hilary agreed with me the food was less than sub-par.'

Dale blew out a breath. 'Apparently the regular chef was off that night. The owner's fired the substitute.' Dale paused and then added, 'He intimated that no one would put much credence in your review anyway, since you're not a professional food critic and you only write a food blog. I told him you were a former professional chef, but it didn't seem to faze him. He wanted us to print a retraction.'

'I hope you told him no,' I bristled.

'I did. I knew you'd stand by what you'd written. He wasn't too happy. I just hope this review doesn't come back to bite you at a later date.'

I frowned. 'Why would it?'

'Because the owner of Ambrosia is Bartholomew Driscoll.'

Ambrosia had been reviewed a lot since then, and they'd all been four-star or better reviews. *In Style* magazine had featured the restaurant (and the smelly sea bass I'd been served) as their 'Pick of the Month' back in July. It's been said that doing well is the best revenge. If that's true, Driscoll has gotten back at me in spades.

So why did I feel trouble brewing?

In the months since that review, my path and Driscoll's had never crossed . . . until now. Why had he agreed to this? He might have decided to let bygones be bygones, but from what I knew of the man I doubted that was a possibility. No, Driscoll had some sort of ulterior motive for agreeing to do this, I was certain of that. Whether or not said motive had anything to do with me, though, remained to be seen.

I sighed. I didn't want to do this. Every fiber in me screamed 'Mistake' but I knew, when push came to shove, I really had no say in the matter. My cell rang. I saw Dale's name pop up. I depressed the answer button. 'What's up? Don't tell me Driscoll backed out?'

'No, sorry. I just wanted to let you know the board gave their blessing to Driscoll's appointment.'

'Big shock there,' I grumbled.

Dale paused. 'You're sure you're fine with this, Tiff?'

I bit back the sigh that rose to my lips. 'It's what's best for the contest, so, yeah, Dale. I'm sure.' *Sure this is destined for disaster.*

As it turned out, I wasn't wrong.

TWO

I put thoughts of Driscoll out of my mind, temporarily at least, and decided to look for a quiet corner where I could sift through the paperwork I'd brought with me. I saw two maintenance men carrying a ladder and flagged them down. 'Try the break room,' suggested the taller of the two after I told them what I wanted. He nodded in the direction of stage left. 'It's back there, behind the kitchen. The Drama Club uses it a lot for breaks during rehearsals, hence the nickname. It's got a few tables, chairs, a couple vending machines. Nothing fancy. It hasn't been upgraded in years, but then again it probably doesn't need to be. It does the job.'

'Thanks.'

I shifted my briefcase to my other hand and was just about to go in search of the break room, when I heard voices behind me. I turned and smiled as I recognized the two people walking toward me – the other judges.

Anastasia Ricci stopped in front of me and blew me air-kisses. The woman was in her late sixties, but she looked more like early fifties. Her hair, a soft ash-blonde, was done in a becoming chin-length style that curled around her neck. Her eyes, a brilliant blue, were as sharp as the wit she was famous for. '*Buonasera*, Tiffany,' she said. 'It is so nice to see you.'

'Yes, it's always nice to see a friendly face.' I smiled warmly at the woman and then turned to the other judge. Giovanni – *call me John* – Ferrante was a beefy, gray-haired man who always reminded me a little bit of Santa Claus minus the beard. His strong arms gripped me in a quick bear hug. 'I understand some of the other faces around here might not be so friendly,' he added, with a meaningful glance at Anastasia.

Oh, ho, bad news really did travel fast. 'I take it you've heard about our replacement judge?'

Both judges' noses wrinkled in expressions of distaste. 'Sì,' said Anastasia. 'Just our luck, eh, Giovanni, to have the devil himself at the judging table with us?'

Giovanni Ferrante's eyes were bereft of their usual sparkle as he shook his head. 'Indeed. I hope the fool remembers this is a contest of amateur chefs, not pros. After all, he's no longer a food critic.'

Anastasia threw her hands up in the air. 'That doesn't matter to him! I was a guest on a cable cooking show shortly before he decided to hang up his critic's cape. I remember it as if it were yesterday. The show was *Home Cooking Today*. He tore apart one of the contestants' recipes, up and down and sideways. The poor girl was trembling when she left the stage.'

Giovanni shook his head. 'The man panned my *vitello tonnato* a few years ago. I had a different chef on that night who wasn't all that familiar with the recipe. It didn't matter to him. "A professional chef must be able to cook every dish on the restaurant's menu at any time," he said.' Ferrante threw a glance my way. 'Sound familiar?'

'It does indeed,' I said grimly. 'Apparently Driscoll doesn't see his own faults, but he certainly has an eagle eye for those of others,' I said dryly. 'I suppose now that he himself is in the restaurant business, he feels those rules don't apply to him.'

'It doesn't matter what business he's in,' Anastasia said as she rolled her eyes. 'The man always has been, and always will be, a *tool*!' She laid a hand on Ferrante's arm. 'And how you can be so calm after what he did to you . . .'

'Now, now, Anastasia.' Ferrante reached out and gave her arm a gentle pat. 'That's old news. Water under the bridge. Best forgotten.'

Anastasia raised an eyebrow. 'Since when? I have never heard you speak so charitably of that slime before?'

Ferrante shrugged. 'That is true, but . . . what good does it do to hold a grudge? It only stirs up negative energy.'

Anastasia rolled her eyes, but I smiled at the chef. 'You're right, Chef. Too bad Driscoll himself doesn't adhere to that policy. I'm afraid he's never forgiven me for my review.'

Ferrante reached out to pat my hand. 'Well, don't give up,

bella. One never knows. After all, he consented to judge the contest, right? And he had to know you were part of it—'

'Enough of talking about that man,' cut in Anastasia. She held up her wrist, tapped at the gold watch she wore. 'We have to get going, Giovanni. Remember, Mr Swenson wanted to meet with us.' She barked out a hearty laugh. 'He probably wants to make sure we won't try to strangle our new judge. He has no worries. We'd have to get in line. A very long one, too.' She reached out to touch my cheek. '*Ciao, bella.*'

Giovanni Ferrante gripped my hand. 'I'm going to throw a small after-party at A Slice of Heaven tonight,' he said. He rubbed his hand across his full tummy as he added, 'I figured that would be appropriate, considering we've been judging pizza the past two weeks.'

I chuckled. 'It is, Chef Ferrante. How thoughtful of you. I imagine the press will be there?'

His face darkened slightly. 'Heck no! None of those vultures. We want to relax and have fun! No, it's just for the judges, contestants, and senior staff of *Southern Style.*' He reached up and gave his ear a tug. 'Believe me, I would like to exclude one particular judge from the guest list, but I suppose there's no tactful way to do that, eh?'

Anastasia let out a snort. 'Since when have you become tactful?'

Ferrante chuckled. 'It's called old age.'

'Oh, neither of you are old,' I assured them. I smiled at Ferrante. 'And I'm sure we'll all have a good time, even if Driscoll comes.'

'Maybe we'll get lucky, and he'll have other plans,' said Anastasia.

'It is possible. Driscoll is a busy man,' Ferrante said with a wry look. He turned to me. 'And now, I'm afraid Anastasia and I must be off. We will see you later, bella! Oh . . . and none of that Chef Ferrante stuff. You can call me John, you know,' he said with a wink.

I smiled at him. 'How about a compromise? Chef John?'

Ferrante grinned. '*Molto Bene!* I like it.'

Ferrante linked his arm through Anastasia's and the two of them walked off, heads close together. I shifted my briefcase to my other hand and went up the short flight of stairs to the stage, past the newly set-up mini-kitchens, and slipped behind the velvet curtain. A passing stagehand directed me up another short flight of stairs, and a few minutes later I pushed open a heavy door and fumbled for a light switch. Dust prickled my nose as lights flickered hesitantly, and then arced on, flooding what was obviously the 'old kitchen', spotlighting generous counter space on which rested several aging appliances. A rickety table holding a blender and a toaster sat square in the middle. Another door was dead center, and I headed straight for it. It swung inward on rusty hinges and I found myself in a room not much bigger than a postage stamp. Two tables and four chairs were wedged in between two old vending machines. In a far corner was a rickety-looking cot and beside it was a sturdy-looking footstool. It wasn't much to look at; then again, to a bunch of high school drama students, it no doubt was more than adequate for their needs and – at the current moment – mine as well.

I went over to one of the tables, pulled out a chair, and started sifting through my paperwork. I'd just started pulling out the release forms that had to be signed by each contestant when I heard the outer door creak open. 'We can talk in here,' said a rough, gravelly voice. 'It seems private enough.'

So much for privacy, I thought. I figured I'd better make my presence known before any conversation was started. I half-rose from my chair when I heard another voice, more well-modulated than the first.

'There's nothing to talk about, Leon. I need your answer today. I can't wait any longer.'

I froze in my tracks. It had been a long time, but I was pretty certain the speaker was Bartholomew Driscoll! He'd called his companion Leon, so I was assuming it was Leon Santangelo. I nibbled at my lower lip as I debated what to do. Revealing myself might not be the wisest course of action. I wouldn't put it past Driscoll to accuse me of spying on him!

Leon spoke, and I could detect an undercurrent of impatience in his tone. 'Why are you bringing this up now? You know my cashflow has been tight.'

'Well, who told you to pony up the entire prize for this cooking debauchery?' snapped Driscoll. In a smoother tone he added, 'I'm sure if you really tried, you could scrape something together.'

'I'm trying to, but I need more time.'

'Sorry, Leon. That's a commodity I can't give you. As I said, I need your answer today.'

My natural curiosity aroused, I tiptoed over to the door. I'd left it slightly ajar, and the opening was just enough for me to peer through without risk of being seen. Driscoll's back was to me, but I had a good view of Leon Santangelo. The pizza dough magnate looked very uneasy, and his gaze darted around the narrow room as if looking for some means of escape. He spread his hands and declared, 'Why are you being so stubborn? I would have expected a more charitable attitude from you, Driscoll. And don't forget, if it weren't for me, you would never have known—'

'Let's not get into that now,' snapped Driscoll. 'Tell me, Leon, do you ever get tired of patting yourself on the back?'

'No, because it's well deserved and you know it,' Santangelo sneered. 'Don't force my hand, Bart. You know I can make trouble for you.'

'More idle threats, Leon?'

The two men stared at each other for a long moment; then Santangelo turned on his heel and walked out of the room. Driscoll balled his hand into a fist, and then slammed it against a nearby counter. A gasp escaped my lips, louder than I'd intended. I drew back quickly, but it was too late. I'd been heard. A second later the break-room door was thrown open, and I found myself face to face with my worst nightmare. I had to admit, the man hadn't changed a whit from our last encounter. He still had the same cold blue eyes, the same well-shaped lips. If the man didn't have such an officious personality, he actually might be quite handsome.

Now those blue eyes widened in surprise, and the corners of his lips turned up in a sneer. He made a slight bow and a motion of tipping an imaginary hat.

'Well, well, if it isn't Tiffany Austin, *Southern Style*'s *esteemed* food blogger. Hiding away here, preparing scathing reviews of other restaurants, hmm? Or perhaps you were hiding here, hoping to get some more dirt to dish on me?'

He was baiting me, and I was determined not to fall for it. It was hard though because, pinned under his laser-sharp gaze, I could feel my confidence slipping away like sands through an

hourglass. 'Mr Driscoll,' I managed to get out. 'No, I haven't
been spying on you. Actually, I . . . I'm happy to see you.'

His eyes widened and he clucked his tongue against the roof
of his mouth. 'Happy, you say? Now why don't I believe that?'

'It's t-true,' I stammered. 'I . . . we – *Southern Style*, that is
– appreciate your stepping up to judge the contest like this,' I
said. 'Not many people would give up some of their time to help
out, and on such short notice, too.'

Now the eyes narrowed to near-slits. 'Consider it my good
deed for the week,' he said at last. 'And you should appreciate
my doing this. Believe me, when I heard you were involved, I
almost refused. Now, if you'll excuse me . . .'

Driscoll turned to leave, and what I should have done was sit
down and shut up, but I admit my curiosity got the better of me.
'Why didn't you? Refuse?' I blurted out.

He turned slowly. The expression on his face was similar to
the one Lily got when she was stalking a plump mouse. 'You
would have liked that, wouldn't you, Tiffany Austin?' he hissed.
'Let me assure you, I've never forgotten what you tried to do to
my restaurant and my reputation.'

Now I could feel my blood pressure rise. 'You make it sound
as if I purposely gave you a bad review, but I didn't.'

Driscoll's eyes became thin blue slits. 'Are you trying to tell
me that hatchet job was your idea of a good review?' he snapped.

I swallowed. 'The truth is, Mr Driscoll, I was extremely
disappointed in the meal that night. The advance buzz on your
restaurant had been excellent, and I'd been looking forward to
the meal. When it didn't turn out as I expected . . . well, I just
wrote how I felt. I'm not going to apologize for having a less
than stellar experience. What I can apologize for is not giving
you a second chance.'

He looked me up and down. 'If you think I'm going to accept
that half-hearted apology, you're sadly mistaken, Ms Austin. You
know what they say,' he said softly. 'Doing well is the best
revenge, and I am doing well. Amazingly well, in fact.'

'I – ah – I'm glad to hear that,' I stammered.

'Are you?' He stroked at his chin. 'Now why don't I believe
that?'

I swallowed. 'Think what you will, Mr Driscoll, but it's the truth. There are no hard feelings on my part. I confess I am curious, though. Why is it you never expanded? I thought your original plan was to open two, three restaurants.'

Driscoll's lips thinned. 'It still is,' he said shortly. 'I just got a bit . . . sidetracked making sure Ambrosia's reputation didn't suffer. Expansion is a situation I hope to rectify sooner rather than later.'

'I see. So then Leon Santangelo doesn't have anything to do with your plans?'

Driscoll expelled a breath, and then he waggled his finger in my face. 'Don't press your luck, my dear. Let me give you a bit of advice. You seem to be doing pretty well yourself. That food blog of yours has gotten quite popular. You should enjoy it while you can. Take a bit of advice. Don't take anything for granted in this life.'

He sounded so wistful delivering that last line – almost human, actually – that I was tempted to press him for more details on his advice. Before I could do so, however, the kitchen door squeaked open and a feminine voice called out, 'Mr Driscoll? Are you here?'

Driscoll tore his gaze away from me. 'In here, Beth.'

A second later the break-room door squeaked open and a girl stood framed in the doorway. 'Oh, there you are Bar . . .' She paused, flustered, as she noticed me in the room and coughed lightly, then began again. 'I'm glad I found you, Mr Driscoll. Peter's looking for you. He said he needs to speak with you. I said I wasn't sure you'd arrived yet, but I'd go look for you.'

Driscoll let out a long sigh. 'Very well, Beth. Where is he?'

'I'm not sure. He stalked off, said he was going to look around for you.'

'Typical of that impatient idiot.' Driscoll lifted his hand, and ran it through his thick crop of wavy iron-gray hair. 'Well, when he shows up again, tell him I can spare him five minutes – no more. Understand? If he balks, tell him it's more than enough time for something that's been done to death already. And be sure you use those exact words.'

'Yes, sir.'

'And tell Mr Santangelo I need to speak with him as well. We haven't finished our discussion.'

'Yes, sir.'

'One last thing. What happened to my water supply?'

'I had them put the cooler just in back of the curtain at stage left so you would have easy access.'

He gave Beth a curt nod, and then pushed past me and out the door without as much as a backward glance. Once he'd gone, I let out the breath I'd been holding and staggered backward.

Beth shot me a sympathetic look. 'Rough encounter?'

'One might say that,' I said. Then, before I thought I blurted out, 'The man hasn't changed. He's just as insufferable, egotistical and hateful as ever.'

To my surprise Beth burst out laughing. 'Yes,' she finally managed to say. 'And those are his good qualities.' She looked at the water bottle in her hand and let out a dry chuckle. 'You should hear how he carries on if his personal water supply isn't available. I forgot it once, and boy did he blast me. He has to have one certain brand of bottled water when he travels anywhere, or all hell breaks loose.'

'Somehow that doesn't surprise me,' I said.

She barked out another laugh, and I took a moment to study the girl. She was definitely young – early twenties was my best guess – and petite. Five one, five two at most, the flat shoes she wore not adding to her height. She had a trim figure, but her simple yellow shift dress did nothing to accentuate it. Her hair, black as a raven's wing, seemed at odds with the pale ivory of her complexion. Her eyes were wide and cornflower blue behind the massive tortoiseshell glasses she wore. She looked timid and unassuming, like a female Clark Kent. Her hand shot out and I took it. For such a tiny person, her grip was surprisingly firm and strong. 'I'm Beth March,' she said. 'I'm Mr Driscoll's personal assistant.'

'Nice to meet you, Beth.' She released my hand, and I flexed my fingers. 'I'm . . .'

'Oh, I know who you are.' She waved her hand in a semi-circle. 'You're Tiffany Austin. I love your blog. I read it religiously, even though . . .' She gave a swift look around and then leaned in closer to me, 'I'd never tell that to Bar . . . I mean Mr Driscoll.'

It was the second time she'd started to call Driscoll by his first name, which made me wonder if there might be more to that relationship than just employer–employee. Beth seemed like a nice girl, and for her sake I hoped not. 'I take it you've heard about my past run-in with your employer,' I said.

She nodded. 'He's never told me the whole story, but there have been enough cryptic comments made so that I was able to piece two and two together.' She shot me a wistful look. 'You can find pretty much anything on the Internet, if you look hard enough.'

'That's true,' I admitted. 'Not a moment has gone by that I haven't regretted that hasty review.'

Beth's eyes widened. 'Why should you regret it? It's how you felt, right? You called it as you saw it.'

'Yes, at the time I did, but in retrospect I should have gone back another night. Every restaurant has their off nights, trust me.'

Beth looked thoughtful. 'That's a very generous attitude, Tiffany,' she said. 'Mr Driscoll isn't quite as charitable – but he's improving.'

She set her water down on a nearby table and pulled a small pillbox out of her pocket. She shook a pill out, popped it into her mouth, and then washed it down with some water. 'Sorry,' she said. 'It's for my nerves. The doctor said it would help to calm them.'

I smiled. 'Working for Driscoll, I can understand that.'

She twirled the water bottle in her hand. 'There have been a few rough moments,' she said. 'I'm new at this assistant stuff, and I do fluff up a bit. But I'd say, on the whole, the experience has been good. Believe it or not, Mr Driscoll has a softer side.'

I goggled at her. 'Forgive me, but I find that hard to believe.'

'I understand completely. It took me a while to figure him out.' She glanced around, and then leaned closer to me. She lowered her voice to a half-whisper and said, 'Trust me, yours wasn't the only bad review his restaurant received. Mr Driscoll . . . ah . . . used his clout and powers of persuasion to tamp the bad ones down.'

That little tidbit surprised me. 'He received other negative reviews? Is that why he never went through with opening more restaurants?'

'No, that wasn't it. There were other factors besides reviews. Things I'm not at liberty to discuss.' She worried her lower lip and a moment later she added, 'It wasn't your negative review in itself that annoyed him, Tiffany. He's done plenty of those himself. It was the fact he considers you a rank amateur at criticizing gourmet food – his words, not mine.'

I drew myself up to my full height. 'He obviously forgets that while I might not be a professional critic, I am a professional chef,' I said with a curl of my lip. 'I consider myself very qualified and far from a rank amateur in that arena.'

'I'm sure you are,' Beth said quickly. She was silent for a few moments and then said, 'I know it's hard to believe, but Mr Driscoll's not always as cranky as he seems. Why, there are times he's downright human – except maybe where his brother is concerned.'

I raised an eyebrow. 'Driscoll has a brother?'

She nodded. 'Yes. Peter Hagen.' She hesitated and then added, 'They're half-brothers, actually. Same mother, different fathers. They both keep their relationship very low-key, although if you ask me, one would never know they were related, let alone brothers. They are nothing alike.'

I thought that was more than likely a good thing, especially for Peter Hagen, but I didn't voice that thought aloud. Instead I said, 'I take it you've worked for Mr Driscoll quite a while?'

'It hasn't been all that long. A little less than a year, actually.' Her lips twisted into a rueful smile. 'Although at times it does feel like forever.'

A young boy wearing a headset popped his head inside the doorway. 'One of you gals Tiffany Austin?' he drawled. At my nod he said, 'Mr Swenson would like you to get those release forms signed before the contest starts, and the contestants are starting to arrive.'

I glanced over at the table and the paperwork scattered across it. 'Tell Mr Swenson I'll get right on it.'

The boy left and I turned to Beth. 'I have to get going. It was nice meeting you, Beth. I hope you enjoy the show.'

'Oh, I'm sure I will.' Beth made a show of rubbing her tummy as she walked away. 'I love pizza.'

I gathered up my paperwork and hurried back onto the main stage area. The first two people I saw were Hilary and her sister.

My BFF was dressed casually, in jeans and a purple sweatshirt. Her short blonde hair was damp, as if she'd just gotten out of the shower . . . and, knowing Hilary's proclivity for tardiness, she probably had.

Her sister was another story. Arleen Hanson looked more like she was getting ready to participate in one of the beauty contests she loved to enter than a cook-off. Today her thick blonde hair curled past her shoulders and there was an extra sparkle in her dark brown eyes. The red tank top she wore matched her high heels and nail polish. She looked cool as a cucumber, but her posture and the way she kept wringing her hands in front of her told me a different story. Hilary looked up, saw me and waved. She whispered something to her sister and then hurried over to me. 'You caught the news about Dumont, right? I texted you the minute I saw it.'

I nodded. 'Yep. It's too bad, but at least it's nothing life-threatening. He's going to be fine.'

Arleen leaned forward and said in a breathy voice, 'I admit, I was a bit worried. I thought maybe they might postpone the contest.'

'That might well have happened, but fortunately Leon Santangelo came up with a substitute.'

Hilary raised a brow. 'Santangelo? That dirty old man? I'd be leery of anyone he recommended.'

'Wise words, especially in this case,' I said with a wry smile. 'The judge he recommended is Bartholomew Driscoll.'

'Driscoll! As in Ambrosia restaurant Driscoll? You're kidding!' Hilary cried.

'I wish I were,' I replied. I glanced over at Arleen. Her sunny smile had been replaced by a deep scowl. 'Arleen, are you OK?'

She looked over at me with a start. 'Oh . . . yes. I was just surprised to hear Driscoll was the judge, is all. I would think he'd be too busy for something like this, what with his TV show and everything.'

She looked more upset than surprised to me, but I decided to let it pass. 'I thought so too,' I said. 'But apparently he had some free time.'

Both Hilary's eyebrows rose to Spockian proportions. She

made an exaggerated motion of fanning herself. 'Mr Wonderful gave up his free time to do this? I didn't think he had any.' She turned and eyed her sister. 'Wasn't he supposed to judge that beauty contest you were in last year?'

'You mean Miss Fulton County?' Arleen asked. 'Yes. He had to back out. He said he had too many commitments.' She gave a hollow laugh. 'He was still doing reviews at the time. I think everyone was relieved.'

'So you met the man?' I asked.

Arleen hesitated, and then shook her head. 'I saw him briefly. He didn't impress me much.'

Hilary shot me a concerned look. 'I was just thinking . . . maybe Driscoll figures this is payback time.'

Arleen frowned at her sister. 'Payback? Payback for what?'

Hilary threw her sister an impatient look. 'I told you about it, Ar. When Tiff first started at the magazine, she gave Driscoll's restaurant, Ambrosia, a bad review.'

'Yes,' I said. 'Apparently he's never forgotten – or forgiven – it.'

'Yeah, someone should tell the old fossil to lighten up,' Hilary said. 'Life's too short for stuff like that.' She threw her sister a wicked glance. 'Maybe you should try talking to him, Ar? You're good at telling guys things like that – and wrapping them around your little finger.'

'Yeah, well, I doubt someone like Driscoll would listen to a nobody like me,' Arleen said.

'You'd be surprised,' Hilary said with a chuckle. 'He's played up in the gossip magazines as quite the ladies' man.'

'Ew,' I gave a mock shudder. 'Wow. I didn't realize there were so many desperate women in the world.'

'You have to admit, the guy's good looking. It's his personality that needs a serious makeover.' Hilary gave her sister a quick appraisal. 'Trust me, Ar, you're just his type. I bet he'd listen to anything you had to say.'

'Don't be fooled by what you read in those gossip rags,' Arleen snapped. 'Bartholomew Driscoll isn't the type to let a pretty face dictate what he will or won't do, or who he will or won't like.'

Hilary eyed her sister. 'Oh, yeah? Since when are you such an expert on Bartholomew Driscoll?'

Arleen flushed. 'You don't have to be an expert on the guy to
see what he's like.' Abruptly she whirled around to face me and
held out her hand. 'Dale said you had some paperwork I'm
supposed to sign?'

I nodded and whipped out the release form. I handed it to
Arleen along with a pen, and she signed her name with a
flourish. Hilary made a tsking sound. 'You didn't read it,' she
admonished.

Arleen shrugged. 'Don't have to. It's standard, right?'

I nodded. 'Pretty much.'

'Well, then.' Arleen rubbed her hands together. 'There's still
an hour before the first leg starts. I'm going to find the ladies'
room and check my makeup. In case you guys hadn't noticed,
there's a lot of press and photographers out there.'

Arleen gave her hair a quick pat and hurried off. Hilary
watched her go, hands on her hips, and cut me an eye roll. 'That's
so like my sister. I knew she'd find a way to treat this like a
photo op.' She reached up and patted her nose. 'My makeup
could use some freshening up too.'

I chuckled. 'You want to keep an eye on her, right?'

'Darn right. I know my sister. She sees photographers and
loses all common sense. I've got to make sure she doesn't do
anything stupid.'

Hilary moved off just as Kurt Howell strode toward me. I
knew that the trucker from Atlanta had impressed the other
judges with his pizza, and I wondered if Driscoll would be simi-
larly impressed. As he handed the release form back to me I said,
'I suppose you've heard about our change in judges.'

'Yep, I sure have.' He grinned and patted his burly chest. 'I
got kidded a lot about my cooking ability when I was in high
school,' he admitted. 'I was one of two boys in the Home Ec
class. Maybe that's why I took up truck driving for a living.'

I looked over his six foot, easily over 200-pound frame and
grinned back. 'I would also imagine it's hard to be taken seriously as a chef, too.'

He waved his hand carelessly. 'None of that fazes me,' he said
confidently. 'Now I don't know much about this dude Driscoll,
other than he has a reputation as a hard-ass critic, but I've also
got one as a hard-ass home cook.'

'I've heard Driscoll likes to eat hard-ass home cooks for breakfast,' I commented.

'Not this one.' Howell turned his hand inward and pointed at himself. 'My dream is to quit my trucking job and enroll full time in culinary school. What I'd like to do is own my own restaurant someday.'

'Wow, that's very ambitious. Would you open it in Atlanta?'

'Nah, too much competition. I'm originally from a small town in Alabama, Reeltown.'

'Reeltown? Sorry, I've never heard of it.'

'I'm not surprised. It's not far from Auburn. I might go back there one day.' He closed one eye in a broad wink. 'Once I take first place, that ten-thousand-dollar prize will go a long way toward making my dream a reality.'

'You sound very confident of winning,' I remarked.

He held up both hands, fingers crossed. 'Let's hope,' he said.

I slid his and Arleen's signed forms back into my folder and had just pulled out the last one when a soft voice behind me said, 'Excuse me, Ms Austin?' I turned around and smiled at Colleen Collins, who'd won the traditional category. Colleen's blue eyes were wide, and I noticed that her hands seemed to tremble just a bit. Probably nerves, I thought. 'Hello, Colleen,' I said. 'I have your release form ready.'

'Thanks. Do you have a pen?'

I whipped a pen out of my jacket pocket and passed it to her along with the release form. The trembling was very evident as she signed her name. She handed both back to me and then said, 'Is it true what I just heard? That Bartholomew Driscoll is now a judge?'

I nodded. 'Yes. We were lucky to get him, or the contest might have been cancelled.'

'Oh.' The corners of Colleen's lips drooped downward. 'Maybe that might have been for the best,' she murmured.

'Not a fan, huh?' I said.

Colleen shrugged. 'You could say that.'

'Well, remember, his opinion only counts for a third of the final score. There are two other judges, and from what I heard, they were pretty impressed with your pie. Will you be making a similar one today?'

Colleen shook her head. 'No, I thought I'd do something different. My first pizza will be a *funghi* pie, consisting of tomato sauce, mozzarella and mushrooms. For my second pizza, I thought I'd do a *quattro stagioni*.'

'A *quattro stagioni*? That's pretty ambitious.' I was familiar with the pie, which was a blend of tomato sauce, mozzarella, ham, black olives, mushrooms, artichokes, peas, salami and eggs. Done correctly, this could be a real game-changer for the woman.

Colleen flashed me a smile. 'I know, but in a competition like this, you've got to take a few risks.'

'Well, good luck.'

'Thanks,' the pretty brunette said. 'I think I'm going to need it.'

Colleen had just uttered those words when the backstage curtain parted and Bartholomew Driscoll, ear to his cell phone, came striding out. For a second, his gaze locked with Colleen's. I saw a look pass between them – what kind of a look exactly was hard to tell – and then Driscoll averted his gaze and continued walking and talking on his cell.

Colleen gazed after his retreating back. 'Yep, lots and lots of luck,' she murmured, so softly I had to strain to catch the words. And then she walked off in the other direction.

THREE

'All right contestants, look alive! The first round of the
final bake-off starts in twenty minutes! You'll have
forty-five minutes to cook your first pizza and present
it to our distinguished panel of judges.'

From my vantage post in stage left, I gave an enthusiastic
thumbs up to the contest emcee, Troy Howard, a local DJ who
hosted his own morning radio show, Troy in the Morning. The
finalists were all bent over their counters, getting their ingredients
ready to prepare the first of the two pies they were to present to
the judges that would decide the grand prize winner. Arleen's
nerves had settled down and I noticed that both she and Kurt
Howell seemed calm and in control as they arranged cheese,
dough and spices on their counters; Colleen Collins, on the other
hand, seemed nervous. She dropped several utensils, and a
container of Parmesan cheese had also found its way to the floor.
Considering what I'd witnessed earlier, I couldn't help but wonder
if Bartholomew Driscoll was the reason for her attack of nerves.

I glanced out at the audience section. It seemed like the entire
town of Branson had turned out to see which home cook would
prepare the best pizza and walk off with the ten-thousand-dollar
prize. The section reserved for members of the press was packed
too, and I noticed two camera crews, one from local news and
another from *Good Morning Branson*, setting up close to the
stage.

In the judges' section, Ferrante and Anastasia carried on an
animated conversation. In contrast, Driscoll sat on the end, his
back to them. He seemed to be pointedly ignoring them, preferring to converse on his cell phone instead. From the dark scowl
that marred his features, I had the idea his conversation was not
a pleasant one. I wondered who he might be talking to? His
brother? Leon Santangelo? I noticed the pizza dough king was
conspicuously absent. Was it because of his earlier argument with
Driscoll?

Two of the backstage crew walked past me. They were laughing. 'Got to hand it to that girl,' one said. 'She sure gave Driscoll what he deserved.'

My ears pricked up at the mention of Driscoll's name. I edged a little closer to the men so I could hear.

'Sure did,' the other one said. 'She twisted out of his grasp so fast I think the old boy was stunned for a second. He really wasn't expecting the little bath she gave him.'

The other man hooted. 'She grabbed that water bottle out of his hand so fast the old coot didn't even have time to duck. Served him right, though.'

'Didn't seem to faze him. He just went and got another bottle of water out of that special cooler he brought with him. I get the feeling it might happen to him a lot.'

They walked off, chuckling. I chuckled myself. I would have loved to have seen that little altercation. Who doused Driscoll, I wondered? Colleen Collins came to mind right away, and so did Arleen. I'd have to ask Hilary later if Arleen had mentioned anything to her.

As if she'd read my mind, Hilary suddenly appeared next to me. She took one look at my face and said, 'OK, I could use a laugh. What's so funny?'

I repeated the story I'd overheard. Hilary shook her head when I'd finished. 'It sounds like my sister,' she said. 'I'll have to corral her and find out.'

'Arleen's not the only likely candidate,' I said. I inclined my head toward Colleen Collins, who had just come up on stage left. 'I sensed something brewing between the two of them earlier. Driscoll sure gave her a dirty look, and she did the same. And she's been nervous as a kitten ever since.'

'Sounds like something's up,' Hilary agreed. 'Although what she could possibly see in Driscoll escapes me.'

'Me too.' I paused. 'Driscoll's been a busy boy. I overheard an argument between him and Santangelo earlier.'

'Hah. What, was he reading Santangelo the riot act for talking him into doing this?'

'No. Actually it sounded more like they were arguing over some kind of business deal.'

'If Santangelo goes into business with Driscoll he's crazier than I thought,' Hilary said. She was silent for a few moments and then said, 'Speaking of crazy, I just talked to Mac.'

Mackenzie 'Mac' Huddleston was a photo-journalist for *Southern Style*. He and Hilary had recently started dating. I noted the expression on my BFF's face as she said his name. Not good. 'What's the matter?' I asked.

'He told me why he was late getting here today. His boss called him in to tell him they're sending him and Bettina Foxworth to Paris to cover International Fashion Week. They leave Monday and they'll be gone for two whole weeks!'

I grimaced. Bettina Foxworth was the new style and local gossip guru, replacing our former one who'd met a rather untimely end. Bettina had come from another online magazine based in Roslyn. She was a shapely platinum blonde who wore designer size zeros and had a reputation as a barracuda with the men. Plus, it didn't help matters that Mac Mackenzie himself, besides being a Superman look-alike, had a reputation as a ladies' man. The two of them together looked like a pair of runway models.

I laid my hand on Hilary's arm. 'Don't worry,' I said. 'You know it's just a job to Mac.'

'Oh, I know. I'm not worried about him. It's her I'm concerned about.' Hilary made a grimace. 'I mean, they're going to be in Paris, Tiff. The most romantic city in the world. And I've heard that once she sets her sights on a man, she doesn't stop till she gets him.'

I refrained from pointing out that up until a few months ago, Mac had the same reputation. Instead I said, 'And you're afraid she'll set her sights on Mac? Have you considered taking some vacation time and tagging along?'

'The thought did cross my mind, and I might except for two things.' She held up her hand and started to tick off on her fingers. 'One, a ticket to Paris at this late date costs almost two thousand dollars. And two, I only have two vacation days left.'

She looked so morose that I couldn't help but feel sorry for her. She really liked Mac. I put a comforting arm around her shoulders. 'I still have seven vacation days left. What if I asked Dale if he'd be willing to transfer a few of them over to you?'

Hilary's expression brightened, but then she frowned. 'Do you think he would? It's against company policy, you know.'

'True, but there are exceptions to every rule. I bet I could convince him.'

'You might convince *him*, but then knowing Dale, he'd run it by the board for final approval. I can just hear them now: "If we do it for her, we'd have to do it for everyone".'

I couldn't help but laugh at Hilary's spot-on imitation of Dale, nor could I argue with that scenario. 'I could still ask,' I suggested. 'Maybe Dale could advance you some time against next year's vacation.'

Hilary shook her head. 'Maybe so, but vacation time isn't my only problem. There are lots of others, money for airfare, for instance. And spending money, of course, for the times when Mac would be on business and I'd be on my own. I just don't have that much spare cash lying around right now.' She let out a giant sigh. 'Had I known this was going to happen, I wouldn't have redecorated my apartment.'

'Yeah, but face it. Your apartment was long overdue for a makeover.'

She twisted her lips into a lopsided grin. 'I'll let my new leather couch comfort me when I'm thinking of Mac and Bettina sipping champagne at the Eiffel Tower.'

I thought of offering my friend a loan, but I knew she wouldn't take it. I slipped my arm around her shoulders and gave her a squeeze just as the pocket of her cardigan vibrated. She reached in, whipped out her cell, and let out a sharp cry. 'Mac's texting me! I've gotta take this.'

My friend hurried off and I turned my attention back to the stage and the judge's area. To my surprise, the seat Driscoll had occupied was now empty. I frowned. Where was the guy? The contest was slated to begin in less than fifteen minutes. No doubt he was searching for someone else to annoy.

I stepped back behind the velvet curtain and looked around backstage. No sign of Driscoll. I glanced at my watch. Five minutes to go. I stood frozen, debating what to do, when I suddenly heard soft voices coming from stage left. I moved in that direction and peered around the corner.

Bartholomew Driscoll stood there, hands crossed over his chest. He was glaring at another man who looked to be a shorter, stockier version of him. He had to be the brother Beth had mentioned, Peter Hagen. 'I never understood why you needed that loan in the first place,' Peter said. He sounded a bit peevish. 'With all the money you make, dear Bart, it's hard to believe you're that strapped for cash.'

'I told you,' Driscoll said impatiently, 'some investments didn't work out quite the way I wanted. If this venture is successful, I should be able to repay you. I just need you to be patient.'

'I have been patient – extremely so, if you ask me. What if this little venture of yours doesn't pan out the way you want it to?'

'Well, then there's always Plan B.'

Peter swiped at his forehead with the back of his hand. 'I should have known. You wouldn't miss an opportunity to ridicule me in print a second time.'

'I hate to break it to you, dear brother, but it's not always all about you.'

Hagen crossed his arms over his chest. 'Look, everything aside, loaning you that money was a good-faith gesture on my part. I should have known better. And as for this "change of heart" on your part – well, we all know leopards don't change their spots.'

'I think, if Plan B comes to fruition, you will be very surprised, dear brother.'

'I doubt that.' Hagen threw up his hands. 'I'm done here. Just be warned. If this turns out to be a repeat of last time, I won't just sit back and take it. You'll be lucky if I don't sue you – or worse.'

'Hard to sue someone for slander when they're telling the truth, Petey. As for doing something worse, well – you need guts for that.'

Peter Hagen's face purpled. For a brief moment I thought he might strike Driscoll, but after a few seconds he turned on his heel and stormed off. I ducked into a nearby alcove just in time to avoid being seen. Peter Hagen barreled past my hiding place, his face looking like a thundercloud. 'No guts huh?' I heard him mutter. 'Well, don't bet on it.'

Peter Hagen clomped off, and a few seconds later Driscoll emerged, his cell phone glued to his ear. As fate would have it, he paused right in front of the alcove where I was hiding. I slunk deeper into the shadows just in case Driscoll should look my way, but his attention – or rather, his wrath – was directed at whoever was on the other end of that phone.

'Look,' he barked, 'I thought I told you not to call me anymore. We have nothing further to discuss.' Another moment of silence and then, 'Press this issue and you'll regret it.'

He snapped the phone shut and then stalked off. Hm, it certainly was a busy afternoon for Driscoll, I thought. No wonder the man always wore a perpetual frown. His people skills definitely needed a makeover. I had to admit I was curious as to the nature of the conversation between the brothers. What was Driscoll considering doing that had upset his brother so?

I waited a few minutes for good measure and then exited the alcove. I wasn't taking any chances on running into Driscoll when he was in such a dark mood. I was just about to return to the main stage when I caught a glimpse of a woman lurking in the wings at stage right. She started walking rapidly in the direction Driscoll had gone, and I had to quicken my pace to overtake her. 'Excuse me,' I called out. 'This area is off limits.'

The woman turned. I judged her to be somewhere in her mid-forties, with eyes the color of a mochaccino. Sleek blonde hair tumbled across broad shoulders, and her fuchsia dress was definitely designer-worthy. A press pass dangled from a black cord around her neck. Her perfectly manicured fingers grasped the cord. She lifted it from around her neck, held it out for my inspection. 'Even to members of the press?' she asked in a soft voice.

I took the pass and looked at the name. *Charlotte Horn. Atlanta Star-Register.* The photo, a small black and white, didn't look recent, and definitely didn't do her justice. I turned the pass over in my hand. 'We've already held a conference for members of the press,' I said.

Charlotte Horn shifted her weight from one foot to the other and angled her chin. 'Yes, I attended that, but it was all standard, general fluff. I was hoping to get an exclusive with one of the judges.'

I handed her pass back. 'Then I'd suggest you speak with my editor, Dale Swenson. I'm pretty sure he could arrange something with one of the judges, either Anastasia or Giovanni. Both are very amenable to interviews.'

Charlotte's tongue darted out, slicked across her lower lip. 'I'm only interested in one judge. Bartholomew Driscoll.'

I shook my head. 'I can't help you, and I doubt Dale could either. Mr Driscoll is . . . ah, rather particular about things such as interviews. Maybe you could approach his assistant.'

Her eyebrow lifted. 'He has an assistant?'

'Yes. Her name is Beth March. She's quite young, dark hair, glasses.'

'Really?' Charlotte Horn's eyes narrowed. 'Now *that* is interesting. Maybe I'll seek her out, offer my condolences. Knowing Driscoll, she'll be looking for other employment before long.' Charlotte pulled a small, pink-covered notebook and a pen out of her pocket and made a notation, then looked over at me. 'You're Tiffany Austin, aren't you?' At my nod she went on, 'I've heard you've had your share of trouble with Driscoll. How do you feel about him judging what people are touting as "your baby"?'

I smiled sweetly at her. I'd been down this road before, and I wasn't about to be baited. 'No comment.'

Charlotte chuckled. 'I can appreciate the diplomatic answer. After all, Driscoll does have a talent for turning people's words around to suit his purposes.'

I made a gesture toward the stage. In as firm a tone as I could muster, I said, 'I think we're done here, Ms Horn. If you'll excuse me, I have to get back out front.'

I turned to go, but Charlotte hurried forward and laid her hand on my arm. 'Just a moment more please,' she said. She glanced swiftly around and then in a low tone said, 'Driscoll's got a particular reason for being in Branson right now. I intend to find out just what that reason is.'

I started to say something and then stopped. I recalled the snatch of conversation I'd overheard earlier between Driscoll and Santangelo. Santangelo had said his recommendation had provided Driscoll with the perfect excuse to come to Branson. Charlotte Horn's accusation could be well founded. But what could his reason be?

Charlotte Horn noticed my hesitation and pounced on it. 'You know something,' she accused.

Somehow I thought it best to keep what I'd heard to myself,

at least for now. I shook my head. 'I really don't. I haven't seen
Bartholomew Driscoll since I gave his restaurant that bad review.
And I certainly haven't followed his career.'

Charlotte Horn nodded. 'I can understand that.'

I had to admit though, she'd piqued my curiosity. 'Why do
you think he really came to Branson?'

'I don't have all the details yet, but I believe it concerns a
woman.'

'I've been told he has quite a reputation as a ladies' man,' I
said. My thoughts drifted to Colleen Collins. 'Would this woman
be one of our contestants?'

Charlotte opened her mouth to answer, then paused and dipped
her hand into her jacket pocket and withdrew her cell phone. She
glanced at the screen, and her smooth forehead puckered in a
deep frown. 'Sorry,' she said. 'We'll have to finish this conversation another time.'

She turned and walked away, phone to her ear. I started to
leave as well when out of the corner of my eye I detected a
movement in the wings, not far from where we'd been standing.
I went and stood behind a nearby pillar and waited. After a
minute or two, Beth March emerged from the wings, a concerned
look on her face. Had she heard what Charlotte had told me?
And if so, would she spill it to Driscoll? Beth started to walk
quickly off in the same direction as Charlotte, and I debated
following them when I heard a shout behind me.

'Tiff! Good, you're still here.'

I turned just as Hilary rushed up to me. 'Mac wants to take
me to dinner tonight. To the Odyssey. I've been dying to go
there. It's supposed to be really good Greek food.'

'It is. I was there reviewing it last week. Try the moussaka.
It's to die for.'

'I will.' She tugged at my arm. 'The competition should be
starting now. Let's go cheer on Arleen.'

'Driscoll's not there,' I said. 'It can't start until all the judges
are in place.'

Hilary pulled a face. 'What are you talking about? Driscoll's
there.'

I followed Hilary's pointing finger. Sure enough, Driscoll was
back in his seat. And then I heard Troy's voice boom over the

microphone: 'OK, contestants! Your pizza baking time starts . . . now!'

'Contestants, you have less than twenty minutes left to finish your pies for the first round of judging.'

From our vantage point in the wings, Hilary and I had an excellent view of the stage and the contestants' entries. Hilary gave me a swift nudge in the ribs with her elbow. 'Look at Kurt Howell's pie. It looks like a work of art.'

I had to agree. The pie that Howell had pulled out of his oven looked like something that should be on the cover of a food magazine.

Hilary gave me another nudge, this one harder. 'Look at Arleen. She seems upset, doesn't she?'

I looked at Hilary's sister. She was looking inside the oven and frowning. She opened the oven, took out her pie and frowned at it.

'It doesn't look like it's cooked, does it?' whispered Hilary.

I shook my head. 'No, it doesn't. Maybe that's why she looks upset.'

Arleen abruptly left her station and walked around to the other side. She bent down and fiddled there for a few seconds, then raced back to her counter and began to swiftly assemble another pie.

'What is she doing?' Hilary cried. 'Making another pie? Does she have enough time?'

I watched as Arleen, who appeared to be cool as a cucumber, quickly rolled out her dough. She spread a generous amount of sauce on top and then grabbed a sharp-looking chef's knife from her counter and sliced tomatoes and vegetables in record time. She assembled her toppings, set them on her pie and slid it into the oven just as Troy Howard sang out, 'Thirteen minutes, contestants.'

I gave Hilary's arm a squeeze. 'A pizza normally takes between eight and twelve minutes to bake. Arleen's should just make it.'

Hilary frowned. 'OK, but why on earth did she have to do a second pie in the first place?'

'I'd like to know the answer to that myself.'

Thirteen minutes later the bell rang, signifying the end of the first round of the bake-off. Arleen had put her pizza in a warming bag and brought it up to the judging table with two minutes to spare. Kurt had placed his there a few minutes before. Bringing up the rear was Colleen Collins. She didn't look at all happy with her pizza, even though I had to admit it looked and smelled yummy. Troy Howard announced a half-hour intermission to allow the judges time to taste, and Hilary and I immediately made our way backstage. Arleen was waiting for us, a grim expression on her face.

Hilary didn't waste any time. 'What happened? Why did you make another pie?'

Arleen's eyes were flashing sparks. 'Because someone unplugged my oven, that's why. I thought something was wrong.' She huffed a blonde curl out of her eye. 'Thank God I walked around to check. It took a little elbow grease to get that plug back in, but . . . actually it might have been for the best. I think my second pie was better than the first.'

'I wonder how that plug came out,' Hilary mused. 'I thought they checked all the equipment before the contest began.'

'They do,' said Arleen. 'Someone waited until my stove was checked, then deliberately unplugged it.'

'No!' Hilary gasped. 'Who would do such a thing?'

'Oh, I know exactly who,' Arleen cried. She whirled around and pointed a finger at Colleen Collins. 'Her!'

FOUR

Colleen Collins's face reddened at Arleen's accusation. 'How dare you,' she cried. 'Are you accusing me of cheating?'

'If the shoe fits!' Arleen got right up in the other woman's face and said, 'Everyone knows you're the dark horse in this competition. You had to do something to get back in the game.'

Colleen's face reddened but she drew herself up straight. 'True, I'm the underdog, but I would never cheat, I assure you. What proof do you have that I did so?'

Arleen backed up a step and ran her hands down the sides of her printed apron. 'None . . . yet,' she grumbled.

'Of course there's none, because I wouldn't stoop that low,' hissed Colleen.

I held up my hand. 'OK, OK, everyone calm down.' I turned to Arleen. 'Arleen, you have no proof that Ms Collins sabotaged your oven, do you?'

'Well, no, but . . . someone did. If not her, then who?' Arleen wailed.

'It could just have been an accident,' Hilary said in a soothing tone. 'The plug in my bedroom fan comes loose sometimes. It happens.'

Arleen threw her sister a black look. 'That . . . plug . . . wasn't . . . loose,' she ground out. 'No one else's came loose, did they?'

I stepped in between the women. 'OK, we don't have enough here for a formal complaint to be filed, so I suggest we all just wait here quietly for the judging results before the second leg of the competition begins.'

'I want my oven triple-checked before the next installment,' hissed Arleen.

Colleen threw up her hands. 'Oh, what's the use?' Her dark eyes flashed as she added, 'I don't know what you're so upset about anyway. It wouldn't matter if your pie were raw. Not when you've got one of the judges in your hip pocket.'

Arleen's head reared up and her lips peeled back in a snarl.
'What did you say?'

'You heard me. I saw you with Driscoll earlier. You were
practically glued to his side, gazing adoringly at him. And he
was looking at you like he wanted to devour you for dessert.'

Arleen threw her shoulders back and tossed her blonde hair.
'Well, you obviously missed the part where he tried to convince
me to visit him in his hotel room after the contest and I threw
a bottle of water in his face. I sincerely doubt after that I have
Driscoll "in my pocket", as you put it.'

'Hah,' Colleen spat. 'That probably only intensified his feelings for you more. Driscoll always wants the unattainable, what
he can't have. It's more of a challenge to him that way.'

'Oh yeah?' Arleen got her face right in the other woman's.
'And just how do you know that, hmm? From personal
experience?'

Colleen's face reddened and she backed up a step. 'Why . . .
why you . . . of all the nerve!'

Arleen was relentless. 'Cat got your tongue, Colleen? Or
maybe it's you who have a judge in your hip pocket. You were
all nerves during the last bake-off. It's amazing you're even in
this competition.'

'Bartholomew wasn't even involved in this contest when I
made semi-finalist,' Colleen shot back. 'And I wasn't the only
one who was nervous. Doris Sharp and Arnie Peck were, too.'

'Ah-*ha!*' Arleen waved her finger under Colleen's nose.
'Bartholomew, huh?'

'Well, that's his name, isn't it?' said Colleen, a trifle too
defensively, I thought. As fascinating as this confrontation had
turned, I was just about to step in between them and intervene
when someone spoke behind us.

'Ladies? And I use that term loosely. What's going on here?'

Everyone turned, and the room grew still as Bartholomew
Driscoll stepped forward. You could have heard a pin drop in the
silence that followed his entrance. He stood there majestically,
staring down both Arleen and Colleen. Colleen looked away;
Arleen stood her ground, her head high, a defiant look on her
face.

Driscoll raised the water bottle he held in his hand and looked straight at Arleen. 'You'll pardon me if I don't let you get too close to this,' he said to her with a sneer. 'In your hands a water bottle is a dangerous weapon.' He raised the bottle to his lips, took a long drag before he continued. 'I could not help but overhear some of your conversation. My dear Ms Hanson, I did not proposition you in any way. You obviously misunderstood my intent.'

Arleen stared at him. 'Really? What part of "would you like to join me for a drink and whatever may follow in my hotel room" did I misunderstand?'

Driscoll clucked his tongue. 'Obviously we both have different interpretations of what might follow. I was anticipating a spirited discussion about cooking.'

Arleen rolled her eyes. 'Oh, *puh-leeze!*'

Driscoll waved his hand, as if Arleen were an annoying fly he wanted to get rid of and turned his attention to Colleen. 'As for you, Ms Collins, nerves obviously do not impair your cooking skills. I thought your pie was excellent.'

I noted that Colleen didn't look Driscoll directly in the eyes. 'Th-thank you,' she murmured.

'Don't mention it.' He patted his jacket pocket. 'I've already scored the entries, you see. And I judge them on their own merit, not on any . . . ah, entanglements I may have with their creators.'

Hilary frowned. 'The judging's over already?'

He turned toward her. In a smooth tone he answered, 'For me it is. The others are still tasting.'

I arched a brow. 'But *you're* done? In less than . . .' I glanced at my watch. 'Ten minutes? When we allotted forty?'

His lips curved in a sneer. 'Yes, Ms Austin. Unlike the others, I know what I want.' His gaze lingered on Arleen for a moment, and then he bowed his head. 'Now, if you'll excuse me. I'm feeling a bit light-headed. I'm going to find a quiet corner and sit down.'

With that, Driscoll tipped his hand and stalked off in the direction of the break room. Arleen stared after him and then turned to me, her eyes flashing. 'Of all the nerve. Did you hear him? He lied! Spirited discussion about cooking, my a—'

'Hey, Ar! Calm down.' Hilary threw her arms around her sister.

'You still have one more pie to bake. Don't let that jerk get you all upset.'

Arleen clenched her jaw. 'Someone needs to teach him a lesson he'll never forget,' she ground out.

Hilary squeezed her sister's arm. 'That's true, someone should, but not you, Ar. Let it go.'

Arleen let out a giant sigh. 'OK, OK. You're right . . . I guess.' She scrubbed her hand over her jaw. 'I must look a mess. I'm going to the ladies' room, freshen up.'

'OK,' said Hilary. 'Want me to come with?'

Arleen shook her head. 'No. I'll be OK.'

Arleen moved away, and Hilary let out a breath. She looked at me. 'Lots of drama, huh?'

I was eyeing Colleen Collins, who was over in the far corner, talking with Kurt Howell. I was reminded again of the earlier exchange between her and Driscoll, and of Charlotte Horn's assertion that Driscoll's 'mission' in Branson had to do with a woman. 'You have no idea,' I told my friend.

'Well, I'm worried about Arleen. I haven't seen her get this crazy, not since she lost the Miss Teen Georgia title. I think this contest means a little too much to her.'

'That, or maybe it's that ten-thousand-dollar payday,' I suggested.

Hilary snapped her fingers. 'You know, I bet that's it. I know she's got tuition bills and that part-time job as fashion consultant at Schuster's really doesn't pay all that great. I guess she's more desperate than I realized.'

'Maybe you should go after her,' I suggested. 'Try and get her to calm down. If she chokes during the second half, she won't stand a chance of beating Kurt.'

'I'm on it.'

Hilary hurried off and I saw that Kurt and Colleen Collins had left the area as well. More people were starting to filter backstage. I walked over to the curtain and peered out on to the main stage area. The tasting area was visible from my vantage point, and I saw Giovanni Ferrante and Anastasia Ricci, each with a pizza slice in their hands, having a lively conversation. *That's how the judging should be*, I thought. *Why does Driscoll have to be so damn antisocial?*

Off to the right of the tasting area, I saw two figures, swathed in shadow, also having a conversation. One moved, and in the dim light I recognized Charlotte Horn. I squinted at the other figure, but it was shrouded too deeply in shadow for me to tell if it were a male or a female. The two figures suddenly melted into the shadows, and I wondered where they might have gone off to. A stagehand walked past, and I reached out and touched his arm. I pointed to where the two judges were still standing and asked, 'Excuse me, but is there another exit out of that area?'

The stagehand nodded. 'Oh, yeah. There's a corridor off to the right that goes all the way back to the break room and kitchen.'

'Thanks.'

There was still a little time. Hilary and Arleen hadn't come back yet, so I turned in the direction of the break room. As I approached the kitchen, I paused. There were voices coming from that direction. Low, intense voices. Curious, I drew closer.

'You're making a huge mistake,' rasped one angry voice. I couldn't make it out, but the tone struck me as feminine sounding. More whispering, then another voice, quivering with rage: 'How dare you threaten me!'

I took a step backward. That voice I recognized. Driscoll! But who was he talking to? Charlotte Horn? Or someone else? I debated moving closer when I heard a loud voice call out, 'Tiffany? Where are you? Are you backstage?'

Immediately the voices in the kitchen silenced. I hurried swiftly back out to the stage area, trying to be as quiet as possible. As soon as I emerged, Hilary ran up to me. 'Arleen's not in the ladies' room,' she announced. 'I hope she didn't take off. She does that sometimes when she gets upset.'

'I'm sure she didn't,' I said reassuringly. My mind was going a million miles a minute. Had the feminine voice I heard arguing with Driscoll been Arleen's? I couldn't say for certain, so I didn't want to voice any concern to Hilary. 'Maybe she just went outside for a breath of fresh air,' I suggested. 'We still have time before the second half. Let's go look.'

We hurried over to the Exit door and outside. We walked around the building and checked the parking lot. Arleen's convertible was still in its place under the shady elm. There was no sign of her, or anyone else for that matter, anywhere in the area.

'I can't understand it,' Hilary grumbled as we made our way back. 'Where could she have gone off to?'

Dale came over to us, and Hilary pounced on him. 'Have you seen my sister? She's missing!'

Dale gave Hilary a puzzled look. 'No she's not. She's onstage. See.'

Dale parted the curtain. Sure enough, Arleen was behind her station, tying her apron. I frowned as I looked at her. Something about her seemed different, but I couldn't put my finger on it.

Hilary put her hand to her breast. 'Thank God,' she murmured. 'She looks pretty calm, too, all things considered.'

I glanced at the other two contestants. Kurt Howell appeared unruffled as he pulled his pizza dough out, but Colleen Collins was grasping the edge of her counter. She seemed a bit short of breath, and I sincerely hoped she wasn't having a panic attack.

Dale's voice cut into my thoughts. 'Has either of you seen Driscoll?' he asked.

'Not recently,' I answered. 'Why?'

Dale pulled a face. 'Mr Wonderful hasn't turned in his scores from the first half, and we need them before the second half can start.' He tapped at his watch. 'Plus, now we're running late and the school needs the auditorium for voting at four, which means we've got to be out by three in order for them to set up.'

'Well, he did say he felt light-headed. He was going to find a quiet spot and sit down, so he's probably somewhere backstage.'

Dale shot me a hopeful look. 'I know he's not your favorite person, but would you help me look for him?'

I opened my mouth to tell Dale that I thought I'd heard Driscoll back in the kitchen, but his cell buzzed. Dale whipped it out of his pocket, mumbled, 'Really? Now?' He held the phone away and looked over at me. 'Thanks, Tiff,' he said. 'I'll join you as soon as I put out this fire.' Without waiting for me to answer he hurried off, phone back to his ear. I squared my shoulders. So, it was up to me to light a fire under Driscoll, huh? Swell. I hoped by now he'd concluded his conversation with his mysterious companion. If not, and I interrupted, I'd most likely get my head handed to me. I glanced out at the judge's area again. It was empty. Apparently both Anastasia and Ferrante had finished with the judging and decided to take a break too. I sighed. I'd better check out the kitchen area before more people started disappearing.

I walked swiftly up the short flight of steps to the kitchen. This time when I approached, the door was closed. I hesitated, then raised my fist and rapped sharply. 'Hello. Anyone in there?'

Silence.

I rapped again, louder this time. 'Hello, Mr Driscoll? Dale wanted me to tell you that we need your scores. You're holding up the second half of the competition. Mr Driscoll?'

Something made me glance down at the floor. Something was caught on the side of the door. I bent down and picked it up. It was a tiny sliver of fabric, a blue, white and purple print. It looked vaguely familiar, but I couldn't place where I'd seen it. I slid the fragment into my pocket and knocked on the door again.

Still no answer.

I twisted the knob. The door opened a few inches, then stopped, as if something were blocking it. I frowned, and pushed harder. 'Anyone in here?' I called. I poked my nose in through the narrow opening, trying to peer around the edge of the door.

The first thing I saw was a black-pants-clad leg, turned sideways beside the round table. I drew a quick breath, took a step back, then flung my full body weight against the door. The door creaked back another foot, enough for me to enter. I eased myself awkwardly into the room, and saw someone had taken the footstool and wedged it against the door. I pushed it aside and made my way towards the leg. My first thought was that Driscoll might have fainted. He'd complained earlier about feeling light-headed. As I drew nearer though, I saw that wasn't the case. I put my hand to my mouth and bit down hard to keep from screaming.

Bartholomew Driscoll lay sprawled across the floor, a chef's knife sticking awkwardly out of the base of his throat. A small pool of dark red had formed around his head. An empty water bottle lay at his feet.

For a minute I just stood, rooted to the spot, staring at the grisly scene before me. Then my feet took me forward, like a somnambulist caught in a dream, overcome by the shock of my discovery. I moved closer to Bartholomew Driscoll and peered down.

In death, Driscoll's eyes weren't wide, but narrowed into slits, glassy like hardened marbles. They were sightless, and I knew he was beyond help, but I touched my fingers to the side of his neck, taking care not to touch the knife, or the blood around the wound. Nothing. I rose and looked down at him. His lips were twisted in a grimace. Shock? Surprise? My gaze strayed to the black handle sticking out of his throat. His assailant had jammed it in pretty deep, but a bit of blade protruded, and there appeared to be symbols – Japanese, perhaps – etched on it. I started to lean down for a closer look when I heard a familiar voice shout, 'Tiffany? Are you back here?'

'I'm in the break room, Dale,' I called back, rising. 'I found Driscoll.'

A moment later Dale stuck his head through the opening. 'You found Driscoll?' he asked. 'Where . . .' His voice trailed off as his eyes settled on the pants leg. 'Oh God,' he moaned. 'Please tell me that isn't what I think it is.'

'Sorry. I wish I could.' And then I did what I knew had to be done. I pulled my cell phone out of my pocket and punched in 911. When the operator answered I said, 'Hello, my name is Tiffany Austin. I need to report a homicide.'

FIVE

Within minutes of my 911 call, two uniformed officers arrived at the high school's back entrance. One waited with Dale and myself in the narrow hallway, while the other pushed through into the kitchen where Driscoll lay. He almost immediately came out again, his cell phone at his ear. He spoke softly into it, listened for a few seconds, then shut it and turned to the other officer. 'Homicide's on its way,' he said. He made a quick motion with his hand. 'We have to see about securing this area. We'll also need a list of people who were allowed back here.'

Dale stepped forward. 'What about the contest?' he asked.

The officer, whose name-tag read Officer Riley, gave Dale a blank stare. 'Contest?'

Dale made an impatient gesture with his hand. 'Yes, that's why we asked you to come to the rear entrance. We're holding the final bake-off in the Bon-Appetempting Pizza Challenge today. We were just getting ready to start the second half. We were waiting for Driscoll . . .' Dale stopped speaking and looked expectantly at the officer.

Riley let out a snort. 'Well, I think you can stop waiting,' he said. He jerked his thumb in the direction of the kitchen. 'If that guy's Driscoll, he's not going to be judging anything.'

Dale glanced at his watch. 'What should I tell people? They'll want to know why the contest isn't starting. And we need to be out of here soon. School board elections are being held tonight.'

Riley frowned. 'That might have to be postponed.' He shot Dale a stern look. 'No one tells anyone anything, and no one leaves the premises until Homicide gets here. Got it?' he barked.

I cleared my throat. Riley looked over at me. His chilly gaze swept me up and down. 'Yes?'

I gave him a disarming smile. 'Pardon me, Officer Riley, is it? I'm Tiffany Austin. I, ah, was just wondering if you knew which Homicide detective is on call today?'

Riley looked at me like I had six arms and three heads. 'No, I'm sorry, Miss Austin,' he said at last. 'Homicide doesn't always inform me of their detectives' schedules. An oversight, I'm sure. The department's been rather shorthanded lately, so there really aren't too many choices. I do hope whichever one they send meets with your approval.'

What I really wanted to do was slap the smirk off his face, but instead I backed up a step, smile still plastered across my face. 'I was just curious,' I murmured. I paused and then added, 'Sorry to bother you.'

Riley grunted and shook his head as he moved away. I saw Dale look at me curiously and I averted my gaze, not wanting to get into a big explanation over just why I was concerned over who might be conducting our interviews. Chances were good I didn't have anything to worry about – after all, what were the odds? Then again, my luck had been pretty lousy lately.

In a sudden burst of sound and movement, new arrivals appeared on the scene. A horde (actually there were four, but it seemed like many more) men and women in overalls barreled through, clutching rolls of yellow crime-scene tape. Two EMTs, emergency medical technicians, a man and a woman – wearing short-sleeved green uniforms and carrying bright green backpacks loaded with equipment – came through next. They were closely followed by two other men, one of whom I recognized: Howard Sample, a former beau of Hilary's and the assistant county coroner. No sooner had they disappeared into the kitchen area than all the hairs on the back of my neck and my arms suddenly started to tingle. A moment later I heard a rough male voice behind me say, 'Well, well. Tiffany Austin.'

Oh God, I thought. Great. More proof of my lousy luck. My worst nightmare was standing behind me.

I can't explain exactly why Detective Philip Bartell makes me feel like an adolescent, star-struck schoolgirl. Maybe it's the dark brown, almost black hair that falls across his forehead in a most appealing way, making me want to run my fingers through it; it could be his strong jaw with just the teeniest of clefts in it; or it could be his eyes, which are piercing and the color of a storm-tossed sea. We have an odd relationship, Bartell and I – in fact, I'd be hard pressed to call what we had a relationship of any sort. We'd met a few weeks ago, when I'd been the top suspect in a murder investigation, and the sparks that had flown between us had been undeniable, although that was what we'd both tried to do – at first. But after an impromptu kiss in a parking garage, both of us were forced to admit there was something between us, although what it was, we weren't exactly sure. Bartell had said he wanted to try and find out, so I'd bitten the bullet and invited him to a party my parents were throwing in my honor. Unfortunately, about an hour after we'd arrived, he'd got a call and had to leave. I hadn't heard a peep from him since, making me think he might have been having second thoughts about getting involved with *moi*.

And now here we were, standing about ten feet away from each other at, of all places, a crime scene.

I turned to face him. 'Detective Bartell,' I said coolly. 'We have to stop meeting like this.'

'That we do.' To my surprise, his perfectly shaped lips curved upward in a smile. 'You do seem to be a bit of a murder magnet, don't you?'

I grimaced. 'I assure you, it's not on purpose.'

His lips thinned a bit and he looked from me to Dale, who stood awkwardly a few feet away. 'So,' Bartell barked, 'who found the body?'

Dale jerked his thumb in my direction. 'Tiffany did. Driscoll was late turning in his scores. He'd gone off somewhere, and Tiffany and I were looking for him.'

Bartell frowned at Dale. 'Turning in his scores?'

The question was directed to Dale, but I answered. 'Yes. He was a last-minute substitute judge for the Bon-Appetempting Pizza Bake-Off. He had to score the pizzas in the first half, and apparently hadn't turned in his scorecard.'

'Ah, yes. The pizza contest. That was today, wasn't it?' Bartell rubbed absently at his forehead, then fastened his laser-sharp gaze on me. 'Go on. Swenson asked for your help in finding Driscoll.'

I shifted my weight from one foot to the other. 'I'd heard him in the kitchen earlier, so I decided to start there. I couldn't open the door at first. There was a stool pushed up against it, but I managed to get it open enough to squeeze through.' I shut my eyes. 'Then I saw Driscoll, lying next to the table. There was a chef's knife sticking out of the base of his throat. I saw symbols etched on the blade when I checked for a pulse, just in case, but . . .' I gave a small shudder and then added, 'Don't worry. I was careful not to touch the murder weapon.'

Bartell had removed a small notebook and pen from his jacket pocket while I was speaking. Now he flipped to a blank page, held the pen poised over it. 'You said you saw symbols on the knife?'

'Yes, a lot of the more expensive chefs' knives have them . . .' I paused. 'Most good home cooks have knives like that – Cangshan, Shun – brands like that.'

'Hm. So I suppose we can rule out someone grabbing an ordinary knife from the pantry, then.'

'I greatly doubt that old kitchen would house a knife like that one,' I said. 'A good chef's knife can cost several hundred dollars.'

'Well, as a former chef you would know.' He riffled a few pages in his notebook, jotted something down. He looked at me again. 'You said you heard Driscoll in the kitchen?'

'Yes, a bit earlier. Someone else was with him. They were speaking in very low tones, so I couldn't identify the other person. I got the impression that it was a female, though.'

'I see. And what gave you that impression?'

I frowned. 'I'm not sure. Something about the timbre of the voice. But I couldn't say for certain. *It might* have been a man – but I don't think so.'

'OK.' Bartell scribbled something down. 'So you didn't hear what they were talking about?'

'I managed to catch a few snippets. The person with Driscoll said, "you're making a big mistake", and then there was some more whispering and I distinctly heard Driscoll say, "How dare you threaten me". He sounded very angry, too.'

'From what I know of Driscoll, I'd say that was par for the course.' His gaze bored into mine again. 'Did you notice anything else unusual?'

OMG, where did I begin with that question? I was debating just where to start when a loud voice behind me boomed out, 'Ah, Detective Bartell. Here you are.'

Did I imagine it, or was there a flicker of annoyance in Bartell's stormy gray eyes as he turned to the newcomer. 'Yes, Hoffman. What is it?'

I took a second to study the new arrival. He wasn't as tall as Bartell by any stretch of the imagination – I'd place him as somewhere in the five foot eight, five nine range tops. His muscular build, though, told me that he doubtless spent a great deal of time at the gym. The tan blazer and matching chinos he wore seemed to be molded to his frame. I'm no pro when it comes to guessing ages, but I put his at somewhere in his mid-to-late twenties. He was what I'd call nice-looking, in a Tom Cruise-ish sort of way – he had a young face, bright blue eyes, a prominent nose and, as he flashed a quick smile, a nice set of teeth. He jerked his thumb in the direction of the stage. 'The crowd outside is getting a bit restless. Do you want me to start getting statements?'

'Hm, addresses and phone numbers should be sufficient. I'd like to keep what happened back here as quiet as possible.' Bartell turned and addressed me. 'Do you have a list of who was author-ized to be backstage?'

'I don't have a written one, but off the top of my head I'd say the staff of *Southern Style*, the judges and contestants, of course. And the high-school maintenance crew as well. I'm sure Principal Jacoby could get you a list . . .' I paused. 'There were several people back here who weren't authorized, and they all spoke with Driscoll.'

Bartell's eyebrow rose. 'Got names?'

'Yes. Driscoll's assistant, Beth March, came backstage a few times. His brother, Peter Hagen, too. Oh, and I caught a reporter lurking about. Charlotte Horn.'

Bartell scribbled something down and then turned to Hoffman. 'Tell Riley and Quinn to station themselves at the exit. Tell them to take people's names, addresses and phone numbers as they leave. If we need their statements, we'll call 'em. We've got to start clearing this place out and get the crime scene secured as quickly as possible.'

'Sure, Detective.'

Hoffman hurried off to find Riley and Quinn, and Bartell looked past me and caught Dale's eye. He motioned for my boss to come forward and once he did Bartell said, 'An announcement needs to be made. I could do it, but then the press will really start sniffing around here, and I'd like to delay that as long as possible.'

'Of course,' Dale said. 'What would you like me to say?'

'Something generic like, "We're sorry folks, but due to unforeseen circumstances we're going to have to postpone the rest of the contest" should suffice – I hope.'

Dale gritted his teeth. 'Sure. I'll do it right now.'

'Dale! Tiffany! There you are!'

We all turned as Giovanni Ferrante strode up to us, his ruddy face creased in an anxious expression. He looked from Dale to me and back to Dale. 'Is everything all right back here? Have you found that swine Driscoll yet? He's holding everything up, and that school principal is pacing back and forth like a nervous Chihuahua.' He paused and stiffened as two uniformed officers walked past him. 'What's going on? Why are the police here? Has something happened?'

'It's all right, Giovanni,' said Dale, taking the man's arm. 'I'm afraid we're going to have to postpone the second half of the contest though.'

'*Madre di Dio!*' The big man wrung his hands in front of him. He caught sight of Bartell standing just behind Dale and his eyes widened. In a whisper he said, 'Something has happened! To Driscoll?'

I touched Ferrante's arm. 'It's nothing you can help with, Chef John. You should go back outside.'

Ferrante motioned toward Bartell. 'I know Detective Bartell. He is a good customer of my Slice of Heaven.' Ferrante paused and then added dramatically, 'Driscoll is dead, no?'

Dale and I exchanged a glance and I laid my hand on the chef's arm. 'Why would you think something happened to Driscoll?' I asked.

Ferrante shrugged off my arm, wiped at his brow. 'It is only logical – no one has seen him for awhile, and he's not exactly the most popular person.'

Bartell stepped forward and paused in front of the chef. 'Hello, Giovanni,' he said. 'Yes, you're right. Driscoll is dead.'

Both Ferrante's eyebrows shot upward. 'Oh, no. What . . . how did it happen?'

Bartell shook his head. 'We're not sharing details at this time.'

Ferrante, however, was obviously not ready to drop the matter. He looked Bartell square in the eye. 'I am not stupid, Detective. You are a homicide detective, no? Then for you to be here, it must be . . . murder.' When Bartell didn't answer, Ferrante shook his head. 'I can't say I'm surprised. The man had many enemies. It was only a matter of time.'

'Driscoll had many enemies, you say?' Bartell's sharp gaze raked Ferrante up and down. 'Would you happen to know if any of them are here today?'

Before Ferrante could reply, Howard Sample approached Bartell. 'I've finished my preliminary investigation,' he said. 'I can tell you that . . .'

Bartell held up his hand. 'Hold that thought, Howard. We'll have that discussion back there, at the crime scene.' He turned to Ferrante. 'I'd appreciate it if you'd stick around, Mr Ferrante. I may have some more questions for you.'

Ferrante made a little bow. 'Of course. Anything for the *polizia.*'

Bartell and Sample moved off. Ferrante pulled a handkerchief out of his jacket pocket and wiped at his brow with it. He seemed nervous, and I couldn't help but recall the remark Anastasia had made earlier, about Ferrante staying calm after what Driscoll had tried to do to him. I also recalled Ferrante's answer, that whatever had transpired between them had nothing to do with Driscoll's bad review of his restaurant. What, then? And was it serious enough to kill over? Ferrante didn't seem the murderous type, but I knew that – when pushed – anyone could be capable of the deed.

Hilary came rushing through the side curtain, Arleen right behind her. My friend raced right over to me. 'What's happening?' she demanded. 'Dale just came out and said that the remainder of the contest is postponed until further notice, and we were all to leave our names and addresses with the men stationed at the exit.'

'Did Driscoll back out of the judging again?' Arleen asked, her tone flat. 'Is that the reason the contest is postponed?'

I shook my head. 'Not exactly.'

Hilary glanced around, seeming for the first time to notice the police officers milling around. She reached out and grabbed my arm. 'Oh, no. The police are here. Does that mean . . .?'

I nodded and pulled both of them into a far corner. 'This isn't for sharing, but Driscoll's dead. Someone killed him.'

Hilary gasped, and Arleen's face went white. She clapped her hand over her mouth. 'Driscoll's dead?' she gurgled. 'Oh my God! I just . . . oh my God.'

I turned to Arleen. 'I know it's a shock, but please, please, keep this under your hat for now, at least until after Bartell makes some sort of statement,' I urged. 'He specifically said that he doesn't want to make Driscoll's demise public yet.'

Hilary's shocked expression changed to one of interest. 'Bartell? Your Bartell? He's here?'

I shot my friend a sharp look. 'He's not *my* Bartell,' I hissed. 'But yes, he's here.'

Arleen sagged against the wall. 'I think I'm gonna be sick,' she moaned.

'Bend down, Ar, and put your head between your knees,' Hilary instructed. As Arleen doubled over, Hilary turned back to me. 'So, what happened when he saw you? Did he say anything about why he hasn't called?'

I stared at my friend in disbelief. 'Hilary, have you lost your mind? This is a crime scene, for pity's sake. He's not going to say anything like that.'

'I know that, but even you have to admit sparks fly whenever the two of you are together. I just thought, you know, that maybe some of those sparks might have ignited when he saw you here.'

'The only thing that got ignited was Bartell's annoyance,' I responded. 'He didn't look at all happy to find me at his crime scene.'

'Well, sure, because he remembers the last time.'

I arched a brow. 'The last time? You mean when I was his number one suspect?'

'No, silly. When you practically solved the case for him. Bartell's a macho man. Maybe he's afraid you'll upstage him again.'

'I greatly doubt that.'

I glanced over at Arleen, still doubled over in the corner. Her face was white as a sheet, and it suddenly occurred to me that *she* didn't have an alibi for the time of death. I frowned. She didn't have a motive, though . . . or did she? Driscoll had come on to her earlier – had he tried it again? And had Arleen lost her cool? Or could it possibly be . . .

'Another woman,' I murmured.

Hilary looked at me. 'What?'

I took my friend's arm and pulled her into a corner. 'That reporter, Charlotte Horn, said she thought Driscoll might be here in Branson because of a woman. I heard him in the kitchen, shortly before he was killed. He was with someone, and even though I couldn't make out the voice, it sounded feminine.'

Hilary's eyes bugged. 'So you think maybe this mystery woman was here today, and she killed him?'

'It's a possibility. I did hear him on the phone a few times, and each time it sounded as if either he were threatening someone, or they were threatening him.' I sighed. 'I'm going to have to tell Bartell this, and I guess the sooner the better.'

I started off in the direction of the kitchen, but I hadn't gotten very far when Dale appeared. He hurried over to me. 'I just talked to Enzo Manchetti. He's not exactly thrilled by the development.'

I swallowed. Enzo Manchetti was the chairman of the board of *Southern Style*. A few weeks ago, I'd helped clear his son from murder charges, and I firmly believed that had weighed a lot in the decision to proceed with the pizza contest. Manchetti, however, was a bit of a straight arrow. I could just imagine how he'd reacted to the news one of the judges had been murdered. 'I bet he wasn't.'

Dale shook his head. 'He's concerned that the publicity surrounding Driscoll's death will affect the contest. He thinks we should try to schedule the second half as soon as possible.'

'I'm for that,' I said. 'I can check with Ferrante and Anastasia, see what their schedules are like. But we'll still need another judge.'

'If we can find one,' Dale said gloomily. 'No one might want to participate now. They might think the contest is jinxed.'

'Jinxed! Don't be silly. Why would anyone think that?'

Dale shrugged. 'It's an angle the press could play up. I wouldn't put anything past them, once they get wind of this. Some of 'em tried to corral me, but I think I stonewalled them pretty good – for now, anyway.' He scratched at his head. 'It won't be long, though, before one of 'em notices the coroner's wagon parked out back, and then all bets are off.'

'Coroner's wagon?'

We turned. Beth March stood there, a shocked expression on her thin, pale face. 'Coroner's wagon?' she repeated. 'What is that doing here?' She looked around frantically. 'Where is Mr Driscoll? I haven't seen him for a while, and he hasn't answered any of my texts. Oh, God . . . don't tell me . . .'

Beth March let out a long, agonized wail. Then she toppled over in a dead faint.

SIX

For a second we just stared, stunned. Then Dale sprang into action, grabbing Beth before her body hit the hardwood floor. He gathered her into his arms and tossed me a helpless look.

'What do we do?' he asked. 'She's out cold.'

I'd taken a first-aid class recently, and I struggled to remember what the instructor had said about fainting victims. 'She should be laid flat on her back,' I said, as Dale started to lower Beth into a nearby folding chair. 'And her legs should be elevated, to restore blood flow to the brain.'

Dale laid Beth gently on the hardwood floor. I took off my cardigan, rolled it into a ball, and thrust it underneath her legs. 'Not great, but it'll have to do,' I said. I tapped at my temple, trying to remember what else the instructor had said. *Loosen tight clothing*, but the simple dress Beth had on definitely wasn't tight – if anything the girl could have taken a size smaller. 'We've got to try and revive her.'

'I think the EMTs are still back in the kitchen with Driscoll's body,' said Dale. 'I'll go look.'

Dale hurried off and I turned my attention back to Beth, who still hadn't stirred. I bent over her. She was breathing, but it seemed to be labored. I racked my brain, trying to remember what the instructor had taught us. I gripped both Beth's shoulders and gave her a vigorous shake.

'Beth,' I said loudly. 'Wake up. Wake up.'

'Uh . . . uhhhh.'

Beth moaned and started to cough. I breathed a sigh of relief, thankful that I didn't have to perform mouth-to-mouth. I helped her to a sitting position. She turned her head, looked at me blankly. 'Wh-what happened?'

'You fainted,' I said. 'You were telling us that Mr Driscoll hadn't returned any of your texts.'

Beth put a hand to her forehead. 'Oh, yes. I remember now.'

Her eyes widened. 'Mr Swenson said something about a coroner's wagon?'

'Yes.' I slid my arm around her shoulders. No sense beating around the bush. Better she found out the sad news sooner instead of later. 'I'm afraid Mr Driscoll is dead.'

'Ooh.' A moan escaped her lips. She made a fist, brought it to her mouth, and bit down on it. She stayed that way for a few seconds, then lowered her hand and looked me straight in the eyes. 'I'm all right now,' she said in a voice that sounded eerily calm. 'Can you tell me what happened?'

Before I could answer, we heard the sound of scuffling feet and then Dale appeared, followed closely by the female EMT. Right behind the EMT was Bartell. The EMT gently pushed me aside and reached inside her backpack. She drew out a portable blood-pressure machine and strapped it to Beth's wrist.

'You really don't have to do that,' Beth murmured. 'I'm fine.'

The EMT, whose nameplate read MAGGIE, cocked her head and bestowed a chilly glance upon her. 'I'll be the judge of that, ma'am. Just extend your arm and be quiet, please.'

Beth didn't look happy, but she did as she was told. I moved back to give them some space and bumped right into Bartell. 'Excuse me,' I murmured.

Bartell was watching Beth and the EMT. 'Swenson said that's Driscoll's assistant.'

I nodded. 'Yes. Beth March. She was upset because Driscoll hadn't returned her texts, and she overheard Dale mention the coroner's wagon. I guess she jumped to a conclusion.'

'An accurate one, too.' Bartell regarded the girl through narrowed eyes then looked at me. 'You met her?'

'Earlier, yes.'

'Seems odd she'd faint like that over an employer. Did they seem to be particularly close?'

'I got that impression,' I admitted. 'She almost called Driscoll by his first name – twice.'

'Hm. Interesting.' He looked at me. 'Do you think it's possible this Beth March could be the woman you heard arguing earlier with Driscoll?'

'It's possible, but offhand I'd say no. Why do you ask?'

'No particular reason. I just thought, perhaps, if there was a bit of hanky-panky going on between them, they could have had a lovers' quarrel.'

I raised an eyebrow. 'So what? You think they fought over something and she up and stabbed him with a knife?'

Bartell's smile was enigmatic. 'I've seen it happen before, believe me. Over very petty things too. There's a lot to that old adage, a woman scorned.'

'Well, I greatly doubt that's the case here. Of course I can't say for sure there wasn't anything romantic between them, but I got the sense it might be more like Driscoll had taken her under his wing, as a sort of protégée.'

Bartell frowned. 'You mean like a Svengali/Trilby sort of thing?'

'Not as intense, but maybe along those lines.'

Maggie had removed the blood-pressure machine from Beth's wrist. She reached into her backpack, pulled out a packet and handed it to Beth. Beth shook her head. Maggie replaced the packet in her backpack, said something else to Beth, then got up and strode over to us. 'She seems fine,' she told Bartell. 'Blood pressure was a bit low, but nothing to worry about. I offered her a sedative to calm her nerves, but she said she has a prescription she can take. She should be just fine.'

Bartell flashed his teeth in a smile. 'Thanks, Maggie.'

Maggie returned Bartell's smile, then left. I gave Bartell a sharp look. 'I hope you're not going to question her right now,' I said. 'Give her a break. She's obviously just been traumatized, and—'

Bartell waved his hand, effectively cutting off the rest of my sentence. 'Give me some credit please, Tiffany. I have no intention of questioning her now. I am, however, going to give her my card and request that she come down to the station to give a statement after she pulls herself together.'

'Along with an admonition not to leave town, right?'

'That's SOP in cases like this.'

I eyed him. 'Yes, I remember,' I said.

He returned my gaze. 'So do I,' he said softly. I felt heat sear my cheeks and we locked gazes for a full minute until I managed to look away. Bartell hesitated, and for a moment I thought he was going to say something more, but then he walked past me and over to Beth. He bent down, said a few words, then pressed his card into her hand. He straightened and walked back toward the kitchen without giving me so much as a backward glance. I took a few deep, calming breaths and then went over to Beth. 'How are you feeling?' I asked.

'Better, I guess.' She twisted Bartell's card in her fingers. 'It's just so . . . it's such a shock. Although I guess it really shouldn't be.'

I stared at her. 'Why would you say that?'

Beth cleared her throat. 'You'll think it's silly, but . . . I had my cards read the other night. They hinted at an impending disaster for a male close to me.' She sighed. 'This sure qualifies.'

'True, but I don't believe in fortune telling.'

'Neither did Mr Driscoll. He laughed when I told him. I was afraid maybe it might be a traffic accident, a fender bender, so I suggested that maybe he shouldn't drive. He poo-poohed my fears.' Her eyes took on a faraway look. 'He sure loved to drive his Mercedes.'

'A Mercedes, eh?' It figured Driscoll would own a high-end luxury car. 'So he drove to Branson?'

'He was planning a brief motor vacation when he got the call to judge the contest, so he decided to just make a small detour to Branson. He wanted me at the contest with him, so I arranged my own transportation here so as not to interfere with his plans.'

'A brief vacation, huh? Any idea where he planned on going?'

She shook her head. 'No. He didn't confide those details to me.'

'How about today? Did you ride here with him?'

Beth gave her head an emphatic shake. 'No. I took a cab here from the hotel. Mr Driscoll came here by himself. He said that he had to meet someone later on, it was better if we came separately.'

'I see.' I patted the girl's arm. 'I'll let you rest a bit, Beth. You've had quite a shock.'

'Thanks Tiffany. I-I guess I'll go back to the hotel and take a nap before I call Detective Bartell.'

'That's a good idea.' I paused. 'Would you like me to go with you, help you get settled?'

She shook her head. 'Thanks for the offer, but I'll be OK.'

I nodded and started to turn away, then looked back at her. 'I'm just curious. What model Mercedes did Mr Driscoll drive?'

'An S-65 coupé.'

Hm, I recognized the model. It was top of the line, and the sticker price was usually upwards of $225,000. It was exactly the type of car I'd figured Driscoll would own. I was also figuring that there probably weren't more than one of them in the parking lot. Chances were slim that the car might be unlocked, but then again, one never knew. I wasn't exactly sure what I hoped to find, anyway. Driscoll was sly . . . it was doubtful he would have left any clues as to his mysterious business in Branson in his car, if indeed he'd come here with an ulterior motive. Still, it was worth a look.

I walked casually out the back door and down the short flight of steps that led to the parking lot where Hilary and I had searched for Arleen earlier. The lot was still packed, no one had started to leave yet. I'd walked halfway across before I finally saw a Mercedes, parked on the far side of the lot underneath a giant elm. I made my way towards the car, glancing around to make sure no one was paying any particular attention to me. It was a beautiful model, a sleek navy metallic color. I laid my hand on the hood, wondering for a brief second just what it might feel like to own and drive such a luxurious car. I walked over to the door, reached for the handle, and stopped as I heard a footfall behind me.

'Just what do you think you're doing?' demanded an angry voice.

SEVEN

I whirled around, and my heart skipped a beat as I found myself staring at Peter Hagen. Close up, the family resemblance was even more evident. Peter, although shorter and heavier, had the same piercing eyes, the same determined chin, the same beak-shaped nose as Driscoll. It seemed he also had the same charming personality. Peter Hagen took a step closer to me and said in a menacing tone, 'I asked you what you thought you were doing?'

I recovered and shot Peter Hagen a wide smile. 'You must be Peter Hagen, Mr Driscoll's brother. I'm Tiffany Austin.' I held out my hand and held my breath.

Peter Hagen's eyebrows rose, and then his manner did an abrupt about-face. '*The* Tiffany Austin? Really?' He took my proffered hand and shook it. 'Well, well, I can't tell you what a pleasure it is to meet *you*.' He gave me a wide smile. 'I remember reading that review you did of Ambrosia and thinking, "Finally, someone has the guts to put Bart in his place and tell it like it ". He sure didn't like being the one on the bad end of a review, can tell you that.'

'I called it as I saw it that night. I'm afraid your brother held against me, though.'

'I wouldn't worry about that, Ms Austin. You're not alone in department, trust me. If I had a nickel for all the people Bart aged to alienate, I could retire early. Maybe I could even rd a Mercedes – a lower-priced model, of course.'

He released my hand. The man had quite a grip and I flexed fingers for the second time that afternoon as I studied his ce. Had he heard the news yet, I wondered. If he hadn't, and spilled the beans, I had an idea Bartell would be more than a little annoyed at me. I looked at Peter Hagen and said, 'So, I imagine you're either here to support your brother, or else you like amateur cook-offs.'

Hagen laughed. 'Well, I can't say I'm here to support Bart,

but I do enjoy cooking myself as a hobby. And I like pizza.' He shook his head. 'That in itself is enough to get me banned from Bart's home, I assure you. Why he agreed to judge this contest is beyond me – no offense.'

'None taken,' I assured him. 'I was surprised myself, to tell you the truth. I didn't think judging a pizza contest was his cup of tea.'

'It's not, believe me.' He cast an eye toward the coupé. 'You didn't answer my question. Why were you trying to break into his car?'

I let my jaw drop and my eyes widen. My lips formed a perfect O of surprise. I pointed at the vehicle. 'This is Driscoll's car?' At Hagen's nod, I took a step backward. 'Oh, gosh. I had no idea. And I wasn't trying to break in. I was just . . . admiring it.'

Peter shot me a somewhat skeptical look. 'Admiring it, eh? Indulging in a bit of dreaming?'

'Frankly, yes. Someone told me there was a Mercedes in the parking lot and I thought I'd run out here and just have a look at it.' I lowered my voice to a confidential whisper. 'It's always been a dream of mine to own one.'

Peter nodded. 'I can relate. It's one of mine too.' He reached out and ran his hand along the hood. 'It's a sure bet, though, that I'd never be able to afford a car like this. Not on a professor's salary, anyway. I guess you have to be a big food critic slash television star to be able to have one of these babies.'

It was impossible not to notice the bitterness in his tone. 'I couldn't afford it on my salary either,' I agreed. 'It looks like your brother kept the car in good shape.'

'Oh, yes, Bart's real good with his toys. When we were kids, my train set was always breaking down. Bart's ran like clockwork, and every piece looked brand new, no matter how old it was.' Peter moved over and peered inside the driver's side window, then motioned to me. 'Have a look.'

He didn't need to ask me twice. I stepped up beside him and peered inside. The interior of the car was beautiful. The black leather bucket seats looked soft and supple, and the car, as far as I could tell, was spotless. There wasn't a speck of dust or a crumb anywhere I could see. There wasn't anything else, either. Nothing in the side compartment, nothing on the backseat or on the floors, except some very expensive-looking floor mats. In truth, the car looked as if Driscoll had just driven it out of the showroom.

So, no clues here to his mysterious mission. Driscoll apparently wasn't a believer of keeping his life in his car like other people I knew; myself, for instance. Files, totes, umbrellas and the like usually littered my backseat.

'Some nice car, huh? It's last year's model, but it looks brand new.' He sighed. 'I wonder if I could talk the old boy into leaving it to me in his will.'

My head jerked up. 'Wh-what makes you say a thing like that?'

He waved his hand. 'Oh, I'm just joking. Bart's in perfect health.' He paused and then added, 'Technically we're stepbrothers. We have the same mother, but different fathers. His lived to be ninety-five. Mine died of a heart attack at fifty-three. Our mother is still alive though. She's eighty-seven and in a nursing home. Has trouble walking, but she's got all her faculties. I keep in touch with her. I don't think she's heard from Bart in years.' He bent down to examine the toe of his shoe, then straightened. 'Unfortunately, my brother will be around for many years to come, reveling in his ill-gotten gains.'

'Ill-gotten gains?'

He waved his hand. 'Just a figure of speech. Make no mistake, Ms Austin, we have our share of disagreements. Why, every time we see each other, we're arguing over something. But I'd never wish him any harm.' He paused and then added softly, 'In spite of everything he's done to me, he's still blood.'

He sounded sincere, and yet I couldn't get the argument I'd overheard out of my mind. 'Everything he's done to you?' I asked. 'It sounds more serious than just brotherly pranks.'

'I suppose you could say that,' Hagen remarked. 'My brother has a vindictive streak a mile wide. He never forgets a slight, as I'm sure you know.' He glanced at his watch and frowned. 'I guess we should get inside. The contest is supposed to start up again, right?'

I cleared my throat. 'Actually it's not. We had to postpone it.'

'Postpone it?' His frown deepened. 'Don't tell me it's on account of Bart. What has the prima donna done now?' He waved his hand. 'No, don't tell me. I don't want to know.' He leaned against the side of the car. 'I'm going to plant myself right here. Bart won't be able to avoid me, not unless he plans on abandoning his car, and I know he won't do that.'

I bit down hard on my lower lip. Either the man was an excellent actor, or he genuinely had no idea his brother had been murdered. I was debating breaking the news when out of the corner of my eye I saw Detective Hoffman approaching, a purposeful look on his face. Time for me to skedaddle.

'I'm sorry, but I do have to get back inside,' I said. 'It was nice meeting you.'

I turned and started to walk back to the high school. I'd taken about a dozen steps when I paused and looked back over my shoulder. Hoffman was standing before Peter and their heads were bent close together. I saw Peter's face pale, and he sagged against the Mercedes. 'Dead!' he wailed. 'Is this some sort of sick joke?'

Brandon murmured something to the man. Peter's eyes widened, and the corners of his mouth drooped down. I turned and retraced my steps back inside the auditorium. I felt bad for Peter Hagen, but I wasn't sure I trusted him completely, either.

Upon returning backstage, the first people I saw were Hilary and Arleen. Arleen appeared to be deep in conversation with a female police officer as Hilary stood nearby, watching. As I drew closer I heard Arleen's anxious voice. 'But that's ridiculous. I need my utensils. Why on earth are you confiscating them?'

'It's not just yours, ma'am,' the officer said patiently. 'We've been ordered to bag everyone's. You'll be advised when you can pick 'em up down at headquarters.'

Arleen crossed her arms over her chest and glared at the officer. 'Ridiculous. I demand to speak with the officer in charge.'

'That would be Detective Bartell, and he's busy right now,' the officer replied.

I moved forward. 'Arleen? Is everything all right?'

Arleen whirled around. Her frown disappeared the instant she saw me. 'Tiffany, thank goodness. Maybe you can knock some sense into these people, or maybe talk to Detective Bartell for me. They won't let me take any of my cooking utensils home. I'd like to take my knife set, at least. It cost me a small fortune.'

I slipped my arm around Arleen's shoulders. 'Don't worry, Arleen, I doubt they'll have it very long. You'll get everything back.'

Hilary touched my arm. 'I tried to tell her it's standard operating procedure in cases like this, but of course she wouldn't listen to me.'

Arleen glared at her sister. 'And why should I? Why should I be treated like a common criminal. I certainly didn't murder the guy – although I can't say he didn't deserve it.'

'Ssh,' Hilary clamped her hand across Arleen's mouth. 'Are you nuts? Don't say something like that at a crime scene.'

Arleen jerked her head free of Hilary's hand. 'Why not? It's the truth. Driscoll was scum.'

'Yeah, and now he's murdered scum. Keep talking like that and you could end up on the suspect list. It happened to Tiff a few weeks ago.'

Arleen crossed her arms over her chest. 'And just like Tiffany, I'm innocent. I was going to make quinoa-stuffed peppers for dinner tomorrow, and you need to chop the ingredients really fine. I was hoping to be able to use my Gyuto knife, but if it's in police custody, I won't be able to now, will I?'

'Oh for pity's sake Ar. It's not the end of the world. Use one of Mom's knives,' said Hilary. 'We'll no doubt be eating at home ourselves now anyway. Dale said that the after-party at A Slice of Heaven was cancelled.'

'Maybe so, but Mom's stainless-steel knives are no match for my Gyuto,' shot back Arleen. 'Maybe we should just go out anyway.'

I held up my hand. 'Tell you what, Arleen. I need to talk to Bartell anyway. I'll ask him when he thinks you might get your knives back.'

Arleen's face brightened. 'Oh, would you, Tiffany! It's nice to have someone care,' she added with a black look at her sister.

'I care, Ar,' Hilary sighed. 'I just don't see the need for the dramatics – or are you practicing for your drama class?'

I left them bickering and walked up the short flight of steps that led to the kitchen break-room area. The first thing I saw was the yellow crime-scene tape, stretched across the kitchen entrance. It made me a little nauseous to look at it, and I took a step backward – straight into Bartell's chest.

'Whoa.' He put out his hands, gripped me by the shoulders to steady me. 'You're right. We've got to stop meeting like this.'

I glanced at the door and then quickly away. 'I guess the body's been removed?'

Bartell nodded. 'Off to the coroner's office for a full autopsy, although Sample's preliminary confirmed that Driscoll was murdered less than an hour before his body was discovered.'

'An hour? That could mean the person I heard him whispering with could well be the killer.'

'It's a definite possibility. Sample also confirmed that the cause of death was a severed artery.'

'In other words, Driscoll bled to death,' I said. That explained the pool of blood I'd noticed around the body. I frowned. 'If that's the case, though, wouldn't the killer have been sprayed with blood?'

'Yes. There were indications in the kitchen, though, that lead us to believe the killer cleaned up after him- or herself.'

'Indications?'

'There are some towels missing from the rack in the kitchen. It's possible the killer used them to clean him- or herself up.' He paused, looking at the expression on my face. 'OK. I can see the wheels spinning. What's going on in that brain of yours?'

'I was just wondering . . . the killer had enough presence of mind to clean up, but left the murder weapon sticking out of Driscoll's throat. Don't you think that's odd?'

'Not really. The knife was jammed in pretty deep. Maybe the killer heard someone coming and didn't want to take the time to try and remove it. That's one possibility.'

'Wouldn't it indicate the killer were male? If it were thrust in that deeply?'

'Not necessarily.' Bartell whipped out his notebook, started thumbing through it. 'You told me that Beth March, Peter Hagen and this reporter Charlotte Horn all were backstage. Beth did speak with me a little bit before she left. She said that Driscoll and the brother were fighting, but she wasn't sure over what.'

'I think it was money,' I said. 'When I overheard their earlier argument, Hagen seemed upset over loaning Driscoll some money. Apparently Driscoll was taking his time repaying the loan.'

Both Bartell's eyebrows winged skyward. 'Money, huh? Always a good motive for murder.'

'I don't know. He didn't act like he knew his brother was dead when I spoke with him. And I saw Hoffman tell him – he seemed shocked at the news, and Hagen didn't impress me as being that good an actor. Charlotte Horn seemed to think—'

But I wasn't destined to tell Bartell Charlotte Horn's theory, because at that moment there was a shout from backstage. Then Hoffman emerged, a plastic bag clutched in each hand. 'Detective Bartell, you'll want to see these,' he cried. 'They were jammed into the garbage pail in the ladies' room.'

Hoffman held the bags aloft. One held what looked to be a bloody towel. But it was the other one that made me gasp. Inside was a swath of printed fabric – and it was covered with blood. I recognized it immediately.

It was the same blue, white and lilac print as the sliver I'd found outside the kitchen where I'd found Driscoll's body.

EIGHT

My 'kids', Lily and Cooper practically knocked me over as soon as I let myself in the back door. Cooper's tail wagged briskly, and Lily thumped her chocolate brown one against the hardwood floor in a greeting. They were happy to see me, and I knew the main reason was hunger. I spooned food into their bowls and then dropped into a kitchen chair. I pulled out the chair next to me, propped my feet on it, slumped down and closed my eyes.

Things had happened quickly after Hoffman's discovery. Bartell had shoved me aside with a murmured, 'We'll talk later,' and the crime-scene boys all descended on the ladies' room, armed with rolls of yellow tape. I realized I wasn't going to get a chance now to show Bartell what I'd found, let alone put in a plea for Arleen's knives, so I went back out onstage to deliver the bad news. Arleen took it better than I thought. 'Maybe they'll finish up quickly and you can get them back by tomorrow,' I suggested.

'I guess I have no choice, do I?' Arleen grumbled. 'I have to be satisfied.'

Arleen and Hilary took off and I went in search of Dale. I found him sitting out front in the judges' section. He looked up at me with a crooked smile. 'Even with an alibi, I still got the *don't leave town* speech,' he said ruefully.

'I guess we all did,' I said on a sigh. 'Have you given any more thought to continuing the contest?'

'Yes. I spoke with Anastasia and Giovanni before they left. Anastasia's schedule is light for the rest of this month, as is Giovanni's. They have commitments booked through the next three months, though, so we're going to have to either reschedule within the next two weeks or . . .'

'Or?' I prompted, even though I had an idea what the alternative was.

Dale's hand shot out to cover mine. 'Or, we're going to have to cancel entirely. I'm sorry, Tiff. I sincerely hope it doesn't come to that.'

I thrust my jaw forward. 'We won't let it,' I said aggressively. 'Let's think positively and announce the winners from the first round, then talk to Principal Jacoby and book the auditorium for two weeks from today. It'll be the Bon-Appetempting Pizza Challenge Final Leg – or bust.'

Suiting action to words, I tracked the principal down and secured the use of the auditorium for two weeks from Saturday. Now all I had to do was find a third judge. That would be the hardest part of all.

My eyes fluttered open and I eased myself out of my chair. As always, when I was faced with a problem, I did what I did best to clear my head and make my thoughts form a cohesive pattern.

I cooked.

I went upstairs where I shed my clothes in favor of a cashmere caftan I'd splurged on when I'd been made full time at *Southern Style*. I pulled the soft, midnight blue material over my head, pulled my auburn hair back into a ponytail, slid my feet into my fur-lined bedroom slippers, and went back down to the kitchen. Cooper and Lily had finished their meal and they both watched me eagerly – hoping for samples, no doubt.

I pulled my giant stockpot and a ten-inch saucepan out of the cupboard, set them on the stove. First things first, though – this afternoon warranted some liquid refreshment of the alcoholic variety. I found a chilled bottle of sweet Riesling in the fridge, as yet unopened. I uncorked it, poured a generous amount into a wineglass, and chugged it down. Refreshed, I refilled the glass and set about making my early dinner.

I was in an Italian mood – brought on, no doubt, by the pizza challenge, so I decided on a favorite of mine. Linguini with white clam sauce. I usually bought fresh clams at the market for this, but I hadn't gotten there this week yet, so the can of diced clams I'd bought at the SaveWay would have to do instead. I got the can out of the cupboard and set it on the counter, then set about preparing the dish. I filled the saucepan and put the water on to boil, then minced fresh scallions and garlic, chopped up parsley. Next I sautéed onions and garlic, followed by the preparation of my white sauce, a recipe I'd learned when I was assistant head chef at a swanky New York hotel. I refilled my Riesling as I added the clams and reserved juice to the pot. I was feeling pretty good when I added salt, pepper, parsley and a pinch of tarragon to the mix. I alternated sips of Riesling with my sauce until I'd decided it had thickened enough. I lowered the burner, covered the pan, and then tossed my noodles into my big pasta pot along with a splash of olive oil and a generous helping of sea salt.

As I waited for my pasta to become al dente, I helped myself to more Riesling, then sat back down and let my thoughts wander to the other events of the day.

Bartholomew Driscoll was a cad; no one would get an argument from me on that point. But did he deserve to die that way? Absolutely not. Someone apparently thought he did, though. Driscoll himself had told his brother that there was a long line of people who would like to see him dead. Peter Hagen had himself admitted to me that he was on that list, possibly heading it. Then there was Bartell's theory that it had been a crime of passion. That made my thoughts drift to Charlotte Horn, and her assertion that Driscoll's reason for being in Branson concerned a woman. An ex-lover, perhaps? Or maybe a business associate or a female chef who's cooking he'd panned? I liked the female chef theory, especially since a chef's knife had been the weapon of choice. She could have brought it with her, or she could have appropriated one of the contestants'?

My laptop was on the kitchen table. I pulled it over, opened it and booted it up. I selected images then typed in 'Chefs' knives with symbols on the blades' and hit enter. I scrolled through the pages of images carefully. I found two that could well be the murder weapon. Both were ten-inch, stainless steel with black handles, and both were Japanese: a Bunka and a Gyuto. I zoomed in on them for a better look. At first glance, I picked the Gyuto. The symbols etched on the blade seemed to be the same, although I couldn't be 100 percent certain. If I could get a look at the crime-scene photos, then I might be able to make a more positive identification, but I doubted Bartell would be in a sharing mood.

I reached for my tote bag, dragged out my notebook containing the contestant information. Each contestant, when they filled out their questionnaire, had to list any equipment they'd be bringing with them for insurance purposes. Kurt Howell's knife set was a Santoku. But Colleen Collins and Arleen both had Gyuto sets.

'Interesting,' I murmured. 'Everyone had their knives out on the counters. Anyone could have picked one up. I guess that's why everyone's utensils were confiscated – to see if one is the murder weapon.' Cooper gave a sharp yip, like he agreed with my assessment. I shut the notebook and tossed it off to the side. Cooper let out another yip and jumped up. His paw snagged the cardigan I'd tossed on the counter earlier, which fell down in a heap in front of the dog. As I bent over to pick it up, the sliver of fabric I'd found earlier fell out of the cardigan pocket. Cooper lunged for it, but I was quicker, snatching it up before the spaniel could lay his paw on it.

'Uh-uh, you can't play with this, Coop.'

I laid the cardigan back on the counter and turned the fabric over in my hand. I nibbled at my lower lip as I thought that I should show this to Bartell. Not only had I found it at the scene of the crime, but its bloody counterpart had been found hidden in the trash can in the ladies' restroom. I couldn't shake the feeling the print fabric looked familiar to me, but for the life of me I couldn't say why.

I started to reach for my cell to call Bartell, but the strident ring of my front doorbell made me pause. Bartell had said he'd talk to me later. Maybe he'd decided to drop by my house on his way back to the station. The buzzer sounded again, more insistent this time. I laid the fabric on the counter underneath the sweater then walked quickly to my front door. Before I opened it, I went over to the side curtain and peered out on to the stoop. The figure standing under the porch light wasn't Bartell, but it was someone else I needed to speak with. I removed the safety chain and opened the door just as Charlotte Horn's finger took aim at my doorbell again. 'Thank goodness you're home,' the reporter said as she breezed past me into the foyer. 'I thought maybe Bartell took you downtown to give a statement.'

I shut the door behind her. 'I haven't given my official statement yet,' I said. 'And how did you find me?'

Charlotte smiled. 'We investigative reporters have our ways of finding out things,' she said.

'Apparently so. Anyway, I'm glad you dropped by, Ms Horn.'

'Call me Charlotte,' she said, and gestured with her hand toward my living room. 'Can we talk in there?'

I hesitated, then nodded. 'Sure.'

I led the way into the living room. I took a seat on my sofa, while Charlotte eased herself into a high-backed chair directly opposite me. 'I'll come right to the point,' she said. 'I think Driscoll's murder is connected to the reason he came to Branson in the first place.'

'You're talking about this mystery woman, right?'

'Yes. I can't reveal my source, of course, but I have it on good authority that an incident Driscoll was involved with twenty-two years ago is now giving him cause for concern.'

I frowned. I'd thought the dalliance more recent. 'Twenty-two years is a long time,' I said. 'What sort of incident are you talking about?'

'I can't go into much detail, because I don't have all the facts yet.' She laced her hands in her lap. 'All I can tell you is that it involves a woman, and a suspicious death.' She scooted to the edge of her seat and leaned towards me. 'I've heard that you seem to have a flair for detection. I was hoping that perhaps we could work together. I think that once this secret of Driscoll's is brought out into the open, we'll also find out who killed him – and why.'

I frowned, considering her words. I thought about the snippets of conversation I'd overheard during the day, and Charlotte Horn's words might actually make some sense. 'You might be right,' I said slowly. 'But acting on the assumption that you are, we'd be deliberately putting ourselves in danger. Wouldn't it be better to tell the police what you know, and let them handle it?'

Charlotte shook her head. 'I've been down this road before and, trust me, the police won't give a fig about a twenty-two-year-old cold case. They've got their hands full with recent murders. But you've got the tenacity of a pit bull, Tiffany. After all, you tracked down Jenny Lee Plumm's killer, right?'

'Yes, but that was different. I was working to clear my own name.'

Charlotte rose and smoothed down her skirt. She reached into her shoulder bag, drew out a small cardboard card and tossed it on my coffee table. 'I have to get going. There's my contact information. If you decide to work with me, call me.' At the door she paused. 'You might not want to be a food blogger forever. A story like this could be a real shot in the arm to your career. Think about it.'

Charlotte swept out without another word. I turned her card over in my hand. OK, I admit I was curious as to who might have murdered Driscoll. And Charlotte Horn's cryptic remarks had the hairs on the back of my neck rising but . . . there was just something about the reporter that set alarm bells off in my head. She seemed the type to do anything for a big story, and she'd admitted her career was in desperate need of one. Would she falsify information to get that big story? Worse yet, would she commit murder to get it?

I started to go back to the kitchen when the doorbell rang again, more impatiently this time. I sighed and flung open the door without even bothering to look. 'Listen, Charlotte, I told you . . .'

I stopped dead in my tracks when I realized it wasn't Charlotte Horn who stood on the other side of the door.

It was Philip Bartell.

NINE

Bartell lounged against my doorjamb, arms folded across his chest, and shot me a quizzical look. 'You were expecting someone else?' he asked.

I paused, flustered, and blurted out, 'Well I definitely wasn't expecting *you*.'

His gaze swept me up and down, taking in the caftan that clung to my every curve, the wavy auburn hair that had escaped the ponytail and now tumbled across my shoulders. 'I can see that,' he said softly. 'Do you have a minute? I do have a few more questions for you about the events of today.'

Conscious of his assessing gaze, I pulled the caftan more tightly around my body. 'Sure. Actually, I'm glad you came by. I have some information for you as well.' I swung the door wide and made a sweeping motion. 'Come on in.'

Bartell entered the foyer, paused, nose twitching. 'Something smells mighty good,' he remarked. He sniffed at the air. 'I detect garlic, onion . . . perhaps a touch of tarragon?'

'I was making sauce . . . Oh gosh! The linguini!'

I raced into the kitchen. Fortunately, I'd had the burner low enough so that the pot hadn't boiled over. I shut off the flame, looked over my shoulder at Bartell, who'd followed me. 'I was making an early supper. It occurred to me when I got home that I hadn't eaten anything all day.'

Bartell rubbed at his slender waistline. 'Now that you mention it, neither have I.'

I saw him look longingly at the pot of pasta and I heard myself ask, 'Would you want a plate of linguini?'

His face split in a genuine smile. 'I thought you'd never ask.'

The corners of my lips tipped up. I'd found out during our last encounter that an appreciation for good food was one thing Bartell and I had in common. I motioned toward the table. 'Have a seat. There's not too much Riesling left, but I could open a Chardonnay. Both go well with seafood.'

'I'm technically still on duty, so if it's all the same to you, I'll skip the alcohol. I'll just have water, or iced tea if you've got that.'

'I have iced tea. Coming right up.'

I went over to the cupboard and pulled down two tall glasses, then reached into the refrigerator for the pitcher of iced tea I'd made yesterday. As I poured the tea into the glasses, I saw Cooper and Lily tentatively approach Bartell, who was leaning against the kitchen counter. He leaned forward, and put his hands between his knees. 'Well hello there,' he said to Cooper. 'Remember me?'

Cooper let out a loud yip, then moved closer to Bartell. He raised one hand and gave the spaniel a scratch behind the ears.

Lily sat back on her haunches, blue eyes narrowed to almost slits. *Meow*, she said.

Bartell turned to the Siamese. 'Hello . . . Lily, is it? You certainly are a beauty.'

Lily let out another throaty meow, then she slowly got up, stretched, and ambled over to Bartell. She rubbed her body against the detective's legs, and he reached down to give her a pat on her head. 'You have such silky fur,' he told the cat, who blinked her big blue eyes at him. Both pets apparently satisfied with the attention they'd received, they turned and retired to their beds in the far corner of the kitchen. I noticed Lily looking a few times in Bartell's direction before turning around twice and snuggling into her bed.

'Looks like you're a hit,' I said lightly.

Bartell shrugged. 'Animals always seem to like me. I had a lot of them growing up in Arizona.'

I wanted to follow up on that offhanded remark, but now wasn't the time. I added a sprig of fresh mint to both glasses and handed Bartell his. I gestured toward the table. 'Have a seat. The food'll be out in a minute.' I paused. 'You said you have questions?'

He took a sip of the iced tea and nodded at me over the rim of the glass. 'Yes, but they can wait until after I taste that heavenly smelling concoction you've cooked up.'

I felt a little swell of pride as I spooned generous portions of linguini on to two plates, then covered it with the delicate clam sauce. When I set Bartell's plate in front of him, he sniffed at it appreciatively before picking up his fork and digging in.

'Oh, man,' he said. 'This is good, Tiffany. Really, really good.'

I speared a clam, popped it into my mouth, chewed. 'You really enjoy food, don't you?'

'Mm-mm,' Bartell said as he shoved a large forkful of linguini into his mouth. 'I enjoy cooking too – although my linguini isn't nearly as delicious as this.'

For the next few minutes we both sat in silence, eating our linguini and sipping the minted tea. At last Bartell pushed his plate back with a contented sigh. I looked at it. The plate was almost as clean now as when I'd taken it out of the cupboard. 'Would you like some more? There's plenty left.'

He patted his waistline. 'Yes, I would, but I'm going to have to pass. I've been putting on a bit of weight lately.'

I eyed his physique, which looked plenty OK to me. 'Not enough exercise at those crime scenes, huh?' I said lightly.

'That, and the endless paperwork. Plus we've been shorthanded the past few weeks. Two men down with the flu, another two on vacation. And I lost my right-hand man, as you know,' he added wryly. 'Captain Pierce did assign me a helper a few days ago but, to be honest, it's turning out to be more of a babysitting job.'

'Let me guess. Detective Hoffman?' At Bartell's pained look I added, 'He seemed to be a bit of a go-getter.'

'He's like a loopy gazelle. Butts in everywhere.' Bartell sighed. 'He's Pierce's nephew. He graduated the academy with honors, and he wants to be a homicide detective. He was working with the men in Senoia, but they don't catch too many homicides. Pierce figured, with Eric gone, this might be the perfect opportunity for me to teach young Hoffman a thing or two.' He reached up and pinched at the bridge of his nose with his fingers, and then he leaned forward so that his gaze locked with mine. 'All this, though, is no excuse for my behavior.'

I frowned at him. 'Your behavior?'

'You know what I mean. My bugging out early on our date and not calling you.'

For a second I just stared at him. I hadn't been expecting to hear an admission like that, and quite frankly I didn't know what to say. When I finally found my voice, what came out wasn't the tirade I'd practiced in front of the mirror. 'You don't have to explain.'

'Ah, but yes, I do. I told you I wanted to spend time with you, see how things between us went, and what do I do on our first date? I take off on business, and then don't call for weeks.'

I shot him a wry smile. 'Well, maybe a party at my mother's house wasn't exactly the greatest place to have a first date.'

He shook his head. 'It was fine. The party was very nice. Your parents were very nice. The problem, unfortunately, is me. My job has always come first, I'm afraid. Sometimes it makes for a sticky time in relationships.'

That remark made me think he might also have had a love affair end badly, but it was none of my business and I didn't want to pry. Instead I said, 'Well, you don't exactly have a nine-to-five job. I have to confess, I'm a bit relieved.'

'You are?'

'Yes. I thought maybe you'd changed your mind about . . . us.'

He reached out and grasped my hand. 'Trust me, Tiffany, I haven't changed my mind. I guess what I'm trying to say is, I'd like to give us another go, if you're willing. Only right now, thanks to Bartholomew Driscoll, I'm just not sure when that second date will be.'

'It figures that Driscoll would manage to screw with me in death, too,' I said. 'I guess the answer is the sooner we solve his murder, the sooner we can have that date.'

Bartell raised one eyebrow. 'We?'

'OK, you. Happy now?'

'I would be if I thought you meant it.'

I resisted the impulse to stick out my tongue at him; instead I rose and started to clear away the dishes. 'I have apple pie for dessert. Interested?'

'Is it home-baked?'

'No, sorry. With the contest and all, I haven't had much time for baking.'

He shook his head regretfully. 'I'll pass, thanks. Although if it had been home-baked I could have been talked into it.'

'I'll remember that for next time,' I said lightly. 'Coffee?'

'That I won't turn down. Milk with two Sweet N Low if you have it, one sugar if you don't.'

I put the dishes in the dishwasher and moved over to the Keurig. I put a mug on the tray and selected a dark roast pod. As the coffee started to drip, I looked at Bartell over my shoulder. 'Now that your tummy's full, you had questions?'

He tented his fingers beneath his chin. 'Yes. Tell me again how you found Driscoll's body.'

I recounted the story as I added milk and one sugar to the stoneware mug and set it in front of Bartell. He took a long pull of the caffeine before he spoke. 'And you didn't notice anyone in the area? Hear anything?'

I returned to the Keurig and set another mug on the drip tray. I put in a pod of light roast and hit the brew button. 'Not when I found the body, no. I told you about hearing Driscoll in the kitchen arguing with someone shortly before that.'

'Right. The unidentified person.'

I added milk to my mug and carried it back to the table. 'Earlier in the day, I overheard an argument between Driscoll and Leon Santangelo. Santangelo was very upset. He told Driscoll not to force his hand, or he'd be sorry.'

Bartell had the mug raised halfway to his lips. Now he set it down, and reached into the jacket he'd draped across the back of the chair for his notebook and pen. 'Were those his exact words?'

I nodded. 'As near as I can remember. Driscoll accused him of making idle threats. Santangelo up and left, and Driscoll punched one of the kitchen counters – then he caught me in the break room and accused me of spying on him.'

Bartell glanced up. 'I imagine that went well.'

'Oh, yeah, real well,' I said dryly. 'I think he might be a bit paranoid. That reporter I told you about, Charlotte Horn, seems to think that Driscoll has a pretty big skeleton in his closet, and she's intent on exposing it – even now, after he's dead.'

Bartell shrugged. 'That's how those gossip rags work, Tiffany. Oftentimes they don't care if the subject is alive or dead, as long as they get a splashy front-page story.'

'She doesn't work for a gossip rag. Her ID said *Atlanta Star-Register*.'

'IDs can be faked. Anyway, her credentials should be easy enough to check out.'

'True. Anyway, she told me Driscoll's secret might be to do with something that happened over twenty years ago. A possible suspicious death, she said.'

Bartell shrugged. 'Sounds to me like she's grabbing at straws, regardless of what paper she's working for. I can tell you from experience, the longer a cold case sits, the tougher it is to solve.'

'Maybe so – but she was backstage right around the time Driscoll was killed. It could have been her I heard arguing with Driscoll.' I paused at the look on his face and added, 'You know, I really do think all this is important information.'

'I'm not arguing with you,' he answered. He pointed to his notebook. 'I'm taking notes, as you can see, and I'll definitely have a word with this Charlotte Horn.' He tapped his pen against the edge of the notebook. 'Anything else?'

I took a sip of coffee, set down my mug. 'Colleen Collins.'

'She's one of the contestants, right? What about her?'

'It's hard to say, exactly. I saw a look pass between her and Driscoll, and the way she spoke about him, I got the sense there might be more going on than met the eye.'

Bartell flipped through his notebook. 'Arleen Hanson accused her of trying to sabotage her entry. She responded by accusing Arleen of consorting with Driscoll.'

'Yeah, well, I think there might have been a little consorting going on between Driscoll and Colleen prior to this contest.' I held up both hands. 'Once again, I'm speculating. No proof.' I paused. 'Have you identified the murder weapon yet?'

'It's still at the lab. Why?'

'I only had a quick glimpse, but judging from the symbols, I'm pretty certain it was a Gyuto knife. Two of the contestants had similar ones.'

'Yes. Arleen Hanson and Colleen Collins.' He paused. 'I can tell you that the ten-inch knife was missing from both their sets.'

I frowned. 'That's odd, right? I mean, why take both knives?'

'Maybe the murderer wanted to confuse the issue.' He leaned back in his chair. 'Anyone else you'd care to share your speculations on?'

'I'm not sure I trust Driscoll's half-brother, Peter Hagen. They had a pretty heated argument backstage too. Hagen passed a remark about suing him – or worse. Driscoll remarked that he'd need guts for the something worse, and then Hagen barreled out of there like a rocket.'

Bartell slid the notebook and pen back into his jacket, then drained the last bit of coffee from his mug. 'I think I've got enough to work on. Thanks for the clarification.'

'You're welcome.' I inclined my head toward the empty mug. 'Want a refill?'

He shook his head. 'Thanks, but I'd better be getting back to the station. I have reports to file, notes to write . . .' He pulled a face. 'And Brandon Hoffman, no doubt, to deal with.'

My eyebrow went up. 'Brandon? That's his first name?'

'After his mother's father. He hates it.'

'The poor kid.' Bartell tossed me a black look, and I pointed to his empty mug. 'Caffeine always makes me feel better. Maybe you should take a cup to go.'

His expression softened. 'Not a bad idea.'

I took the mugs over to the dishwasher and slid them inside, then reached into the cupboard for my stainless-steel Thermos. I set it underneath the Keurig and slid in a pod. When it was done brewing, I looked at Bartell. 'Need any milk or sugar?'

'Black's fine, thanks.' He walked over to me and placed both his hands on my shoulders. 'Tiffany, I know how much you love to channel your inner Nancy Drew. This time, though, I'd really like it if you did me a big favor and restrained yourself. You remember what happened the last time you played detective, right?'

'Right.' I shot him a smug look as I snapped the lid on the Thermos. 'I solved the case.'

He scratched absently at his forehead. 'That you did, but you also ended up on the wrong end of a .45 revolver.'

'But I also managed to overpower our perp – before the cavalry arrived, I might add.'

Bartell's hands dropped from my shoulders to my waist and he pulled me against his chest. 'I also recall your saying you couldn't have held him off much longer, you were glad I arrived.'

'Well . . .' I pushed lightly against his chest. 'I didn't want to hurt your feelings.'

'Very funny.'

'Don't worry, Detective,' I said. 'I can't help it if I'm naturally curious, but I assure you, I have no desire to interfere in your investigation.'

Bartell sighed. 'You might not have a desire right now, but you just said it. You're naturally curious. You can't help yourself. It's like a disease with you.' He raised one hand, crooked it under my chin and tilted my face up to his. 'You do have good instincts, Tiffany. I admit that. But you're not a trained detective or police officer. I can't be around twenty-four seven to protect you. Just promise me that if you should come across anything you think might be pertinent, call me day or night. I'll follow up on it.'

I cocked an eyebrow. 'Is that an official order?'

'As a matter of fact, it is.' He gazed into my eyes. 'I need you to stay safe and in one piece. How can I take you to dinner at Chez Marcel otherwise?'

'Chez Marcel,' I squealed. 'Really?' The posh eatery had recently opened in Atlanta. Its owner was Marcel DuPres, a popular chef who'd worked in many Michelin-starred restaurants. 'I've been dying to review it. I heard the lobster Newburgh there is to die for – and expensive as sin.'

Bartell grinned, a slow, easy one. 'Right on both counts. But I can't think of a better place to atone for botching up our first date, can you?'

'Well, gee . . . no. But honest, you don't have to . . .'

'Yes, Tiffany, I do.' His steely gaze bored into mine. 'There is one tiny condition, though.'

I threw up a hand in protest. 'Yeah, no sleuthing. I get it.'

'OK, two conditions. No working on our official first date. You'll have to review their food another time.'

I let out a soft whoosh of air and smiled. 'Oh, I think I can handle that.'

He arched a brow. 'Both conditions?'

I hesitated, then nodded. 'Yeah. Well, definitely the second. I'll try very hard for the first.'

'Try exceedingly hard.'

He looked at me for a long moment and then he leaned down. His lips covered mine in a soft, sweet kiss that was all too short, in my opinion. When he raised his head, he ran his thumb along my jawline.

'Trust me, I'm going to work as hard as I can to solve this case as quickly as I can so we can have that date. And I'll work a lot better and faster if I know you're safe and not out gathering clues and interrogating possible suspects, putting yourself in danger.'

I placed my hand over my heart. 'OK. I promise I won't go out of my way to get involved in Driscoll's murder.'

'OK.' He gave me a long, searching look, then leaned down again and gave me another swift kiss on the lips. Then he was gone, out the back door and into the night. I leaned against the closed door and remembered I'd forgotten to tell Bartell about the fabric. I jerked the door open in time to see his car taillights disappearing down the street.

I went back inside and closed the door. Cooper and Lily were huddled in front of me, heads cocked. If animals could give accusing stares, I'd have been pinned to the wall. 'OK, OK, so shoot me. I forgot, I really did,' I said. 'I'll do it tomorrow for sure.' I paused. 'Honest.'

Cooper let out a sharp yip, and Lily sat back on her haunches, waved one paw in the air. I leaned over and gave each of them a pat on the head. 'I knew you'd understand,' I said.

I wasn't a bit sleepy, so I got out my trusty laptop and decided to work on my column for the week, but the words just wouldn't come. At last I set the laptop off to the side and went to the hall closet. I returned a few minutes later with a small whiteboard and markers tucked under my arm. Lily and Cooper watched me curiously as I propped the board up on the kitchen counter.

'I was going to set this up and put recipes for the week on it, but now I've found a better use,' I told my pets. I uncapped the black magic marker and wrote 'Bartholomew Driscoll' right in the center of the board. I tapped at the name with the edge of the marker. 'There's our victim. Now, who might have had reason to want him dead, you know, besides the hundreds of people he gave scathing reviews to? Best to limit it to those we know.'

Above Driscoll's name I printed Leon Santangelo. 'They were arguing pretty heatedly over something. I heard Driscoll tell

Santangelo not to threaten him. What if Driscoll pushed him too far?'

Underneath Santangelo's name I wrote down Peter Hagen. It was pretty obvious to me, from the argument I'd overheard, that there was bad blood between the two. I remembered, too, Hagen's reaction when Driscoll said he needed guts. Had Hagen taken the challenge seriously?

I tapped the marker against my chin as I considered my next suspect. I wrote down Colleen Collins. I couldn't forget the look that had passed between her and Driscoll, nor her nervous demeanor in the competition. There was something, some history there. Just what that history was, and if it could have led to murder, remained to be seen. And Bartell seemed to like the 'woman scorned' angle.

After a moment of debate, I wrote Charlotte Horn's name underneath Colleen's. I couldn't explain it, but I had a gut feeling there might be more to Charlotte Horn's crusade against Driscoll than merely getting a scoop to revitalize her flagging career. After another minute I wrote Beth March's name underneath Charlotte's. There was something more to her relationship with Driscoll than just employer and employee, I was certain. After another minute I wrote LS – for long shot – after Beth's name.

Next I wrote down Giovanni Ferrante. 'Anastasia hinted at bad blood between Ferrante and Driscoll, and not because of that scathing review he gave his eatery. There might be more to that, as well.' I stood back and surveyed my handiwork. 'To be continued, I'm sure,' I told the animals, 'but these are a start, anyway. Every single one of them was backstage at some point, and any one of them could have pilfered one of those knives.' After a moment I wrote down one final name – Mystery Woman.

Both Cooper and Lily opened their mouths in a yawn, then they each padded back to their respective beds. Apparently my powers of deduction were boring them tonight. Well, maybe a little more sleuthing was in order. I remembered Beth March's words: *You can find almost anything on the Internet, if you know where to look.* Now I was going to put that theory to the test.

I plucked my laptop off the counter and took it over to the kitchen table. I called up a search engine, typed in Charlotte

Horn's name and hit enter. Quite a few entries came up, so I narrowed it down by adding 'reporter'. I found no less than ten Charlotte Horns, reporters on LinkedIn. I clicked on a few profiles before the photo told me I finally had the right one.

Charlotte Horn turned out to have a very impressive résumé. I should have made a bet with Bartell on the woman's employment. Charlotte was definitely employed as a reporter on the *Atlanta Star-Register* and had been for the past three years, specializing in crime. She'd also moved around . . . a lot. Before the *Atlanta Star*, she'd held down an investigative reporter post at the *Augusta Chronicle*. Before that, she'd been a crime reporter for the *Macon Bugle* and a beat reporter for the *Valdosta Sun* before that. Two of her in-depth exposés had won journalistic awards. Charlotte Horn was certainly no lightweight in the field of investigative reporting.

Next I typed in Driscoll's name. A Wikipedia page popped up, so I clicked on that. The photo displayed there was definitely him, only about twenty years younger. I had to admit, the man was devilishly handsome. Too bad he had the personality of a wet dishrag. I read the article with interest. His parents had both been English professors at his alma mater, Georgia State University. After his father's death, his mother had remarried. His brother, Peter Hagen, held a doctorate in Biology and taught at Augusta University.

Driscoll himself had graduated from Georgia State with a degree in English. He'd attended the Wiregrass Georgia Technical College in Valdosta and obtained a degree in Culinary Arts. He began his career as a part-time food critic for the *Valdosta Sun*, then graduated to higher-grade full-time positions on the *Macon Bugle* and the *Augusta Sun-Times*. His rapier wit and discerning palate had earned him both fans and critics alike, and he did publish two cookbooks, *The Art of Cooking* and *Trust Your Palate*, while working as a freelance food critic. At the bottom of the page was a short disclaimer: *Driscoll has apparently retired from being a food critic to concentrate on his new career as a restaurateur. He runs a trendy restaurant, Ambrosia, located in downtown Branson, Georgia.*

I frowned. I couldn't help but wonder why Driscoll had chosen Branson to open his restaurant in, when he could have had his pick of much larger cities. Maybe he'd just decided to try it out in a smaller venue first.

I looked the article over again. According to it, twenty-two years ago Driscoll would have lived in Augusta. I typed in the city and the year, and then the words, 'accident' and 'suspicious death'. I got several hits, but nothing of particular interest. Five auto accidents, three drug overdoses, two hit-and-runs. Nothing out of the ordinary, and the perpetrators had all been arrested. All of the cases were closed. None of them mentioned Bartholomew Driscoll. Well, I'd hit a dead end. Charlotte, though, apparently hadn't. I made a mental note to ask the woman for more details – although I doubted she'd share them.

I went back and printed out Driscoll's bio, then I went back to Charlotte Horn's résumé on LinkedIn and printed that out too. I went into my den, got them, returned to the kitchen and put them side by side on the table. After a few minutes of studying them, I realized what it was that had bothered me.

Charlotte Horn had worked in the same cities at the same time as Driscoll. What's more, they both started their careers on the same paper, the *Valdosta Sun*. No doubt that was where they'd first become acquainted. Judging from this, maybe using the term 'stalker' in reference to Charlotte Horn and Driscoll was more than accurate.

I went back to the laptop, typed in Leon Santangelo-Santangelo Pizza Dough and hit enter. Quite a few hits came up. I clicked on one article that focused on the official opening of Santangelo Pizza Dough. Midway through the article was a mention of a 'silent partner' being instrumental in Santangelo's setting up his business.

'Now that's interesting,' I murmured. It also made me wonder: could Driscoll's selection of Branson as the site for his restaurant have anything to do with Santangelo? There seemed to be more connect-the-dots here than met the eye.

A soft meow made me lift my head, and I saw that Lily had left her bed and was now sprawled across the side of the kitchen table, her head resting on one paw, blue eyes trained on me. Cooper, not to be outdone by his feline sibling, hopped up on to the chair next to mine and reached out a shaggy paw to touch my arm. I patted his paw absently and murmured, 'Santangelo has a silent partner. Wow. What if it were Driscoll? Could that have been what they were arguing about?'

Or maybe it had something to do with Ambrosia?

I wondered just how I could confirm that. I doubted Santangelo would tell me. I continued sifting through the other articles. They were mostly reprints of interviews given by Santangelo to food magazines, mainly praising his 'superior pizza dough'. There was nothing of real interest there, so I found his LinkedIn profile and clicked on that. A few minutes later I sucked in my breath.

Santangelo had started out as an apprentice in a pizzeria in Valdosta, then moved on to assistant chef and head chef positions at pizzerias located in Macon and Augusta before deciding to enter into his own business, Santangelo Pizza Dough, located in Branson. He maintained a home in Branson as well as Marietta. He'd also lived in Atlanta for a brief time. It listed his marital status as 'divorced'. I Googled *Santangelo divorce* and came up with the information that he'd married his high school sweetheart, the former Dolores Carlson, right after becoming head apprentice at the Mamma Mia Pizzeria in Valdosta. The couple had no children, and had gotten divorced a little less than a year ago. The article intimated that Dolores had received a fairly hefty settlement in an uncontested divorce.

I pushed back my laptop and laced my fingers behind my neck. It couldn't be a coincidence that Driscoll, Santangelo and Charlotte Horn all lived in the same places, at roughly the same times. No, I was willing to bet an entire month's salary that there was a deeper connection there, but what? I pulled the laptop in front of me again and this time typed in Dolores Carlson Santangelo. I was pleasantly surprised to find that not only did she have a Facebook page, she was on Twitter and LinkedIn too. I clicked on her LinkedIn page, where I found out that Ms Carlson had her own interior design business under her maiden name. There was a short list of clients shown there, and I gave it a quick glance, then I did a double take and leaned in for a closer look.

Nope, I wasn't seeing things. The name right in the center of the short list screamed up at me. It was a name I knew well, someone who not only wrote the Household Tips N Tricks column for *Southern Style*, but who was also considered somewhat of a gossip maven around the magazine.

Twyla Fay Thorpe. Who knew? I shut down my laptop and went upstairs to my bedroom, feeling encouraged. With Twyla Fay's penchant for digging up gossip, she just might be able to fill in some of the blanks that bothered me.

TEN

'Goodness, Tiffany, are those blueberry buttermilk muffins from Goodson's Bakery I smell?'

I stood in the doorway of Twyla Fay's office at *Southern Style*, gray and pink bakery box in hand. Compared to my little cubbyhole, Twyla Fay's office seemed as large as the Falcons' Mercedes-Benz Stadium. It held a massive cherrywood desk, a state-of-the-art computer on a separate, wood-grain computer table, a small glass-topped table, four leather chairs, and three cherrywood file cabinets – with enough room left over to fit a king-sized mattress, if Twyla so chose. At her greeting, I waved the bakery box aloft. 'Sure are,' I said with a bright smile. 'There's also cinnamon, banana, and pumpkin/chocolate chip as well.'

Twyla Fay held out her hands, wiggled her fingers. 'Ooh. Well, don't just stand there. Bring it here, girl.'

I walked over to the desk, conscious of my heels sinking into the plush magenta carpeting and held my offering out. Twyla Fay's chubby fingers closed around the box. She set it down right in front of her and, without a minute's hesitation, plucked a blueberry buttermilk muffin from the selection. She carefully peeled away the muffin's bright yellow wrapper and took a large bite. 'Oh, so good,' she mumbled, her mouth full. She leaned over to peer at the contents. 'Well, I'll be. There's also blueberry/ cream cheese, Bailey's and chocolate, cran/orange, cheddar cheese . . . these are all my favorites.'

I perched myself on the other edge of her desk. 'Yes, I know.'

Twyla Fay took another bite and closed her heavily made-up eyes. Today she was dressed in a bright lemon and fuchsia tent-style dress, made of a flowy material that came down to her ankles. The bright pink five-inch heels on her feet were a designer brand that probably cost more than I made in a month, but thanks to her late husband's wise investments, Twyla Fay could easily afford them. Her eyes popped open and she reached up to pat her well-lacquered beehive hairdo. She shot me a sly look. 'OK, spill it. Why do you come to my office bearing gifts? What do you want?'

I widened my own eyes. 'Why, Twyla Fay! What makes you think I want something?'

Twyla Fay let out a boisterous laugh, so loud it made the dangly pink and yellow crystal earrings in her ears sway back and forth. 'Oh, honey. I know bribery when I see it. So, give. What's up?'

I eased myself off the edge of her desk and into the leather chair in front of it. 'I see I can't fool you,' I said, propping my elbows up on the desktop. Leaning forward, I lowered my voice to a half-whisper. 'I'm looking for some information.'

'Information, huh?' Twyla Fay preened as she reached for another muffin. 'Well, you've come to the right place. Information is my specialty. Who are you looking for intel on?'

'Well, I'm thinking of doing some redecorating, and I happened to notice that you used the services of Dolores Carlson.'

'Ah.' Twyla looked a bit disappointed as she took a large bite of the banana muffin and set the rest on her desk. 'Well, I can tell you that she's top-notch, very thorough . . . and expensive.' Her gaze swept over my tailored navy skirt and polka-dot blouse, right down to my comfortable Mary Janes. 'No offense, dear, but I doubt you could afford her.'

'Oh, I've been saving up,' I said lightly. 'Correct me if I'm wrong, but wasn't she married to Leon Santangelo?'

Twyla paused, her muffin halfway to her lips. 'Yes, she was, poor thing. She's well rid of that loser, let me tell you.' She set the muffin down and leaned toward me. 'Those stories about him being a womanizer aren't fiction, you know. If it had cute legs and wore a skirt, Leon Santangelo went after it.' She picked the muffin up again and looked me up and down. 'You had dealings with him about the contest, right? You mean to tell me he didn't try and make a pass at you?'

'Actually, Dale was his point of contact for everything. I didn't have to deal with him at all. As a matter of fact, I only met the man at the bake-off for the first time.'

'Lucky you.' Twyla smirked. 'I bet that rattled Santangelo's chain. Dale is definitely not his type, but you sure are, honey.'

'Thanks . . . I think.'

Twyla waved her hand. 'Getting back to Dolores – she put up with it for years, and finally put a PI on him. She caught him in a compromising position, with some very revealing photos. I understand her settlement was in the high six figures.'

I let out a low whistle. 'That much? It must have put a terrific strain on Santangelo's cashflow?'

'Oh, yeah.' Twyla Fay leaned even closer to me. 'Dolores told me, in confidence, that he had to get a silent partner for his pizza dough business to recoup some of that money. His business seems to be doing fine now, though.'

'Interesting,' I said. 'I don't suppose Dolores knows who this silent partner might be?'

'I doubt she cares, as long as she has her money.' She looked sharply at me and waggled a finger in the air. 'OK, enough. You can't fool me, Tiffany Austin.'

I swallowed. 'Fool you? I don't know what you're talking about, Twyla Fay.'

'Oh, you don't have to pretend, dear.' Twyla Fay reached behind her desk and whipped out the morning edition of the *Branson Bugle*. She laid it on the desk and the headline screamed up at me: FORMER FOOD CRITIC AND RESTAURATEUR TAKES LAST BITE. Below the headline was a large photo of Bartholomew Driscoll.

Twyla Fay tapped at the paper, then waggled a finger at me. 'You're playing detective again, aren't you? You're trying to figure out who killed Bartholomew Driscoll!' She placed a hand over her heart. 'Don't tell me you're a suspect again? Because, you know, of your history with the deceased?'

'Thank goodness not this time. But I confess I am curious over who might want the man dead.'

Twyla Fay let out a snort. 'You can't be serious! Honey child, everyone who ever met the man wanted him dead!'

I had to chuckle at that. Even Driscoll had alluded to that possibility. 'I'm just wondering about the relationship between Driscoll and Santangelo. I thought maybe they were more than just business associates. After all, Santangelo got Driscoll to agree to step in as judge pretty quickly. Plus, it seems they lived in a lot of the same places at the same times.'

'We-ell,' Twyla Fay selected another muffin from the box,

started to peel away the wrapper. 'It was never confirmed, but I did hear rumors that years ago Dolores stepped out on Leon herself – with Driscoll.'

'Really?' Now that was interesting. Could Dolores Carlson be the mystery woman Driscoll had come to Branson to see?

Twyla Fay shrugged. 'Of course, it's just a rumor. And if you're thinking maybe Santangelo killed Driscoll over Dolores, I doubt that. Anyway, I've got a way better suspect than him.'

'Yeah? And who might that be?'

Twyla Fay scooted to the edge of her seat and said in a conspiratorial tone, 'I just happened to be near the stage area during that brief intermission, right after the introductions? I was just about to go over to tell Anastasia how much I enjoyed her latest cookbook, *Recipes from My Sicily*, when out of the corner of my eye I detected a slight movement behind the curtain. I casually wandered over and parted them, just a tad. Guess what I saw?' Without waiting for an answer, she rushed on, 'That cad Driscoll had his arm around Colleen Collins's waist. He had her fairly glued to his side, and she didn't look like she wanted to get away anytime soon.'

I tapped at my chin. 'That's interesting. Colleen accused Arleen of pretty much the same thing.'

'Hmpf,' said Twyla Fay. 'She was probably just trying to divert suspicion from herself.'

'I did see them exchanging dirty looks. Maybe Driscoll's advances weren't as wanted as one might think.'

Twyla Fay hesitated a moment before answering. 'Maybe, but according to Minnie, Colleen isn't above playing fast and loose to close a few real-estate deals, especially with men.'

'This comes from Minnie, huh?' Minnie Mae Draper was the owner of the local hair salon and Twyla's best friend. She was also a notorious gossip, way worse than Twyla Fay. Unlike Twyla, though, Minnie Mae's gossip usually held a kernel of truth. 'I guess it's possible.'

'Exactly,' Twyla Fay said smugly. 'They probably had a lovers' spat and Colleen hauled off and let him have it good.'

'Funny,' I murmured, 'Bartell said pretty much the same thing, only he cast Driscoll's assistant, Beth March, in the role of the wronged female.'

'That mousy little thing?' Twyla Fay waved her hand in a deprecating motion. 'I greatly doubt it. Not only is she too young, she definitely wasn't his type. Colleen, yes.' Twyla Fay paused. 'Or Arleen.' At my sharp intake of breath she added, 'Arleen's a beautiful girl, just the type Driscoll always went for.'

'Arleen thought Colleen sabotaged her oven during the first half,' I said. 'Colleen denied it, but she accused Arleen of having Driscoll in her corner.' I shook my head. 'Arleen didn't act like she wanted anything to do with Driscoll. As a matter of fact, he did make a pass at her. She threw a bottle of water in his face.'

Twyla clapped her hands. 'Good for her,' she said. 'As for Colleen's accusation, it sounds like the old bait and switch. Accuse someone else to take the heat away from you. That would be her style,' Twyla remarked. 'Like I said, Colleen's been known to bend a few rules in her day. She's a definite possibility, if you ask me. Or you can ask Minnie Mae.' She shook her hand in a circle. 'Has that girl got stories!' Twyla Fay glanced at her watch and let out a gasp. 'Oh my, look at the time. I've got a meeting down in the Art department.'

We both rose. Twyla Fay opened her middle desk drawer, fished around, and pulled out a small cardboard card which she passed over to me. 'That's Dolores Carlson's information,' she said. 'In case you were sincere about wanting to redecorate.' She closed an eye in a broad wink. 'Of course, if you just wanted to pump her for some info on her ex, she probably would be more than willing to oblige. Just tell her Twyla sent you.'

Back in my office, I noticed that I had three missed calls. Two were from a number I didn't recognize, and one was from Dale. I returned Dale's call first. Callie Johnson, his admin, answered on the first ring. 'Hey, Tiffany. Dale would like you to come to his office at eleven, to go over the photos of the contest for your weekend blog.'

'Great. Tell Dale I'll be there.'

I hung up and then dialed the other number. It rang three times and then a pre-recorded voice greeted me: '816-555-0987 is currently unavailable. Please leave a number for a return call.'

I hung up, then turned to my computer and called up a phone lookup site I had a membership on. I typed in the number, and a few minutes later got back the information that the number was registered to a pre-paid cell phone from a carrier who didn't require owner registration. I grabbed my tote bag and fished around in it, finally pulling out the card Charlotte Horn had given me with her contact info on it. I compared the phone number. Not a match.

Interesting. Apparently either whoever called me wished to remain anonymous, or it had been a wrong number.

I decided I'd ask Bartell about it when I saw him next (whenever that might be) and pulled out the card with Dolores Carlson's info on it. I dialed the number and a few minutes later a pleasant voice answered. 'Dolores Carlson Designs.'

'Hello, Ms Carlson?'

'No, I'm sorry. Ms Carlson is unavailable at the moment. I'm her assistant, Mimi Krupa. How can I be of service?'

'My name is Tiffany Austin. I was recommended to Ms Carlson by Twyla Fay Thorpe.'

'Oh, yes. Mrs Thorpe. You're a friend of hers?' Mimi's bored tone underwent a distinct change.

'Ah, yes. We were talking today, and I mentioned that my home needs refreshing. Mrs Thorpe said Ms Carlson was the best around. I'd like to make an appointment to speak with her, if I might.'

'Certainly.' I heard pages being riffled. At last Mimi spoke again. 'Ms Carlson is fairly well booked, but seeing as you're a friend of Mrs Thorpe's . . . how is one o'clock tomorrow?'

'I suppose that would be all right, but I was hoping for something sooner . . . like today, if possible?' I paused. 'My home really is in *dire* need.'

More pages were riffled, and then, 'Well, she could squeeze you in at six, but you'd have to be done by six thirty. Ms Carlson has a dinner engagement at Rafferty's at seven fifteen.'

'That will be fine. I'll be there at six.' I hung up and entered the appointment in my phone's calendar. Then I spent the next hour and a half working on my blog post, which I'd titled 'Pizzacraft 101'. Before I knew it, it was time to head down to Dale's office. As I pushed open the glass door marked DALE A. SWENSON, EDITOR IN CHIEF, I got a pleasant surprise – Chef Frederick Longo was standing beside Callie's desk, chatting with her. He looked up and gave me a wide smile as I approached.

'Tiffany, my dear.' The former world-class chef, who was now a member of *Southern Style*'s board, had known me back in the days when I was an assistant chef at a swanky New York hotel. He took my hand, planted a soft kiss on my upturned palm. 'It's good to see you.' He sobered instantly. 'I'm sorry to hear about what happened at the contest. I understand you are the one who found Driscoll?'

I nodded. 'Yes. It wasn't exactly a pretty sight. He and I had our differences, but I never wanted anything fatal to happen to him.'

Longo blew out a breath. 'The board's in quite a tizzy about it. They would like to press on with the contest as quickly as possible.'

'I know. I feel the same way. I booked the high school auditorium for two weeks from this past Sunday. I figured that should give us plenty of time to find another judge to fill Driscoll's place – unless, of course, you have time to step in?' I asked hopefully.

Longo shook his head. 'I would if I could, but I already have a commitment at the International Food Show.'

I laughed. 'I understand. I'd pick Venice over Branson too.'

He chuckled. 'Venice is lovely, but not all it's cracked up to be, especially when you are dealing with temperamental chefs.' His eyes twinkled as he added, 'I understand that there is a food show coming right here to Branson in the next few weeks. The National Foodie Association Convention.'

My head snapped up. 'Foodie Fest, right?'

'Right,' Longo said. 'They're fairly new. This is only their second convention. Frankly, I'm surprised one wasn't started sooner, what with all the rising enthusiasm among foodies over the past few years.'

'Foodies are a loyal bunch,' I agreed. 'I'm sure I can attribute the success of my blog to them.'

'Never underestimate a loyal foodie,' said Longo with a wry grin. 'It's to be a four-day convention and if it's as successful as their last attempt two years ago, I'm sure it will turn into an annual event. There will be food samples, food trucks, and some manufacturers will debut new items not yet seen in stores. I believe there are a few contests as well. Industry experts, premier chefs and restaurant owners will converge to discuss the latest trends in food . . . among other things,' he added with a wink. 'I thought about attending it,' Longo continued, 'But unfortunately the timing is not good for me.' He looked me straight in the eye. 'Does it sound like something that would interest you?'

'Does it ever,' I squealed. 'I think I could get quite a few articles for the blog out of an event like that.'

'I agree.' He tapped idly at his chin. 'I think I'll put a recommendation in to the board for you to cover it.'

'That would be wonderful,' I said. 'But do you think they'll go for it? I know Marcia said the other day Manchetti was complaining about sluggish revenue and the numbers being down.' Marcia was Marcia Allen, Enzo Manchetti's admin and virtual right-hand woman who always seemed to have her finger right on the pulse of whatever was going down at the magazine.

Longo waved his hand carelessly in the air. 'Enzo is always complaining about the revenue and the numbers,' he said. 'However, I don't see as he'll have much to complain about in that area with this. After all, the convention being held locally spares the expense of air fare and hotel. It's just a matter of the registration fee and your meals.'

'I hope you're right,' I said. 'But with Manchetti you never know.'

Longo shot me a look that indicated he didn't think refusal was a possibility. 'In the meantime, I'll ask around to see if I can find someone willing to take on the judging task here at the pizza contest.'

'Would you?' I touched his arm. 'That would be a great help.'

'Of course. You know I'll do anything I can to help you, my dear.'

The intercom on Callie's desk buzzed, and she gave us a bright smile. 'Dale will see you both now,' she said.

Chef Longo and I went into Dale's office. Dale rose from his chair as we entered. I noticed that the top of his desk was covered with glossy prints.

'Glad the two of you could make it,' he said. He gestured toward the photos. 'Tiff, I need you to look through Mac's photos and mark down the ones you want to accompany your article.

They're numbered on the back. Fred, I need to talk to you about that Venice show. Let's go into my conference room.'

'Excellent,' said Longo. 'I have a few things I'd like to run by you too.'

Longo tossed me a wink before he and Dale disappeared into Dale's small conference room and shut the door. I went over to the desk, pulled out the chair and sat down. As usual, Mac had missed nothing. His photos, besides being astonishingly clear, seemed to capture every single minute of the competition. He'd taken photos of the contestants as they arrived at their workstations; as they donned aprons and unpacked utensils; as they mixed pizza dough, rolled it out, put it in the oven. He'd even snapped a photo of Arleen re-plugging her oven.

I turned to the photos Mac had taken of the judges. Anastasia and Ferrante looked pleasant in each and every one, while Driscoll maintained a scowling countenance. Quite a few shots showed the man with his cell phone glued to his ear, and each and every one practically screamed *I don't want to be here!* I picked out one that showed all three chefs at the beginning of the bake-off, and then selected one that showed Arleen and Kurt bent over their ovens, before Arleen noticed something was wrong. As I lifted the photo up, I saw there was one underneath it, of Colleen and Arleen tying on their aprons. I glanced at the timestamp at the bottom of the photo. It was dated just before the second half was slated to begin.

I frowned as I looked at the photo. Something was off. I reached for the photo of Arleen and Kurt at their ovens, and looked at it.

In that photo, Arleen was wearing a print apron. But in the later photo with Colleen, she had on a white apron. She'd switched her apron? Why? I picked up another photo which showed all the contestants at the end of the first half. Arleen's apron appeared to be clean, unless she'd spilled something on it afterward . . . and that's when it hit me.

I grabbed my photos, including the one of Colleen and Arleen, and hurried out of Dale's office and back up to my own. I went inside my office, shut and locked the door, tossed the photos on my desk, and grabbed my tote bag. I opened the zipper compartment and withdrew the piece of fabric that I'd found outside the kitchen, right before I found Driscoll's body. I'd meant to give it to Bartell last night, but had forgotten. As I laid the fabric next to the photo of Arleen in the printed apron, I was glad I had.

They looked to be an exact match. Which could well mean Brandon Hoffman's discovery of the blood-covered printed fabric in the ladies' room could end up implicating Arleen in Driscoll's murder.

ELEVEN

Hilary's mother and sister lived in a small white bungalow on the outskirts of town. It was usually a short trip from *Southern Style*'s offices, but thanks to a water-main break a few days ago, the street was being repaved, down to one lane for traffic, which doubled travel time. After almost a half-hour of stop and go, I finally reached the Brighton Hill Road turnoff that led to the house. As I pulled up in front, I saw Arleen's white sedan in the driveway. She was home. Good. With any luck, Hilary's mother would be out, and I'd get a chance to speak with Arleen alone. I had an idea she might not be as forthcoming with answers to my questions if her mother were around. I parked and hurried up the short walkway to the front porch, where I rang the bell and waited. I heard footsteps and a few minutes later my heart sank a bit as Mrs Hanson opened the door.

'Tiffany. What a nice surprise.' A widow in her late fifties, Hilary's mother could easily pass for forty. Her skin was clear and unlined thanks to a regular regimen of moisturizers and mudpacks, and today her trim figure was encased in a soft lemon-yellow pantsuit. Her pale blonde hair curled around her face, and her blue eyes, so like Hilary and Arleen's, looked at me curiously. 'What can I do for you?'

'Actually, I'm here to speak to Arleen. It's, ah, about the contest. There are some final details about rescheduling I need to go over with her.'

'Oh, yes, the contest.' Mrs Hanson's nose wrinkled just slightly. 'Such a shocking thing to happen! I'll certainly miss Mr Driscoll's morning segment on *Good Morning Branson*. I looked forward to it every week.' She gave her head a brisk shake. 'Arleen stepped out. She said she had an important errand to run, and she took my car since it was blocking hers. She should be back soon, though, so if you'd care to wait . . .'

'I would, thanks.'

Mrs Hanson stepped aside and motioned for me to enter. As I stepped into the foyer, I noticed the copy of the *Branson Bugle* on the hall table in the entryway. It was face up so that its headline, FOOD CRITIC TAKES LAST BITE, screamed up at me. Mrs Hanson followed my gaze, walked over and flipped the paper over. She motioned toward the living room. 'Have a seat, dear. Can I get you anything? Coffee, tea, water?'

'I'd love an iced tea, if you have it.'

'I have instant.'

'That's fine.'

Mrs Hanson disappeared into the kitchen, and I went into the living room. Every aspect of the room radiated cozy, from the red and brown plaid sofa and loveseat to the framed photos and knick-knacks on the fireplace mantel. I seated myself on the edge of the loveseat and idly glanced at the array of magazines that littered the mission-style coffee table in front of me. There were several fashion magazines interspersed with popular gossip magazines I'd seen at the supermarket checkout counter. A small stack on the end were devoted to food and recipes. Arleen's, no doubt. The magazine on top, *Foodie International*, had an article titled, 'The 51 Best Pizza Recipes'. I started to reach for it when I heard the front door open and close, and a second later I heard Arleen's voice, raised in frustration.

'What do you mean, you don't know? Surely you must have some idea . . . yes, yes, I know it's all considered crime-scene evidence, but . . . OK, OK. Fine.'

I heard a muffled oath, and then Arleen herself stood framed in the living-room doorway. Her eyes popped as she saw me sitting on the sofa, and her hand went to her throat. 'Tif-Tiffany,' she finally managed to croak. 'Wh-what are you doing here?'

'Arleen! Don't be rude, dear. Tiffany came to see you about the contest.'

Mrs Hanson appeared in the doorway behind her daughter, balancing a tray on which rested a large glass of iced tea and a plate of cookies. She walked over, set the tray on the coffee table in front of me, and turned to her daughter. 'Would you like a glass of iced tea, too, dear?'

'Yes, Mother.'

Mrs Hanson nodded and disappeared into the kitchen once

again. Arleen shed her light jacket and tossed it over the back of the loveseat before she plopped on to it. 'Sorry if I was rude,' she said to me. 'It's been an incredibly frustrating morning.'

'So I gathered.' I looked her straight in the eye. 'I couldn't help but overhear your phone conversation as you came in.'

Arleen shot me a sheepish look. 'Guess that was my fault. Well, it's no secret. I called the police station. I wanted to know when they think they'll be releasing my cutlery set.'

'That's hard to say. I know they packed up everything that was lying around.'

'Yeah, evidence in a crime scene, or something like that, at least that's what the officer who took my call said. But geez, it's not like I killed Driscoll or anything. I really don't see why they have to hang on to my stuff.' She blew out a breath. 'I'd like to practice, you know, and it's hard without my knives. I went down to Bigelow's to see if I could find something similar – no such luck.' She made a little growling sound deep in her throat. 'All their knives are bargain-basement quality, and even if I had the money, there's no time to order another custom set.'

'Well, Driscoll was killed with a chef's knife, and it was a home chef cook off, so it's only logical they would want to rule out everyone's knives as the murder weapon.' I paused. 'According to the insurance form you filled out, your knife set is a Gyuto, correct?'

Arleen frowned. 'Yes, but what does that have to do with it?'

'I saw the murder weapon,' I said. 'It was a black-handled, ten-inch chef's knife, and the blade had symbols etched on it.'

'So? What does that . . . oh!' Arleen's puzzled expression morphed into one of sudden understanding. 'You don't mean . . . the police can't possibly think that my knife is the murder weapon? Surely there are other knives around that fit that description.'

'I doubt there are any fancy knives like that in the high school break-room pantry. And the only two contestants with Gyuto knives were you and Colleen Collins. Kurt Howell's set is a Santoku.'

'So? Santoku's also have symbols etched on their blades.'

'True, but the handles on Howell's set were stainless steel. I noticed it particularly because they were different from the other knives.'

Arleen shifted in her seat. 'Look – Driscoll annoyed me, I admit that. He tried to come on to me, and I didn't appreciate it. But kill the guy over it? Get real! Why, if I killed every guy who made unwelcome advances toward me, I'd have about thirty back-to-back life sentences.'

I reached across the coffee table and grabbed her hand. 'I'm not saying that you killed Driscoll, Arleen. I'm just telling you why the police are holding on to everyone's cutlery. There is something I did want to ask about, though . . .'

'Here we are, dear.'

We both looked up as Mrs Hanson returned with a tall glass of iced tea. She plucked a coaster from the rack in the center of the coffee table and set the glass on top of the coaster in front of Arleen. 'Can I get you girls anything else?'

Arleen waved her mother away. 'No, we're fine, Mother. If you could just give us a little privacy?'

Mrs Hanson looked a little miffed at the rebuff, but she just said, 'Of course. I need to go to the store anyway. You girls can chat, and I'll be back soon.'

Mrs Hanson pulled a jacket out of the hall closet, and a few minutes later we heard the click of the front door closing. Arleen shook her head. 'I love my mother, but at times she can be very overprotective . . . not to mention nosy.'

I couldn't suppress a smile. 'I remember Hilary telling me the exact same thing.'

The corners of Arleen's mouth turned downward. 'To be honest, that's one of the reasons I wanted to win the contest. If I had that prize money, I could make a good-sized dent in my student loan and maybe get my own apartment.' She slapped her hand down on the couch. 'Well, I know you didn't come here to listen to me grouse about my problems. My mother said you came to see me about the contest?' A look of sudden panic crossed her face. 'They haven't changed their minds about continuing it, have they?'

'Oh, no. We reserved the auditorium for a week from this coming Saturday. We figured it would give time for all the negative publicity surrounding Driscoll's death to die down – and to find another judge. I'll mention all that in my Saturday blog.' I let out a breath. 'Which brings me to the reason I wanted to speak to you. When I was looking over the photos to accompany my article, I couldn't help but notice you put on a different apron for the second half.'

Arleen's head snapped up and her eyes narrowed. 'Say what?'

I opened my crossbody bag and pulled out the two photos I'd taken from Dale's desk. I laid them side by side on the coffee table in front of Arleen. 'See. This is one that was taken right before the first half of the contest started. You're wearing a blue, white and purple printed apron. Now at the start of the second half . . .' I tapped the photo showing Arleen and Colleen tying their aprons. 'You have on a plain white one. I was just wondering why the switch?'

Arleen stared at the photos. One hand balled into a fist, and she clenched it so tightly that the knuckles bled white. Finally she looked at me. 'It was no big deal,' she said. 'I just felt like switching. I thought maybe the white apron might bring me luck. It did once before.'

I reached into my bag again, drew out the sliver of printed fabric and held it up. 'But can you explain this? I found it snagged on the door leading to the kitchen, right before I found Driscoll's body. This is from your apron, isn't it?'

Arleen's lips moved but no sound came out. Then she lunged across the coffee table and grabbed at the fabric. Fortunately, my reflexes were faster than hers. I shoved the bit of apron back into my purse and looked at her.

'Believe me, I'm trying to help you, Arleen. If you killed Driscoll in self-defense—'

'I didn't kill Driscoll,' Arleen cried out. She reached up and rubbed at the bridge of her nose. Then in a quieter tone said, 'I didn't kill anyone, Tiffany. There's a logical explanation for that fabric being there.'

'OK.' Now it was my turn to sit back and fold my arms over my chest. 'I'm listening.'

Arleen rose and moved over to sit next to me on the sofa. In a low tone she said, 'I did have an argument with Driscoll, but I didn't kill the man, I swear it. You know that he tried to make a pass at me, and I threw water at him. After he denied it and said all those mean things, well, it made me mad. I went looking for him, and he was just going into that kitchen. I told him that just because he was a famous food critic, he couldn't intimidate me.' She shook her head. 'The creep tried to make another pass at me. I point-blank told him if he tried anything like that again, I'd start blabbing that he and Colleen Collins were a lot closer than a judge and a contestant should be. I saw them earlier, in a pretty tight clinch.'

I nodded. That fitted in with what Twyla Mae had told me. Aloud I said, 'I'm sure that didn't faze Driscoll.'

'Nope, not a bit. He just laughed and told me I had no proof. That's when I lied.' She lowered her gaze. 'I told him I'd snapped a photo on my phone, and he could just explain it to the press.'

'And what was Driscoll's reaction to this?'

'He said that he didn't respond well to threats. Then he demanded I give him my phone so he could delete the photo. I went to leave, and he grabbed my apron. I tried to jerk away, but he was pretty strong. I finally gave it one good tug and I guess that's how it ripped. I didn't look for the missing piece, I just hot-tailed it out of there.'

'Did anyone see you?'

'No, I don't think so.' She paused. 'I just wanted to get away. I was afraid he'd follow me. I bet he would have, too, but someone else came into the kitchen after I left.'

'Really? Then they must have entered through the back way, through the break room.' I leaned forward. 'Do you know who it was?'

Arleen shook her head. 'I don't know. Whoever it was didn't say anything. I just heard Driscoll say, "What are you doing here?" and he didn't sound too thrilled. I didn't hang around, I just beat it. Then I saw my apron was ripped, and I knew I couldn't go back onstage with it. I always keep a spare apron in my tote, just in case I spill something on it, you know? I was so angry I just ripped the apron off and threw it down on the floor under one of the tables in the break room. Then I went for a short walk outside in the parking lot to cool down.'

'Hilary and I looked for you out in the parking lot. We didn't see you.'

Arleen shrugged. 'You must have just missed me. I came back inside pretty quick, because I knew I had to dig that apron out of my tote bag.'

I closed my eyes, replaying the scene in my mind. The voice I'd heard with Driscoll could have belonged to Arleen, or to the mysterious person she'd claimed had entered after her. But how to prove it? I opened my eyes and looked at Arleen. 'Detective Hoffman found that printed apron, along with a towel, in the trash bin in the ladies' room. They were both covered in blood.'

Arleen put her fist to her mouth and stifled a gasp. 'Oh my God! That makes it look bad for me, doesn't it?'

I nodded. 'Especially if it should turn out to be your knife that killed Driscoll, yes.'

'My knife . . . oh golly!' Arleen's normally rosy complexion turned white. 'Everyone's knives were spread out on their counters. I guess anyone could have walked by and picked one up.' Her eyes sparked. 'Maybe it was that Colleen Collins. I still think she's the one who tried to sabotage my oven.'

'Murder is a far cry from sabotaging an oven,' I said.

'Well, maybe she had a history with Driscoll. She was pretty quick to accuse me of having one.'

I looked Arleen straight in the eye. 'Do you?'

She gave her head a quick shake and looked away, twisted her hands in her lap. I had the distinct feeling Arleen was holding something back, but I could also tell she wasn't going to reveal anything more. 'Well, I have to get going,' I said.

She looked at me. 'Are you going to show that piece of fabric to Bartell?'

'I'm going to have to, at some point.' I laid my hand on her arm. 'I'm going to give you some advice, Arleen. You don't have to take it, but I would strongly advise that you contact Detective Bartell and tell him just what you told me, about your argument with Driscoll and him ripping your apron. It's only a matter of time before they will identify it as yours, and it's far better if you come clean before they approach you.'

Arleen nibbled at her lower lip. 'You might be right. I-I'll think about it.'

I gave her arm a quick squeeze. 'Here's some more advice. Don't think too long.'

TWELVE

I had some time before I was expected at Dolores Carlson's, so I sent Hilary a text. *Got time for a latte? Got something urgent we need to discuss.* My BFF texted right back: *Sure. The usual spot?*

I texted back *fine*, and fifteen minutes later I walked through the door of Jumpin' Java, a cozy little coffeehouse on the ground floor of a red-brick building about two blocks away from *Southern Style*'s offices. Hilary was seated at a marble-topped table in the rear of the store. She saw me the minute I walked in and started waving madly. I waved back and stole a quick glance at the counter. The line was pretty long, so I made my way across the freshly waxed wood plank floor to her table, where a pleasant surprise awaited me – namely a steaming mocha latte and a large chocolate nut brownie. I slid into the seat opposite Hilary and reached for the brownie. 'Aw, you remembered,' I said, taking a large bite. I closed my eyes and a blissful sigh emitted from my lips. 'Delicious.'

'I remembered you raved about those in your review.' She pushed the large slice of coffee cake on the plate in front of her around, and I noted she had yet to taste it. 'I ordered two extra-strength lattes, too. I figured we might need 'em.' She pushed her latte off to one side and leaned forward. 'So, don't keep me hanging. What's the something urgent?'

I quickly told her about finding the sliver of Arleen's apron in the kitchen doorway just before I discovered Driscoll's body, and Hoffman's subsequent discovery of the bloody apron. While I talked, my friend was silent – a condition rare for her. When I finished, she stared at me for a moment, then dropped her head into her hands. 'I knew something was up with her,' she muttered. 'She was trying not to show it, but I know my sister. Driscoll's presence was upsetting to her.' She raised her head and looked at me, and I could see tears starting to form in her eyes. 'But Tiff – she's not a killer.'

'I know that,' I said soothingly. 'I don't think she killed Driscoll either, but she is hiding something.'

Hilary frowned. 'Hiding something? Like what?'

I picked up my latte, took a sip, set the cup down before I answered. 'I think she knows Driscoll a lot better than she let on. Remember he had to bow out of judging that beauty contest she was in last year. I think something might have transpired between them before that.'

My BFF's frown deepened. 'You think maybe he made a pass at her then?'

I shrugged. 'It's possible. Arleen's a beautiful girl, and from all accounts, Driscoll was quite a ladies' man.'

Hilary sighed. 'I guess it's possible. Ar never mentioned anything like that, though.'

'Maybe she felt ashamed.'

'Or she was afraid to bring it up around our mother. Mom would have driven right down to Driscoll's TV studio, walked onstage when he was on the air and read him the riot act.'

I couldn't suppress a smile, because Hilary's mother would indeed do something like that. 'Well, once Bartell realizes that bloody apron is Arleen's, he'll pull her in for more questioning. I suggested she beat him to it, go down to the station and tell him just what she told me.'

'I get what you mean. Not saying anything makes her look guilty, right?'

'Right.'

Hilary shook her head. 'It's good advice, but I can tell you right now, Ar won't take it. She's stubborn. I'd try and talk some sense into her, but believe me, she won't listen to me either.'

'Well, there is a ray of hope. Arleen told me she overheard Driscoll say, "What are you doing here?" to someone after she stormed out of the kitchen. Unfortunately she didn't hear the other person speak, so she has no idea who it was.' I leaned forward and lowered my voice. 'What I'm really afraid of is that the murder weapon will turn out to be Arleen's knife.'

Hilary paled. 'Oh my gosh, I never thought of that!'

'It could either mean that the killer just snatched the first knife available, or someone's deliberately trying to frame Arleen.'

'Maybe Ar will get lucky and the murder weapon will belong

to that Colleen Collins,' suggested Hilary hopefully. 'After all, they both had the same set of knives.'

'She's a definite possibility,' I agreed. 'I keep thinking about what Charlotte Horn told me, that Driscoll had a big secret in his past, something that had to do with a woman.'

'You think the woman was Colleen Collins?'

'Maybe. I was thinking of something else, though.' I told Hilary what I'd discovered about Driscoll, Charlotte and Santangelo all living in the same cities at approximately the same time. 'Maybe Charlotte knows more about this "big secret" than she lets on.'

Hilary looked puzzled, and then her expression cleared. 'Oh, I see what you're getting at. You think maybe Charlotte Horn herself is this mystery woman?'

'It's possible. She might have made up that story about Driscoll being involved in a suspicious death and her looking for a "big scoop" story to divert suspicion away from herself. Who knows, maybe she and Santangelo are both in on it. I can tell you that Santangelo was none too pleased with Driscoll, and vice versa.'

Hilary ran her finger along the rim of her coffee cup. 'I doubt Charlotte Horn will tell you anything,' she said. 'The woman's a crime reporter. She's too slick.'

'Oh absolutely. She'd never admit to anything directly. Anyway, I wasn't thinking of asking her,' I said. 'I've got someone else in mind.'

'Who?'

'Santangelo's ex-wife, Dolores Carlson. I've got a six o'clock appointment with her.'

Hilary gave me a sidelong glance. 'So much for your promise to Bartell not to investigate, huh?'

'That was before all this happened with your sister. You know I'm going to do everything I can to make sure Arleen doesn't get railroaded for a crime she didn't commit.'

Hilary smiled at me. I could see the tears glistening in her eyes. 'Thank you for doing this,' she murmured. 'Even though I know you making like Nancy Drew will steam Bartell.'

'He'll get over it,' I said. I shot her a grin. 'If we have any shot at a relationship, he's going to have to get used to me whipping out my deerstalker hat and magnifying glass on occasion.

Which reminds me, I've got about four hours to bone up on interior decorating for my meeting with Dolores Carlson.'

'Do you really think you can get anything useful out of her?'

'It's worth a shot. From what Twyla Fay told me, there's no love lost between Dolores and her ex, so if she's privy to any of his secrets, she just might be amenable to spilling them – or, at the very least, putting me in touch with someone who could.' I paused. 'And, of course, there's another possibility.'

'What's that?'

'That Driscoll's mystery woman could be Dolores Carlson.'

I returned to my office and divided my afternoon between interior design research and polishing up my weekend blog. By five thirty I was ready to leave to keep my appointment with Dolores Carlson. I hadn't heard from Arleen, not that I expected to. I texted Hilary, but she hadn't heard from her sister either. I wondered if she'd taken my advice and had gone to see Bartell, but somehow I doubted she would. She'd seemed too frightened.

Five minutes to six found me parking my convertible in front of the address on Dolores Carlson's business card. The house was nothing like I'd expected. It was a small bungalow style with a sloping porch, tucked back in a shady corner on a quiet street lined with huge elms and flowering shrubs. I locked my car and went up the neatly trimmed walkway, up the porch steps and rang the front doorbell. A few minutes later the door opened to reveal a demure-looking woman with short medium-brown hair that had streaks of gold running through it. Her eyes, behind wire-rimmed glasses, were a bright hazel with flecks of gold in the center of their irises. She had a wide, full-lipped mouth that was parted in a smile, revealing a nice set of bright white teeth. She had on a U-necked LBD, which was the perfect foil for the thick braided gold chain around her neck. I'm terrible at guessing ages, but I put Dolores Carlson in her middle fifties – a very well-kept middle fifties. She pushed her glasses down on the bridge of her nose and held out a well-manicured hand.

'You must be Tiffany Austin. Please, come in.'

I stepped over the threshold and she wiggled her fingers, indicating I was to follow her. We went into a room that I took to be the parlor, and she turned on a lamp with a fringed shade. One glance around told me that Dolores Carlson's reputation as a high-end interior designer was well founded. The delicate rose color of the walls was a perfect contrast to the soft white sofa and loveseat combo. The material had little metallic threads of rose and gray running through it, and throw pillows in the same colors were strategically placed on both pieces of furniture. The carpet, thick and plush, was a perfect compliment with its swirl pattern of rose and gray. There were built-in bookshelves lining one wall, filled with leather-bound volumes. A massive Steinway piano sat off to the left of a marble fireplace. There were some framed photographs on top of the piano. I glanced at them as I walked past. One photograph in particular caught my eye. It showed Dolores with her arm around a slender teenager wearing large black glasses. Something about the younger girl struck me as familiar, but I couldn't place just what that was.

'Sit, sit,' said Dolores. She waved me toward the loveseat, and she took a seat in a high-backed Queen Anne chair upholstered in the same material positioned directly opposite me. 'I'm sorry I can only give you a half-hour. I have another business engagement.'

'Yes, your assistant mentioned that.'

'So.' Dolores Carlson leaned back in her chair and pushed her glasses farther up on her nose. 'Twyla Fay Thorpe recommended me to you?'

'Yes, yes, she did. Twyla Fay said you were just the person I was looking for.'

'Well, isn't that sweet.' She leaned forward a bit in the chair. 'What exactly were you looking to do? A complete redecoration? One room?'

Oops. Good question. 'Ah . . . I was considering an entire facelift.'

'I see.' I could almost see the dollar signs reflected in the woman's irises as she leaned back and tented her fingers beneath her chin. 'You live in an apartment, dear?'

I shook my head. 'No, a house. I inherited it from my aunt, along with all the furnishings. It's quite charming, but not very modern.'

'I see,' she said again. She rose and walked over to a

Chippendale desk in the far corner of the room, returning a moment later with a notebook and pen. She balanced the notebook on one knee, held the pen aloft. 'What sort of house is it?'

'A Tudor-style cottage.' A mental picture rose in my mind's eye of my home, complete with arched doors, a thatched roof, cross gables and even a small turret. 'The furniture is very sturdy. A damask sofa and loveseat in the living room, oak table and chairs in the dinette. A nice four-poster bed with a canopy and cherrywood dresser and vanity in the master bedroom.'

Dolores looked up from her scribbling. 'It actually sounds divine. You might not need an entire makeover, dear. To be honest, lots of times my clients are looking for exactly what you're thinking of changing up.' Her lips curved in a half-smile. 'Modern isn't always what it's cracked up to be, you know.'

I scooted to the edge of my seat. 'You know, you're right. Twyla Fay seemed to think I should stick with what I have too.'

She took off her glasses, twirled them in one hand. 'Now, I'm not saying don't redecorate at all. Maybe you just need to rearrange some things, or maybe get one or two more quality pieces here and there for a fresh look.'

'You might have something there,' I said. 'I was thinking perhaps of replacing the old oak coffee table with something in a mission style. Maybe spruce up the dining room with a mission style banquette, too.'

'Those are good ideas.' Dolores Carlson's tone was approving. 'What about the ceiling? Box beams or coffered ceiling tiles?'

'Ceiling tiles.'

'Hm, they're usually stained dark like the other woodwork. You could paint the ceiling to make the room lighter.'

'I could paper the walls too, right?'

'Yes, but I don't really like to do that. I know a manufacturer that sells coffered ceiling tiles that can be installed with a drop grid in a variety of colors.' She scribbled something in her notebook. 'What color is your carpet?'

'It's an Oriental. Done in tones of black, blue and red.'

'Hm, Orientals are nice, but far too dark for my taste. Maybe a nice mauve carpet might give the place some punch. You have a working fireplace?'

'Yes, a marble one.'

Dolores nodded. 'How about lighting?'

'There's a couple of sconces in the living room. Most of the house just has standard fixtures, but above the dining area off the kitchen there is a darling stained-glass chandelier.'

'Do you have a formal dining area?'

'Yes, but I hardly ever use it.'

'You might if it were spruced up. I could visualize a tiered fourteen-candle chandelier, maybe a bright brass. I'd need to see the interior, of course, before I make a final assessment. I don't suppose you took some photos on your phone?'

'That would have been a good idea,' I said. 'Truthfully, I didn't think of it.'

'No matter. You can take some and e-mail them to me. I still want to do a hands-on assessment, though, but with the photos it will give me more of an idea what we can do.'

She set the notebook and pen on the table, walked back to the desk, returned a minute later with an iPad. 'I have next Wednesday at seven open. Would that be good for you?'

Finally! My opening! 'I . . . ah, I'm not sure, actually. You see, we're in the middle of this contest right now for my blog, and things are a bit unsettled right now.'

One perfectly penciled eyebrow rose. 'Contest?'

'Yes. Maybe you've heard of it. It's a pizza bake-off.'

'Pizza bake . . . oh, of course.' She put a hand to her head. 'Twyla mentioned it to me a few times. Now I know why your name seemed familiar. You write that food blog, correct?'

'Right.'

'Tiffany Austin.' The look she shot me bordered on apologetic. 'I should have recognized your name, of course. I'm much better with faces. I'm afraid I don't have much time for reading, but I do like your blog. I've found many good restaurants through it, and stayed away from lots of duds.' She smiled. 'You do a good public service for foodies who like to eat out, my dear.'

'Thank you.' I shifted in my seat. 'I thought perhaps you might have heard about the contest from your husband. Leon Santangelo is one of the sponsors.'

Dolores's smile didn't falter, but I noticed that her eyes turned cold and hard. 'You mean my *ex*-husband, dear. We've been divorced a while. A good long while, in fact.' She paused and then added, 'I heard what happened to Bart Driscoll. I imagine that's what put your little contest in flux?'

'Yes, it was . . . shocking.'

She replaced the glasses on her nose. 'Do the police have any idea who did it?'

I shook my head. 'Not yet. They're still investigating.'

Her lips thinned. 'I'm sure there are no shortage of suspects. Bart Driscoll wasn't exactly the best-loved man around.'

'No, he wasn't.' I hesitated, then plunged forward. 'I guess you knew him quite well?'

Her brow lifted. 'What makes you say that?'

'The way you referred to him as Bart, not Bartholomew.'

Dolores Carlson's smile faltered just a tad as she answered, 'Did I? It's just that Bartholomew is such a mouthful, I just shortened it for my own convenience. I knew the man by reputation only, thank God.' She glanced again at her iPad. 'So, you will let me know if Wednesday is good for you? If not, I have some slots open the following week.'

I sensed the woman was about to bring our interview to a halt, and I stole a quick glance at my watch. Heck, I still had fifteen minutes left!

'I guess your ex-husband was better acquainted with Driscoll,' I went on blithely, ignoring her question. 'After all, he is the one who persuaded him to step in as judge after Pierre Dumont's attack.'

Dolores Carlson looked at me over the rim of her glasses. 'I'm sure that if Leon did that, there was some benefit in it for him. My ex rarely does favors without an ulterior motive.'

'Oh? I thought it was because they'd known each other quite a while. Augusta, Macon, Valdosta, Atlanta.' I ticked each one off on my fingers. 'I just assumed they were either friends or had some sort of work relationship.'

Dolores removed her glasses, laid them on the coffee table before she spoke. 'Leon was never friends with Bartholomew Driscoll – at least, not that I was aware. But, of course, there was a great deal my ex kept from me.' She let out a soft guffaw. 'I suppose they could have met over some business deal. Maybe Driscoll wanted to start serving up pizza at that fancy restaurant of his?'

I decided to try another tack. 'Are you acquainted with a woman named Charlotte Horn?'

This time I got a much different reaction. Dolores Carlson's eyes widened just a bit, and she sucked in a breath sharply. She twisted her hands in her lap. 'Charlotte Horn?' she repeated. 'I'm sorry, that name's not familiar.'

'She's an investigative reporter for the *Atlanta Star-Register*, but before that, she worked crime beats on the *Augusta Chronicle* and the *Macon Herald*.'

Dolores's eyes narrowed. 'She's an *investigative* reporter?'

'Yes. I thought, maybe since you'd lived in the same places, you might be familiar with her work.'

'Well, I'm not,' she snapped.

'You wouldn't happen to know if your ex-husband was acquainted with her, would you?'

'If she's good-looking, there's a fair chance,' Dolores replied. 'My ex always did like the ladies, perhaps a bit too much. Probably not, though, if her specialty is crime. The only crime my ex has ever committed is adultery, and I doubt she's interested in that.' She angled her head at me. 'You ask a lot of questions, Ms Austin. Tell me, are you moonlighting for a local gossip rag in addition to your food blog?'

'Hardly.' I waved my hand in a careless gesture. 'I guess it's just my natural curiosity coming to the fore.'

'Oh.' Dolores picked up her glasses, repositioned them on her nose and then fixed me with a level stare. 'You do know what they say about curiosity, don't you? It killed the cat, after all.' She glanced at her watch and rose, smoothed down the side of her dress. 'I'm sorry, Ms Austin, but I have to end this meeting. As I said, I have another engagement that I can't be late for.'

She paused and looked at me expectantly. I couldn't think of another premise to prolong things, so I rose as well. 'I'll let you know about next week as soon as I can.'

'Yes, yes, do that,' Ms Carlson said. She took my elbow and practically shoved me down the hall to the front door. 'It was nice meeting you.'

'You too,' I said, and then the door closed right in my face. I started to go down the porch steps, when out of the corner of my eye I caught a glimpse of Dolores Carlson through the large picture window. She was standing beside her desk, punching a number into her cell phone, and the expression on her face was hard to read: Annoyance? Fear? I crept over to the window, which fortunately was open a crack. I made sure I stayed in the shadows just in case Dolores happened to turn and look my way. She didn't, though, and a few seconds later I heard her say, 'Thank goodness you're in. We have to talk. Meet me here in ten minutes. Come around back.'

Dolores snapped her phone shut and I slunk off the porch and moved quickly over to my car. I sat behind the wheel for a few moments to collect my thoughts. Who was Dolores in such a hurry to meet before her big appointment? Had my questioning gotten to her? I'd thought I'd struck a nerve when I mentioned Charlotte Horn. She'd denied it, but it had certainly seemed to me as if she might have known the woman.

I paused as another thought struck me. Maybe the person she'd called to meet her was Charlotte Horn! Well, there was only one way to find out. I turned the key in the ignition, slowly glided away from the curb. There was a side street just off to the right, a dead end. If I parked right at the edge, I could see the back entrance to Dolores's house. I turned down the street, made a quick U-turn in a driveway, and pulled up right to the edge. I cut my lights and slumped down in my seat. I didn't have long to wait. A few minutes later, a small Ford sedan came slowly around the corner. It stopped a few yards from the side entrance to Dolores's house. A slender figure got out, slammed the car door, and hurried down the winding driveway. It was dark, but fortunately the person had parked near a streetlamp. When they exited the car, I got a good, clear view of the face. A gasp of surprise escaped my lips.

Dolores's mystery visitor wasn't Charlotte Horn.

It was Colleen Collins.

And before I had a chance to process this development, my cell phone pinged with an incoming text. I fished my phone out of my pocket and read the brief message from Hilary:

Hoffman took Ar in for questioning. On my way to the station. Meet me if u can.

THIRTEEN

Parking was at a premium, but fortunately I found a space just across from the police station, a large gray edifice that always seemed to evoke images of Rikers Island in my mind. I parked and hurried across the street, up the short flight of stone steps and pushed through the double glass doors. A quick glance around assured me the police station hadn't changed much since my last visit. The biggest difference was the walls. Instead of the horrible grayish-green I remembered, now they were a light eggshell color – still dull but a tad more inviting. There was a small cluster of chairs on the far left side of the room, and I saw Hilary hunched in one of them, cell phone at her ear. She jumped up as I approached and jammed the phone into her jacket pocket before enveloping me in a bear hug. 'Thank God you're here,' she mumbled into my chest. 'I'm going nuts.'

I gently pushed her back into her chair and sat down beside her. 'What happened? I take it Arleen didn't get in touch with Bartell like I told her to.'

'I don't think so. I got home a little after six and she was slumped in front of the TV, eating a bag of Cheetos. I started to ask her about her conversation with you, and she said she didn't want to talk about it, she had a lot on her mind. Then the front doorbell rang. It was that Detective Hoffman. He said that Detective Bartell wanted him to bring Arleen in for questioning. Arleen got upset, wanted to call a lawyer, but Hoffman told her that wasn't necessary, she wasn't under arrest, Bartell just needed to ask her a few questions. I pulled her aside and told her it would look bad if she refused to go, so she went. I texted you and then came straight here.' Hilary looked almost ready to cry. 'They won't let me see her.'

I gave my BFF's arm a comforting squeeze. 'That's standard,' I reassured her. 'I'll bet Bartell has identified the apron. It would have been so much better if Arleen had gotten to him first and told him what happened.'

Hilary looked at me anxiously. 'Do you think you could find out what's going on? Maybe do some damage control?'

I knew the chances of Bartell telling me anything were slim to none, but Hilary looked so woebegone that I didn't have the heart to disappoint her. Besides, I still had to hand over the fabric I'd found at the crime scene. I put on a game face and gave my friend's arm a squeeze. 'I can't promise anything, but I'll do my best.'

Hilary slumped back in her chair and I walked up to the wide, walnut-wood reception desk where a bored-looking woman sat. She wore a starched denim blue shirt, and her long blonde hair was pulled into a braid that hung over one shoulder. She eyed me warily as I approached. 'Can I help you?' she asked in none too friendly a tone.

I drew myself up to my full height and said in an authoritative tone, 'I'd like to see Detective Philip Bartell.'

The receptionist gave me a chilly stare. 'Detective Bartell is busy at the moment,' she said, her tone clipped.

I leaned across the counter and said, in as firm a voice as I could muster, 'Yes, I know he's busy, but I have some information for him that concerns the witness he's interrogating. It's imperative I speak with him *right now*.' I pounded my fist lightly against the counter to emphasize the last two words. 'Detective Bartell told me to call him day or night if I came across anything pertinent,' I added. 'Check with him yourself if you don't believe me.'

She shot me a wary glance, but she pulled the desk phone closer, picked up the receiver. 'What did you say your name was?'

'Tiffany Austin.'

The woman dialed a number and after a few seconds said, 'Detective Bartell. There's a Tiffany Austin here to see you. She says she has *pertinent* information about the witness that was just brought in.' She listened for a few more seconds and I saw her cheeks redden a bit. Then she mumbled, 'Yes, Detective Bartell. OK. I'll do that.' She replaced the receiver and swiveled around in her chair to face me. 'Detective Bartell said he'll see you right away. He said to take the elevator at the end of the hall and you'd know where to go.'

'I do, thanks.' I tapped the edge of the desk with my nail. 'I know exactly where to go,' I muttered under my breath. I shot Hilary an encouraging smile, then hurried down the hall to the elevators. One was just opening, and I slipped inside, hit the button for the second floor. The ride was quick, and I exited and walked down the familiar hallway to the door at the end marked 'Conference Room 1'. I pushed open the door, half-expecting to see Arleen sitting in one of the leather chairs, looking scared and vulnerable, but the only person in the room was Bartell. He was seated in the same chair as when I'd first met him, at the end of the conference table that took up almost the entire length of the room. When he saw me, he rose and walked right over to me. His lips were tight, his expression guarded. In short, he had his cop face on.

'I'd offer you a seat, but you're not staying,' he said. 'What's this information you have for me about Arleen Hanson?'

'Before I tell you that, I have to show you something,' I said. I reached into my pocket and pulled out the sliver of printed fabric, held it up.

Bartell's eyes widened, then narrowed. 'Where did you get that?'

'I found it snagged on the door leading to the kitchen right before I found Driscoll's body.'

The eyes widened again. 'You *what?*'

'Calm down,' I said. 'I was going to tell you last night, but we started talking about other things and it slipped my mind.'

'Slipped your . . .' He reached up, lightly massaged his fore-head. 'You do recognize this, right?'

I nodded. 'It came from the bloody apron Hoffman found.'

'A bloody apron that belongs to Ms Hanson.'

My spine tingled. I'd been right. Aloud I said, 'It didn't take you long to identify it.'

'All in a day's work. Now let me get this straight. You found this snagged in the doorway right before you found the body?'

'Yes.' I drew in a breath. 'I know it doesn't look good, but . . . I asked Arleen about it, and she had a perfectly reasonable explanation.'

Bartell's left eyebrow winged upward. 'She did, eh?'

'Yes, she did.' I felt it best not to go into too much detail, so

I just added, 'The gist of it all is, Arleen said she didn't kill Driscoll, and I believe her.'

Bartell nodded. 'Of course you do.'

Now it was my turn to raise an eyebrow. 'What's that supposed to mean?'

He shrugged. 'It's only logical you would believe her. After all, she is the sister of your best friend.'

'That's true, but it's not the only reason I believe her. She – Arleen – doesn't seem the type to commit murder.'

He threw me a patient look. 'We've been down this road before, Tiffany. Anyone can be pushed to murder, you know that. I do appreciate your coming forward with that, though.' He pointed to the fabric that I still clutched in my hand. He walked over to a small desk in the corner of the room, and returned a few minutes later with a small plastic bag and a pair of tweezers. He plucked the fabric out of my hand with the tweezers and dropped it into the baggie. 'We might not be able to get too much from it, but I'll run it through the lab anyway.' He set the bag and twee-zers on the conference table and looked over his shoulder at me. 'Look, I know you're worried about your friend's sister. If it will set your mind at ease, Arleen isn't the only person we've brought back for questioning.'

'Good. You should be trying to focus elsewhere, because Arleen has no motive.'

Bartell's eyes narrowed. 'Did she tell you that?'

I swallowed. 'She didn't have to. I know that apron looks bad, but Arleen really had no motive to kill Driscoll. She didn't know him.'

'Are you certain about that?'

Something in Bartell's tone made me look at him sharply, but the man's face was a stone mask. 'You think she did?' I countered.

'He was a judge in a beauty contest she was in. And before you ask how I knew that, let me remind you that knowing things like that is my job – which people tell me I'm quite good at.'

'But he wasn't a judge,' I protested. 'Driscoll bowed out before the contest began. Arleen couldn't have been that well acquainted with him.'

'Is that what she told you?'

Something in his tone made my antennae rise. 'You know something you're not telling me,' I accused. 'What exactly are you implying?'

'I believe we've had this conversation before, but it bears repeating. I do not have to share information pertaining to an open case with a civilian, nor do I have to share any opinions or conclusions I may have reached with said civilian.'

'Even when the civilian is trying to help you solve a murder?'

'Right now the civilian is trying to draw suspicion away from her friend's sister. It's a very different scenario.'

'The civilian is trying to keep her temper, which is difficult because the detective is being pig-headed,' I snapped.

'I am not . . .' Bartell broke off his sentence, took a deep breath and reached up a hand to rub at the bridge of his nose. 'Once again . . . I'm not at liberty to share any details with you right now. If that makes me pig-headed, well, so be it.'

'Fine,' I said through clenched teeth. I started to move towards the door, then stopped. I turned around and jabbed my finger in the air. 'The murder weapon, the knife. Have you identified it yet?'

Bartell nodded. 'We have.'

'It was Arleen's, wasn't it?' At his pained look, I held up my hand. 'I know, you can't answer me. But I can make an educated guess. Those knives were lying in plain sight on the counters. People were back and forth – anyone could have taken it.' I shot him a pleading glance. 'It looks to me like someone's deliberately trying to frame Arleen.'

'Tiffany . . .' Bartell blew out a breath, swiped his hand across his forehead. Then he reached out and put his hands on my shoulders. 'You have to be the most infuriating, stubborn female I've ever known.' His lips split in a smile. 'Maybe that's the attraction, huh? Who knows?'

I found myself smiling back at him. 'Could be. Stranger things have happened.'

He lifted his hands from my shoulders, then caught one of them in his. 'Look, there's a lot going on here, things I'm not at liberty to share with you. All I can say right now is Arleen isn't being charged with anything . . . yet.'

The door to the conference room suddenly opened, and

Brandon Hoffman strode in. 'Oh, good, here you are, Detective Bartell. Mr Sample said to tell you that report will be ready in a few hours . . .' He broke off abruptly as he caught sight of me standing there. 'I'm s-sorry,' he stammered. 'Did I interrupt something?'

Bartell let out a sigh. 'No, Hoffman. Ms Austin was just leaving.' Bartell took my elbow and piloted me right through the door and into the hallway. 'Thank you, Tiffany, for your co-operation.' He leaned in a bit closer to me. 'Please, please, remember what you promised me.'

'I remember my promise,' I said through clenched teeth. 'Whether or not I keep it, though, is another story.'

And then I turned on my heel and walked out, slamming the door behind me. I headed straight for the door marked STAIRS and power-walked down them. When I reached the bottom I turned and walked back up again, taking them two at a time. I walked up and down about five more times before I finally felt calm enough to push through the door back into the lobby. Hilary was still in the same chair. She looked up anxiously as I approached. She took one look at my face and her own fell.

'Bad news?' she asked. 'Is Bartell going to arrest her?'

'No – at least, not yet,' I muttered. I dropped down into the chair next to her and started tapping my fingertips against its arms. 'Bartell knows more than he's letting on.'

'He does? What could he know about Arleen?'

'I don't know, but he knows something, and he wouldn't tell me – or he couldn't.' I raised my hand, rubbed at my forehead. 'Bartell knew about Driscoll being a judge at that beauty contest Arleen was in. He gave me the impression that she might have known Driscoll a little better than we thought.'

Hilary nodded. 'I hate to say it, but he might be right. She got so jumpy whenever he was around, and she snapped at me when I mentioned it. I just attributed it to nerves, but now I'm not so sure myself. But even if that's so, Tiff, I doubt that anything happened between them that would drive Arleen to murder him.'

'Let's hope not,' I said. I pushed my hand through my hair. There was no way to sugarcoat what I had to tell Hilary, so I just came out with it. 'Bartell said they identified the murder weapon. He didn't confirm or deny, but I know it was Arleen's knife.'

'Swell.' Hilary shot me a dejected look. 'So, what do we do now? If Ar has to spend the night in jail – heck, how do I tell my mother?'

'I don't think she'll have to go to jail; at least, not yet. Bartell said he had other people to question. But . . .'

'But what?' Hilary prompted as I hesitated.

'But circumstantial evidence seems to be piling up against her, and I also know from experience that if enough of it points to her as the killer, the police will stop looking for anyone else.'

'But Bartell wouldn't do that, would he?' my friend asked anxiously.

'He might not have a choice, if the DA feels a strong enough case can be made. That's where we come in. We need to formulate a plan of attack. We have to help steer Bartell in the direction of the real killer.'

'And just how do we do that?'

I let out a long sigh. 'Honestly, Hilary? I wish I knew.'

FOURTEEN

Hilary decided to hang around a bit longer and wait for Arleen. 'Mom won't be home from her book club meeting till eleven,' she said. 'Hopefully Ar and I can beat her there.'

I left Hilary there, a copy of *People Magazine* unopened on her lap, and went straight to my car. I drove home, pulled into my driveway and then just sat there, trying to sort out my jumbled thoughts. Someone had killed Bartholomew Driscoll, someone who might possibly have wanted to incriminate Arleen, because her knife had been used to do the deed.

The most logical person, in my mind, was Colleen Collins. She and Arleen had been none too friendly, and it seemed that Colleen herself had a history with Driscoll.

And she'd been the person Dolores Carlson had called, who she'd said she had to talk to. What was up with that?

I exited my car and went inside my house. As usual, Lily and Cooper were there to greet me. After I got a sloppy doggie kiss from Cooper, and Lily rubbed up against my legs, I gave them both treats and went over to the kitchen table where I'd left my laptop. I booted up my computer and typed in Colleen Collins-Branson and hit enter. Several hits came up. I selected Colleen's website and clicked on that. It was a simple, home-made one. The title page had a brief bio of Colleen, and the second page, titled 'Accomplishments', listed various real-estate sales. There were several pages, so I decided to scroll through all of them, just in case. On the third page I found what I was looking for. Underneath the caption, 'Recent Properties Sold' was a photograph of Colleen and Driscoll standing in front of Ambrosia.

I sat back. Well, there was the connection. Colleen had met Driscoll before – she was the real-estate agent who'd gotten him the property for his restaurant. I played through some scenarios in my mind. Colleen and Driscoll could have embarked on an affair, and most likely Driscoll dumped her – that might account for Colleen's attitude toward him. But had the break-up been bad enough to murder over? Maybe I shouldn't be so quick to diss Bartell's 'woman scorned' theory.

The other thing that bothered me was the fact Dolores had called Colleen to meet her. Why? I went back to Colleen's website and found my answer two pages later . . . she had helped Dolores Carlson find her current home. That would explain how they knew each other, but why the secret meeting? Dolores had seemed to get upset after I mentioned Charlotte Horn . . . maybe there was some connection between the three of them?

I typed in Colleen Collins slash Dolores Carlson slash Charlotte Horn. I got a few hits, but nothing that linked the three women together. Next I typed the same names, but added Driscoll to the list. I got ten pages of hits, and I scrolled down each page carefully, scrutinizing every one. On the eighth page I found an article labelled, 'Macon Reporters Accept Good Citizen Award'. There was a group of five reporters all being honored by the Case Foundation for being exemplary role models for journalism students. Standing right in the front row, clutching his brass plaque, was a smiling Bartholomew Driscoll. Next to him was a reporter named Everett Carlson, and beside him Louis Collins. Over on the far left stood a young Charlotte Horn. Charlotte Horn wasn't looking at the camera, but rather at Driscoll. There was no mistaking the besotted look on her face. It was pretty clear from that photo that Charlotte had harbored romantic feelings toward Driscoll.

I studied the photo. Had Charlotte declared her feelings of love and been rebuffed by Driscoll? The more I thought about it, the more sense it made. Charlotte Horn could have made up that story about Driscoll coming here to confront some woman from his past. Or, perhaps, the woman he was going to confront was Charlotte herself! I sighed. It was a pretty good theory, but that was all it was: a theory. If I wanted to clear Arleen, I had to have absolute proof.

I decided to try a different tack and turned my thoughts instead to Peter Hagen. I remembered during their argument he'd mentioned being ridiculed in print. When I'd researched Driscoll I'd come across two books by him, and they were both cookbooks. Surely he hadn't mentioned his brother in those? I went over to

Amazon and typed in Bartholomew Driscoll. The same two cookbooks came up. I frowned. Maybe he'd used a pseudonym? How in the world could I find that out? I tapped my fingernail against the table, and suddenly it came to me. Many authors published books using just their initials.

I went back to Wikipedia and looked up Driscoll's full name. Bartholomew James Driscoll. I went back to Amazon and typed in B. J. Driscoll. This time I got one hit. This wasn't a cookbook, however, but rather a work of fiction entitled, *Full Disclosure*. I read the brief description. It was the story of a young boy, persecuted by his father, unloved by his mother, who'd grown up in the shadow of his smarter (or so everyone thought) slightly younger brother. What defined the boy was his desire to become a world-renowned chef, but when he couldn't fulfill that ambition, he sought fame and fortune and achieved it as a food critic.

I scrolled down to read the reviews, most of which were three stars. One four-star review touted the book as a 'work of literary art', and I strongly suspected it might have been written by either Driscoll himself, or else he'd paid someone to do it. I kept scrolling and finally found one that had been posted by Leon1963. One line in the book stood out: *The main character, Burton Draper, effectively gets his final revenge on his dapper brother by publicly revealing the fact that the man had an affair with his married boss at an awards banquet.*

I sat back, thinking. Was this what Peter Hagen had meant when he said he'd been ridiculed? As a tenured professor, I could understand why Hagen wouldn't want that facet of his life made public, particularly if there were any truth to it. And knowing Driscoll, he'd done it in the most embarrassing way possible. Whatever had gone down, from what I'd overheard, it continued to be a very sore spot between them.

The name of the poster also intrigued me. Leon1963. Could that possibly be Leon Santangelo? Or a coincidence? It was indeed possible he'd written this review. I frowned as another thought occurred to me. Hagen had said something like 'wasn't ridiculing me once enough for you?' to his brother. Driscoll had hinted at something big brewing. Had Driscoll written yet another novel? And was he planning to reveal something else about his brother; something else that Hagen didn't want revealed?

To my mind, that would be a swell motive for murder.

I glanced at my watch. It was just a little after eight thirty. Not too late to pay a call on someone who might be able to shed some light on Driscoll's newest book, if there was one.

His assistant, Beth March.

I remembered Callie, Dale's assistant, mentioning that Driscoll was staying at the Haverford Inn. I'd been surprised at that, because it was situated on the edge of town, in an area of gas stations and fast-food restaurants. Definitely not the sort of five-star hotel Driscoll usually frequented. Callie had explained that with the Botanical Convention in town, it had been the only hotel available for the last-minute reservation. I'd figured Driscoll had been none too happy about that development.

I found an empty space near the front doors, parked, grabbed my purse, and hurried up the front steps. The lobby wasn't particularly inviting. The carpet was badly worn, the few armchairs scattered around were tattered, and there were cracks visible in the ceiling. A small alcove off to my right advertised a complimentary breakfast. I glanced idly at the brochures grouped on a display rack. The usual touristy things.

A short, overweight woman stood behind the front desk. As I approached, she glanced up at me with a wary expression. 'Hello,' I said. 'I'm not checking in. I'm just looking for a woman who's a guest at this hotel.'

The clerk raised both her overplucked and overdyed eyebrows. 'And who might that be?'

'Her name is Beth March. She might be registered under Elizabeth March.'

The clerk typed the name into the computer. After a few seconds she looked at me, her frown deepening. 'Sorry. No Beth March registered here.'

I nibbled at my lower lip. 'She might have been registered under Bartholomew Driscoll's name. She was his assistant.'

The clerk gave me a sharp look. 'Oh, yes. I do remember her now. She and Mr Driscoll were both in the Presidential Suite.'

I wondered just what the Presidential Suite might look like, considering the rest of the hotel. 'Do you know if she's in right now?'

'Hm, hard to say. I know the police came and got her, took her downtown a while ago. I'm not sure if she's back or not.'

That made sense. Bartell had told her to call when she felt better so he could finish questioning her. I shot the clerk a disarming smile. 'Could you ring her room and check? Please?'

The clerk hesitated. 'I don't know . . .'

I reached into my pocket, pulled out a folded twenty-dollar bill, slid it across the counter. The clerk looked at it, then picked it up and slid it into her pocket. She picked up the phone and dialed a number. After a few minutes, she hung up and turned to me. 'I guess she's not in. She's not answering. Did you want me to send someone to check the room?'

I frowned, remembering that the EMT had suggested Beth take something to calm her nerves. Maybe she had, and it had knocked her out. It was possible the girl was just sleeping soundly, after all the stress she'd undergone. If that were the case, I didn't want to disturb her. 'That won't be necessary. I'll just leave a message.'

The clerk passed me a pad and pen, and I deliberated just how wordy I should be in my message. After I moment I decided to keep it simple:

Beth, please give me a call. There is something I'd like to discuss with you about your employer. Tiffany Austin.

I jotted down my cell number, folded the paper, wrote Beth March across the face, and passed it back to the clerk. I saw her tuck it underneath her computer as I turned to leave, and I hoped that Beth would indeed get the message. If I didn't hear from her by noon tomorrow, I'd make a return visit.

I'd only taken a few steps when another thought struck me, and I retraced my steps to the counter. 'Sorry to bother you again,' I said to the clerk, 'but could you tell me if you have a Charlotte Horn registered here?'

The clerk sighed, then tapped on her keyboard once more. She squinted at her computer screen, then at me. 'Sorry. No one by that name.'

I thanked her and made for the exit. Of course, Charlotte could have used a phony name. When I came back to see Beth, I'd do a little more investigating. In the meantime, I needed to find someone else who might be able to give me the answers I wanted – and I knew just the person . . . or rather 'persons'.

I drove back to town, parked my car in the *Southern Style* employee lot and walked the two and a half blocks to Po'Boys Anonymous. I knew that on Mondays, Twyla Fay and her bestie, Minnie Mae Draper, had dinner here after Minnie Mae finished up at her beauty parlor, Lavish Locks, at eight o'clock. As I approached the low-slung gray slate building, I could see through the large plate-glass window that it was extremely busy for a Monday night, which is normally a restaurant's 'off' night (usually because potential customers have overindulged on the weekend). Nearly every table was full. There was a counter in the side window that had stools facing the street, and that was almost full as well. I paused before the picture window and peered in at the dining area. I saw Twyla Fay and Minnie Mae huddled at a table in one corner. My quarry sighted, I pushed open the front door and walked in, and almost immediately a cheery voice called out 'Tiffany Austin, welcome!'

I smiled as a petite, dark-haired woman carrying a large platter of catfish hurried toward me. Nita Gillette walked right up to me and gave me an air-kiss on each cheek. 'Bob and I were wondering if you'd find time to stop by.' She lowered her voice. 'We heard what happened at the contest. What a shame – although both Bob and I said the guy had it coming.' She wrinkled up her pert nose. 'Bartholomew Driscoll was a real stinker.'

'Yes, I haven't found anyone yet who's too broken up about his death, except possibly his assistant.'

Nita rolled her eyes. 'That man had an assistant? Good Lord! The poor thing. So, what's going to happen to the contest now?'

'The board wanted us to push forward, so we've made arrangements for next Saturday. We need another judge. You or Bob interested?'

'To help you out? I'm pretty sure one of us can be available.'

'Great. I'll talk it over with Dale and let you know.'

'Sure thing. So, what can I get you tonight? Takeout?'

'Actually, I see some friends over in the far corner. I'll see if I can join them.'

I weaved my way through the tables and, when I was about a foot away, Twyla Fay lifted her head and saw me. 'Tiffany!' she waved me over. 'Hey, what are you doing here?'

'I lost track of time and thought I'd drop in for a late supper.' I glanced around the crowded restaurant. 'Who would have thought it'd be packed on a Monday?'

'It's usually not,' Twyla Fay said, 'but they have some pretty good specials tonight. Say, you can sit with us if you want. We haven't even ordered yet.'

Minnie Mae smiled at me. She and Twyla Fay were about as different as night and day. Minnie Mae was a tiny woman, a size zero if that. Unlike Twyla, Minnie wore conservative clothes in conservative colors. Tonight she had on black slacks and a black-and-white sleeveless top. Her hair was always perfectly coiffed in a sleek pageboy that curled underneath her prominent chin. 'Yes, do join us, Tiffany,' she said in her soft Southern drawl. 'It seems like ages since I've seen you. You haven't been to Lavish Locks in a while.'

I slid into the seat opposite Minnie, and my hand went up to pat my hair a bit self-consciously. 'I've been letting it grow a bit,' I said, 'but you're right. I really should stop by for a trim.'

'Anytime. You're always welcome,' Minnie Mae replied.

'I was just filling Minnie in on all the recent happenings,' said Twyla. She leaned forward and said in a lower tone (at least, low for Twyla), 'Word on the street is Bartell's close to making an arrest. I figured chances were good you knew that, you know, considering your relationship.'

It seemed as if everyone thought Bartell and I had a relationship except Bartell and me. 'I didn't hear anything about an arrest,' I said. 'I do know he's pulled several people back for questioning.'

'Oh, yes.' Twyla Fay's head bobbed up and down. 'I know for a fact Colleen Collins was there earlier today.'

'Speaking of Colleen Collins, I found out something interesting about her today,' I said. 'She got Driscoll the venue for Ambrosia.'

'Oh, that.' Minnie Mae waved her hand in the air. 'That's old news, dear. I thought everyone knew that.'

Twyla Fay looked at her friend. 'Well, I didn't know that! See, I knew there was something going on between them.'

'Hmpf,' Minnie snorted. 'It was just business, so far as I know. Any romantic interest would have been on Colleen's part, and I doubt that. In that respect, she and Driscoll were two of a kind. The love 'em and leave 'em type.'

'Yes, I heard that Driscoll was quite the ladies' man,' I said. 'It's hard for me to believe.'

'Well, believe it,' Minnie Mae said with feeling. 'That man left a trail of broken hearts behind him longer than the San Andreas Fault. Any woman who got involved with him had to know what she was getting into. There was only one woman he ever wanted.'

'Really?' I leaned forward, propped my chin in my palm. 'Who was that?'

The two women exchanged a glance, and then Minnie Mae said, 'It happened a very long time ago – oh, it had to be twenty years or so, right Twyla?'

Twyla nodded. 'At least. His career as a critic was just starting to take off and he'd just published his first book.'

'His first cookbook?'

'Oh, no. They came later. This was fiction, a piece of trash called *Full Disclosure*. Gives me the chills thinking about it.' Twyla shook her head so hard the ends of her bob wiggled back and forth. 'It was *supposed* to be fiction, but I think it was more . . . personal.'

I looked at her. 'You read it?'

She shot me a sheepish grin. 'Sure. My customers all did, so in the end I had to as well. It was kind of *Peyton Place*-ish, if you get my drift, except for the unrequited romance part. That actually seemed heartfelt.'

'You thought so?' Twyla Fay's nose wrinkled. 'I thought it was vindictive, myself.' She turned to me and said, 'If you ask me, that was the whole reason for outing the brother. He wanted his girlfriend.'

I frowned. 'I thought the girlfriend was married.'

Twyla clucked her tongue. 'Oh, not that girlfriend. It was another girl he was going with at the time and she was single. She came from a pretty strict family. Needless to say, the fallout over that book broke them up. Peter took it pretty hard.'

Minnie let out a snort. 'If you ask me, Driscoll put that in his book on purpose. Even though he insisted it was a work of fiction, people who knew them could see the parallels. Driscoll hoped it would end his brother's romantic relationship, and it did. Driscoll swooped right in, but it didn't last long. She broke up with him.'

Twyla gave her head an emphatic shake. 'No, no. He broke up with her.'

'No, I think you're wrong. Driscoll was devastated over it.'

'The character in the book who was supposed to be Driscoll was devastated. In real life it was business as usual for the crumb.'

As the two of them bickered back and forth, I sat lost in my own thoughts. If the book was based on real-life events, then it was entirely possible that Peter Hagen had lost someone he'd cared deeply about, because his brother had exposed his dalliance, one he regretted, with another woman. And then Driscoll had gone on to woo the woman himself. Small wonder a lot of resentment had built up between them over the years, but was it a possible motive for murder?

Maybe.

'Tiffany, did you hear me?'

I jumped. 'Oh, sorry, Twyla. I guess I was daydreaming.'

'I was just telling Minnie that I heard Bartell pulled in Leon Santangelo for a grilling, although I don't know why. Santangelo is a cheat and a letch, but he hasn't got the guts to kill anyone. Just ask his ex-wife, she'll tell you. Speaking of which . . .' Twyla turned toward me with a knowing smile. 'How did your meeting go? Did you find out everything you wanted?'

'I tried,' I admitted. 'Unfortunately we were interrupted. Dolores showed me the door because she had another visitor. You'll never guess who.'

Twyla Fay put her finger to her lips. 'Let's see – Brad Pitt?'

Minnie Mae laughed. 'Heck no. Hugh Jackman is more Dolores's type.'

'Well, you're both wrong. It was the last person I ever expected to see her with. Colleen Collins.'

Twyla Fay and Minnie Mae exchanged a glance, and then Minnie Mae covered my hand with hers. 'Not so unexpected, dear. Colleen is Dolores's niece.'

'Her niece,' I cried. 'You're kidding.'

'Oh, no dear,' said Minnie. 'Colleen is Dolores's sister Ada's daughter. Ada married Nathan Collins, and they had two children: Bradley, who's a doctor in Valdosta, and Colleen. Colleen helped her aunt find that gorgeous house of hers after her divorce.'

'Yes, I saw that on her website,' I admitted. I frowned. It might make sense, now, why Dolores might call her niece. Maybe Charlotte Horn was investigating one or both of them as Driscoll's mystery woman. I'd gotten the definite sense that at the very least Dolores was acquainted with Charlotte, even though she denied it. How well all these women knew each other, though, remained to be seen.

Well, I might not have gotten anything out of Dolores, but Charlotte Horn was another story. If the woman wanted my help, as she claimed, she was going to have to come across with some answers, and soon.

We finished up with dinner around nine thirty. I'd had the giant catfish and oyster po'boy which had been delicious . . . and filling. Twyla Fay had chosen the fried clams, while Minnie Mae opted for traditional roast beef. We all declined dessert, and I was actually glad of the short walk from the restaurant back to *Southern Style*'s parking garage. It would definitely help my waistline.

I entered the garage and was just starting for my car when I heard a loud 'Psst' behind me. I whirled around, but could see nothing in the shadows. I started walking again and once again I heard a 'Psst. Tiffany. Over here.'

I squinted, and this time I made out a dark figure, hunched next to a sedan in the shadows.

'Who's there?' I called out. My hand fished in my pocket, closed around my cell phone. I had Bartell's cell on my speed-dial and, in spite of the strain between us, I wasn't hesitant at all to dial the number.

The figure straightened, walked into the dim light, and I saw who it was.

Charlotte Horn.

FIFTEEN

C harlotte moved toward me, a relieved look on her face. 'Tiffany, thank goodness. I saw your car here. I've been waiting over an hour for you to show up.'

'Why are you sneaking around in the dark like this?' I demanded. 'You could have come to see me at my house, like you did last night. Or you could have called, and I could have met you somewhere.'

Charlotte shook her head. 'It's not safe.'

'Not safe? What do you mean, not safe?'

Charlotte took a step closer to me. 'Keep your voice down,' she commanded. 'I told you, I'm still on the trail of Driscoll's mystery woman. I think . . . I think I'm getting close. Very close. It's just a bit more complicated than I'd thought.'

I'd had about enough of this. I put my hands on my hips and said, 'Knock it off, Charlotte. There is no mystery woman, is there? The mystery woman is you.'

She looked puzzled. 'Me?'

'Yes, you. I did some internet research, I found a photograph of you and Driscoll, taken when you were both reporters starting out. There's no mistaking that look of love in your eyes.'

Charlotte stared at me, and then she sagged against the sedan and started to laugh. 'Oh my God, you really believe that,' she gasped. 'You really think I was in love with Bartholomew Driscoll?'

'I've been in love myself, Charlotte. I know the look.'

The reporter sobered instantly. 'I'm sorry, I didn't mean to laugh, but . . . that infatuation was so long ago that I forget, sometimes, that I thought those feelings were real, genuine. It seems a lifetime ago.'

'So you admit that you are the mystery woman?'

Charlotte's eyes flashed. 'I admit nothing of the sort. I was infatuated with Driscoll for a short time, I admit it. OK, maybe

I mistook those feelings for love. But no way am I his mystery woman.'

I folded my arms across my chest. 'And I should believe you because . . .?'

Charlotte's shoulders lifted in a shrug. 'There's no reason on earth why you should believe me. I can understand why you would be suspicious of me.'

'I'm glad you see my point of view,' I said. 'I don't know you. I have no idea what lengths you might go to for a story.'

Charlotte's eyebrow quirked. 'I've been known to go pretty far, but I draw the line at murder, if that's what you're thinking,' she said. 'And speaking of that, I understand the police are waiting for the results of a toxicology report, and then they're primed to make an arrest.'

I frowned. 'Toxicology report? I thought the cause of death was a severed artery?'

'Well, there was a water bottle found by Driscoll's body. The police – specifically Detective Bartell – thought Driscoll might have been drugged. There was no sign of a struggle, and some witnesses said he'd complained of feeling light-headed earlier.'

'That's true, he did. I never thought of that angle.' I looked Charlotte straight in the eyes. 'Do you know Dolores Carlson?'

Charlotte's head jerked up. 'Leon Santangelo's ex-wife, right? I've met her,' she said carefully. 'Why do you ask?'

'I mentioned your name and asked if she was familiar with your work. It seemed to upset her that your background was in crime reporting. Right after that, she called Colleen Collins and had a confab with her.'

Charlotte's eyes widened. 'I did speak with Colleen at the contest, tried to draw her out a bit about Driscoll. No doubt she confided in her aunt, and when you mentioned my background, she felt obligated to tell her.'

'Why do you think she would feel obligated?'

Charlotte shrugged. 'I was asking Colleen some pointed questions. She most likely wants her to exercise caution.'

'These questions – were they about Dolores?'

'Dolores? No, why would you think that?'

'I thought Dolores could possibly be Driscoll's mystery

woman. I've heard rumors that she and Driscoll were romantic-ally involved years ago. I met with her earlier and hinted around about it, but she denied knowing him.'

Charlotte waved her hand. 'Well, she's been acquainted with him recently. Driscoll was talking to her about decorating his newest restaurant.'

'His new restaurant,' I cried. 'So he was expanding?'

'He wanted to. It was all being kept very hush-hush. On account of Leon.'

'Santangelo? What did he have to do with it?'

'Well, for one thing his liquid cash had been tied up in Santangelo's business. For another, he didn't want Leon finding out he was considering using Dolores.'

'That could have been what they were arguing about when I overheard them.'

'Could be. Rumor has it that Driscoll got himself into a bit of a financial pickle with his financial advisor. He supposedly lost a huge bundle of money. He wanted Santangelo to buy out his interest. He needed the cash for the new restaurant. But Santangelo was strapped himself. Driscoll, though, wasn't taking no for an answer. He threatened Leon with selling his interest off to someone else.'

My eyes widened. 'Not Dolores?'

'No – Giovanni Ferrante.'

My jaw dropped. 'You're kidding! I had the impression Ferrante wasn't too fond of Driscoll.'

'He wasn't. There was some bad blood between them, but Ferrante is first and foremost a businessman. Owning a control-ling interest in a pizza dough business would have been a sweet deal for Ferrante. But Santangelo wasn't going down without a fight.' Charlotte let out a breath. 'Santangelo wanted Dolores to help him buy out Driscoll.'

I raised an eyebrow. That explained why Santangelo had begged for more time. 'And Dolores wouldn't do it?'

'She was considering it. I think she was trying to figure out which was the lesser of two evils, Driscoll or her ex.'

'Leon might have figured Dolores was going to turn him down. Plus, I overheard Driscoll tell him he was out of time. That could have meant Driscoll had decided to sell his interest to someone else, which would have made Leon pretty desperate,' I said. 'It could have driven him to take action. And he was backstage . . . a lot.' I started to hurry towards my car. 'I've got to go to Bartell and tell him all this. Why don't you come with me?' I coaxed. 'Bartell might pay a bit more attention to this information if it comes from someone other than me.'

She shook her head. 'No, I'm working on another angle. I've got to lie low.' She shot me an encouraging smile. 'I'm sure you can handle Bartell.'

'That makes one of us,' I said. 'This other angle you're working on – would it have anything to do with the fact that Driscoll stole his brother's girlfriend?'

Charlotte let out a chuckle. 'You read *Full Disclosure*, huh?'

'No, but some friends told me about it. This girlfriend – is she the mystery woman?'

'There's a connection,' Charlotte said slowly. 'And that's all I can say right now.'

I threw up my hands. 'OK, fine. I'll give you a call, let you know how I make out. I still have your card with your contact information.'

'Don't bother with that,' Charlotte said. 'I lost my cell and had to get one of those disposable ones. I tried to call you and tell you, but I got interrupted both times.'

Well, that solved the mystery of those two burner-cell calls. 'What's the number?'

She shook her head. 'It's safer for you if I'm the one who initiates contact.' She glanced around anxiously. 'I've stayed here too long. I've got to go.' She turned and walked away swiftly, melting into the shadows like a wisp of smoke.

'Wait,' I called after her. 'Can't you at least tell me where you're staying?'

No answer. Charlotte had disappeared.

I got in my car and made tracks back to the police station. There was a different woman behind the desk now, a chunky girl with curly hair who was chewing what seemed like an enormous wad of gum. I asked to speak to Detective Bartell and gave my name. She didn't even bat an eyelash, just picked up the phone, dialed a number. Five minutes later I found myself back in Conference

Room 1, only this time Bartell wasn't sitting there. The room was empty.

I didn't have to wait long. Bartell came in about five minutes later. There were deep circles underneath his eyes, and he didn't look at all happy to see me. 'Tiffany,' he said. 'What can I do for you? Or have you uncovered something else you think I need to know?'

'I heard you're about to make an arrest,' I blurted out. 'But I've got information that could change everything.'

He stared at me. 'What sort of information?'

'Leon Santangelo has a beauty of a motive. Driscoll was going to sell his controlling stake to—'

'Ferrante, Leon's rival,' Bartell finished my sentence. 'Yes, I know. And I agree, it's an excellent motive, except for the fact Santangelo has an alibi for the TOD.'

My face fell. 'He does?'

'Yes. He was chatting with Anastasia Ricci at the time. Several of the reporters who were there have them on tape, and even *Southern Style*'s photographer got a shot of them. Date- and time-stamped, so there's no chance of error.'

I grabbed Bartell's arm. 'You're going to arrest Arleen, aren't you?' I said, my voice hoarse.

I expected him to evade my question, but instead Bartell met my gaze. 'Yes.'

I shook my head. 'You're making a mistake, you know. She's not guilty.'

'The evidence says otherwise,' he said softly.

'What evidence, exactly? The fact that her knife was the murder weapon?'

'That, and more.' He sighed. 'I may as well tell you, because it will be public knowledge soon anyway. The knife used to kill Driscoll was hers. The only prints we found on the handle belonged to Arleen.'

'Doesn't mean anything,' I said brusquely. 'The killer could have worn gloves.'

'True, but there's more. Remember that water bottle that was near the body? Beth March told us that Driscoll always took his own stash of bottled water with him wherever he went.'

'That's true,' I said. 'He kept it in a cooler backstage.'

'Well, we had the water bottle tested as well. There were traces of Natrol in it.'

'Natrol? That must mean someone deliberately drugged him, most likely so he couldn't fight them off. But that doesn't mean it was Arleen. That cooler was backstage and it wasn't locked. Anyone could have picked up a bottle and tampered with it.'

'True, but Ms Hanson has a prescription for Natrol. She uses it to calm her nerves. There was a half-empty bottle of Natrol in her purse. When you combine that with the bloody apron, Arleen's prints on the murder weapon, their confrontations that day . . .'

'I know,' I sighed. 'It doesn't look good.'

'That's putting it mildly.' Bartell paused. 'Then there's a little matter of Arleen threatening him at the pizza contest.'

'What?'

'Colleen Collins said in her statement that Arleen said, quite vehemently, that someone should teach him a lesson. She said you and Hilary were both there.'

My stomach sank. 'Yes, I-I do remember her saying something like that. But she didn't mean it.'

'Well, the DA likes her for Murder One, and wants us to wrap this up quickly.'

My head was spinning, but I struggled to remain calm. 'Listen, Bartell, I hear what you're saying, but it's a frame. Trust me, there are far better suspects.'

'I'm sure there are. But none of them have their fingerprints on the murder weapon, or a prescription for drugs they carried found in the victim's system.' He reached out and touched my arm. His expression was unreadable. 'I'm sorry, Tiffany. Really sorry.'

We looked at each other for a few minutes, and then Bartell turned and walked out of the room. I reached up to dab at the moisture accumulating in my eyes, when my phone pinged with an incoming text. I pulled it out and read the message from Hilary:

Help! Hoffman here to arrest Arleen.

SIXTEEN

I texted my friend back: *Am at police station. Will wait for U.* Then I made my way back to the lobby area. I didn't have to wait long. About fifteen minutes later, a haggard-looking Hilary burst through the front door. She saw me sitting over by the far wall and made a beeline for me. 'Oh, Tiff,' she cried. 'It was awful. Poor Ar!'

I took my friend's arm. 'Sit down and tell me what happened.'

'Well, Ar was pretty sullen after her earlier visit here. She didn't want to talk about it, and I thought it best not to press her. So we ordered takeout from Lampoon's – you know, that cute little Thai place – and then we watched some TV. Arleen was just getting ready for bed when that Detective Hoffman came back. When he started to read her her rights, I thought she was going to faint!' Hilary gave her head a brisk shake. 'She was calm – it was eerie. I've never seen her so quiet. I have to say, though, that Detective Hoffman was pretty decent. He talked to her in a quiet tone, then waited till she got changed. He didn't even handcuff her or anything, just took her arm and walked her out to the squad car.'

'They must have come in the rear entrance,' I said. 'I've been sitting here since you texted me and I haven't seen them.'

'Something happened to make them change their minds,' Hilary wailed. 'To actually arrest her.'

'Something did happen,' I said. I pulled my friend off to one side and quickly filled her in on what Bartell had told me. 'It doesn't look good,' I finished. 'Especially the part about Driscoll's water being drugged. It screams premeditation.'

'Ar does have a prescription for Natrol,' Hilary admitted. 'She was real nervous at the first bake-off, but she calmed down since. I don't think she's taken five pills out of that bottle.'

'Well, the purse was in a locked drawer where no one could get at it.'

'Locks can be picked. Heck, we've picked 'em. Someone's

framing her,' Hilary declared. Her blue eyes flashed sparks. 'Arleen's silly and spoiled, and most of the time she's a giant pain in my you-know-where, but my sister is no killer, Tiff.'

'I know that, and I think Bartell knows that too. But the circumstantial evidence is pretty powerful, at least in the DA's eyes.'

'Hang 'em Hartford? Swell!' Melissa Hartford, our current DA, had gotten the nickname of 'Hang 'em' because of her reputation for seldom losing a case. Right now her win record was 98 percent. She was pretty much the Perry Mason of DAs, at least in Fulton County.

Hilary turned to me with an anxious glance. 'I'm so confused, Tiff. What should I do?' She gasped as a sudden thought occurred to her. 'Oh my God. My mother should be home now. She must be wondering where we are.'

'You should call her,' I said. 'Tell her the news before she hears it somewhere else. Arleen is going to need a lawyer, too.'

'A lawyer. Geez, I hadn't even thought that far.' Hilary ran her hand through her spiky crop of hair. 'I guess I could call Dave Brewster, he's our family lawyer.'

I knew Dave Brewster. He was a nice enough guy, but wills and real-estate matters were his specialty. 'Arleen is going to need someone who's had experience in criminal trials. I don't know anyone offhand, but maybe Dale does.'

I started to whip out my phone, but stopped as a male voice shouted, 'Hilary!' We both turned to see Mac Mackenzie striding toward us. He swept Hilary up in his arms in a massive bear hug.

'Mac,' Hilary breathed when he finally set her down. 'How . . . how did you know I'd be here?'

'I heard about Arleen's arrest on my police scanner.' Mac was a big radio buff, and kept a police scanner because, as he put it, he wanted to be first on the scene to get exclusive photos. 'What happened? Is this about Driscoll?'

'They've arrested Arleen for his murder,' I said. 'The evidence is all circumstantial, but the DA apparently thinks she can make a solid case.'

'Old Hang 'em Hartford is at it again, huh?' The corners of Mac's lips drooped down. He reached over and chucked Hilary underneath the chin. 'How are you holding up?'

'As well as can be expected. I've got to tell my mother the news, though, before she hears it from someone else.'

'That's a good idea,' Mac said. 'I saw some reporters lurking around outside when I came in. News like this will travel fast, especially when it concerns a celebrity like Driscoll.' He laid his hand on Hilary's shoulder. 'I'll drive you to your house,' Mac offered. 'We can come back for your car later.'

Hilary flashed him a grateful look. 'Thanks, Mac.' She glanced over at me. 'I guess I should call Dave Brewster first, though.'

Mac sniffed. 'Dave Brewster? He's a good family attorney, but Arleen will need a good criminal lawyer. Someone who can make a good argument for getting her out on bail. I bet my Aunt Maggie knows a few. Let me make some calls.' Mac's Aunt Maggie was Margaret Huddleston, a wealthy dowager who was on *Southern Style*'s executive board. If anyone had connections, it was her.

Hilary looked at him worshipfully. 'Oh Mac, would you? That would be so great.'

'Yes, it's very generous of you,' I said. 'You really are a Superman, you know that?'

Mac waved away my compliments with one hand, and tightened his grip on Hilary's waist with the other. 'It's the least I can do for my girl.'

I couldn't miss how Hilary's eyes lit up at Mac's pronouncement. At least something good was coming out of this gigantic mess. I laid my hand on her arm. 'Do you want me to come with you when you break the news to your mom?'

Hilary hesitated, then shook her head. 'No. Mac's here. I'll be fine. I won't be at work tomorrow, but I'll give you a call, let you know how things are going.'

I gave her a hug. 'Don't worry. Things will work out. I'm not about to let Arleen be the fall guy for someone else.'

'I know you won't.' Hilary squeezed my arm and managed a wink. 'I'll try not to worry, not when I know Detective Austin is on the job.'

It was almost midnight when I finally got home. Cooper and Lily looked up sleepily from their beds as I entered. 'Go back to sleep, kids,' I told them. 'No sense in all of us staying awake.'

I peeled off my jacket, tossed it on the kitchen counter, and flopped down at the table. I pulled out my phone to check my messages. There were three: one from my father, one from Twyla and one from Dale. None from Beth March or Charlotte Horn. I listened to Twyla's first. 'Honey, I just heard about Hilary's sister,' Twyla said. 'Let me know if there's anything I can do.'

I sighed. Apparently Mac had been right: bad news travels fast. I sincerely hoped Hilary had been able to reach her mother. Dale's message was short, crisp and to the point: 'I just heard Arleen Hanson's been arrested for Driscoll's murder. Be in my office at nine sharp. We have to talk about how this affects the contest.'

Swell. I hadn't even gotten that far in my own thinking, but it was true. This would definitely throw a monkey wrench into the already embattled contest. I picked my laptop up off the kitchen table and went into the living room. I kicked off my shoes and tucked into my loveseat, balancing the laptop on my knees. I dug the remote out of the cushion where I'd stashed it and switched on the local news channel. The first thing I saw was the serious face of KPTX local news anchor, Darla Gravesend. She had a solemn expression on her face, microphone in her hand. The caption on the screen read 'Reporting Live' and I recognized the building in the background – the Branson police station.

'This is Darla Gravesend, coming to you live from the Branson PD, where we understand they have made an arrest in the murder of noted food critic Bartholomew Driscoll. The police have arrested Arleen Hanson, twenty-five. Ms Hanson is a finalist in the *Southern Style* Bon-Appetempting Pizza Bake-Off, which Mr Driscoll was slated to judge. Sources tell us that the evidence against Ms Hanson is overwhelming. The DA, Melissa Hartford, was quoted as wanting a "swift conviction" so that "justice might be served".'

I sighed and shut the TV off. That sort of publicity was exactly what we didn't need right now. I picked up my phone and dialed my parents' number. My father answered on the first ring. 'Honey, I'm sorry I didn't call you earlier, but your mother and I just got back from visiting your brother. We just heard about Driscoll being murdered at your pizza contest.'

'Yes, it's been quite an eventful few days.'

I brought my father and mother (who was listening in on the extension) up to speed. When I'd finished my mother said, 'I can't believe Arleen did it. She's such a nice girl.'

'I don't think she did it either, Mom, but the circumstantial evidence is pretty bad.'

'Well, you just be careful,' my father cautioned. 'I hate to speak ill of the dead, but that Driscoll wasn't exactly a nice guy. I remember when he worked on the paper in Valdosta – he wrote a lot of columns and made a lot of enemies.'

'Dad, you don't by any chance remember ever hearing his name mentioned in connection with any sort of scandal, do you? It would have been awhile ago – twenty-two years, to be exact.'

'Twenty-two years?' My father chuckled. 'I'm lucky if I can remember yesterday. But to answer your question, not that I can recall.'

'It would most likely have been right when his career as a food critic was starting to take off, and it might possibly have involved a woman.'

'A woman, eh? Well, where Driscoll's concerned that's doubtless a given. Why are you asking about this? Does it have something to do with his death?'

I sighed. 'Maybe. To be honest, I don't really know. This reporter, Charlotte Horn, is pretty convinced that Driscoll came to Branson on account of some mystery woman, and it has ties to something that happened twenty-two years ago. She also hinted at a "suspicious death".'

'A suspicious death, you say?' My dad was silent for several seconds, and I could almost see the wheels turning in his head. Finally he said, 'I can't think of anything offhand, but if either of us do, we'll let you know. And you be careful. I know you're digging into this to help Hilary's sister. Your mother and I don't want to have to worry about you.'

'I promise,' I said. We exchanged good nights and I rang off. Since I wasn't a bit sleepy, I decided to do some research. I grabbed my laptop, booted it up, typed in Beth March's name and hit enter. I was still a bit wary of the relationship between Driscoll and his assistant. I had a feeling that they were a lot closer than Beth claimed.

I got many hits for Beth March, including the usual references to the character from the classic *Little Women*. I weeded those out and scrolled through the rest carefully. None of them resembled the young woman I'd met in the least. I decided to try Elizabeth March, but I fared no better with that. Next I tried images. Lots of photos of lots of Beth or Elizabeth Marches, but none who resembled Driscoll's assistant. Nothing on Facebook or Twitter either. Now that was really odd. Talk about keeping a low profile, hers was nonexistent.

I switched gears and decided to concentrate on Peter Hagen. He was a likely suspect, in my mind at least. No love lost between him and his brother, and I thought Hagen had an excellent motive. I had to think for a moment to remember the title of his book and then I typed in, Driscoll-*Full Disclosure* and hit enter. Lots of hits came up, most of them sites where the book was available. I clicked on a couple of the review sites. While most critics panned the book, people who'd read it (mostly women) gushed over it. One site had a detailed synopsis which I read eagerly. The gist of the story was that the main character, Joseph B. Drackle, was madly in love with his brother Pierre's girl, Sally. He won Sally by comforting her after he revealed Pierre's affair with a married co-worker, but then after a while Sally saw through Joseph's machinations and cheated on him, the result being a bitter breakup and Sally's leaving town. I noted that the name of the man that Sally had the affair with was 'Lee', and I couldn't help but wonder if that might be a veiled reference to Leon Santangelo. On a hunch I typed in Sally-suspicious death-and the year. Nothing.

I sifted through more articles on Driscoll and his novel, and finally came across gold: an interview with Driscoll himself on a site called LiteraryGossip.com. I clicked on the article. It was only about two months old, and basically a rehash of an older article about Driscoll's career as a food critic and his first book. The last part, however, proved interesting:

> *Reporter: Mr Driscoll, rumor has it that you're working on a new book?*
> *Driscoll: Yes, I've been working on a collaborative cookbook. I'm taking some of my own recipes in addition to*

ones from cooks I've interviewed on my show over the
years. It should be good.
Reporter: That's interesting, but there's been talk you're
planning to write another work of fiction. Is it true
you've been in talks with an editor at Appleseed Press?
Driscoll: Sorry, at this time I have no comment.

Appleseed Press seemed like an excellent place to start. I entered
the name into the search engine and the site came up. I clicked
on the 'About Us' tab and found a list of editors. Twenty, to be
exact. I combed through the list and narrowed it down to eight
who specialized in fiction, then dashed off a quick e-mail to each.
I explained that I was from *Southern Style* magazine, and I was
doing an article on Bartholomew Driscoll – his life and accomplishments. As part of the story, I needed confirmation on the
release date for his second novel. I doubted any would answer,
and if they did, they probably wouldn't tell me anything, but hey
. . . it was worth a shot.

I closed the laptop and sat for a moment, my hands folded on
top of it. What if the reason Driscoll had come to Branson had
something to do with this second book? Suppose this 'mystery
woman' was featured in it, and the portrayal was less than flat-
tering? She might have wanted a showdown with Driscoll? Things
might have turned ugly. I remembered, too, the snippet of conversation I'd overheard between Driscoll and Peter Hagen. Had
Driscoll revealed another secret about his brother? There were
other possibles too: Colleen Collins, Santangelo, even Chef John.
All could have been mentioned in Driscoll's newest tome.

What it all boiled down to was this: Was what Driscoll put in
his second book serious enough to commit murder over?

SEVENTEEN

Nine a.m. the next morning found me in Dale's office. My boss, who usually looked like he stepped off the pages of *GQ*, didn't look so hot today. His eyes were bloodshot, and he sat slumped in his chair, a defeated look on his face. He waved me to take a seat in front of his desk as I entered.

'I know, I know, I look a fright,' he said once I was seated. 'I've been up most of the night, doing damage control with the board. Almost all of them blew a fit when it came out that one of the leading finalists in our pizza bake-off was arrested for Driscoll's murder.'

'It's all a terrible mistake,' I hastened to assure Dale. 'Arleen didn't do it.'

Dale raised an eyebrow. 'Not according to every news station in town. Apparently the DA gave a statement, hinting at a sure conviction.'

'Oh, Hang 'em Hartford needs some publicity,' I grumbled.

'Melissa Hartford has a near perfect track record. I doubt she'd go so far as to make a statement unless she felt she had an airtight case.'

'But it's all circumstantial.'

Dale shot me a patient look. 'Do you know how many people are convicted each year on circumstantial evidence? More than we can count.' He raised a hand, rubbed at his eyes. 'Have you spoken to Hilary?'

I shook my head. 'Not since I left her at the police station last night. Mac Mackenzie was going to try and get Arleen a lawyer.'

'I spoke with her about an hour ago,' he said. 'I told her that she could have all the time off she needed, with pay.'

I jumped up and impulsively threw my arms around him. 'Dale! That's so generous of you!'

He made no move to disengage himself from my grasp. 'Yeah,

well, Hilary's been a loyal employee. This whole thing isn't her fault.'

I released him and took a step back. 'Did she mention anything about Arleen?'

'She did. Apparently Mackenzie managed to secure the legal services of Tad Bronson.'

My eyes popped. Tad Bronson was a major criminal attorney, whose record for wins rivaled that of Melissa Hartford's for convictions. I was certain the man wasn't inexpensive, either.

'No doubt Mac's aunt played a major role in that acquisition,' Dale went on. 'Tad did manage to get Arleen out on bail, released into Hilary's custody. I understand Hartford's pushing for a speedy trial – like, the beginning of next week.'

I gulped. 'You're kidding? So fast?'

'That's how certain she is of conviction.' Dale hesitated. 'There's more, I'm afraid. The board wants the pizza bake-off to proceed quickly. They want us to push it up from next weekend to this Sunday.'

'This weekend – but that's next to impossible,' I cried. 'That would only give us four days to lock down a venue, get another judge . . .'

'Enzo Manchetti has already taken care of the venue,' Dale said. 'He managed to get Principal Jacoby to rearrange the senior class annual revue so that we can have the high school auditorium this Sunday from one to three.'

'OK, but how about a judge? We still need another one, don't we? I did enquire at Po'Boys, and Nita Gillette said that either she or her husband would be happy to help out—'

'Already taken care of,' Dale said in a clipped tone. 'I called Fred Longo, and he managed to secure the services of Emmanuel Fargoni.'

'Fargoni! Really!' Emmanuel Fargoni was an Italian chef, based out of Los Angeles. He had half a dozen restaurants, most of them Michelin three-star, and had authored at least a dozen cookbooks. The man was semi-retired, and a legend. As far as I knew, he no longer traveled, preferring to stay local and manage his little empire from his palatial estate in Bel Air.

'He had to call in a favor, but he got Fargoni to agree. Of

course, *Southern Style* is footing the bill for his travel and hotel,' Dale added with a wince.

I folded my arms across my chest. 'I'm betting his accommodations won't be at the Haverford Inn.'

'No. The Hilton. Longo pulled a lot of strings to accommodate us, so it's the least we can do.' He paused and looked me straight in the eye. 'You know what I'm going to say next, don't you?'

I sighed. 'Yes. That we have to start afresh with the scores, and Arleen's spot will have to be given to the next runner-up.'

'Which would be Doris Sharp. Do you want to notify her, or shall I?'

I reached across the desk impulsively and grabbed Dale's hand. 'There's still five days. Arleen is innocent, Dale. It would be a shame if she had to give up her place in the contest over this. Can't we hold off on notifying Doris Sharp?'

He gave me a thin smile. 'That's my Tiffany – always hoping for a miracle.'

'They do happen,' I said. 'Give me till noon Friday. That'll still give Doris Sharp a day and a half to prepare. She's a long shot at best anyway. We both know that.' I shot him a pleading glance. 'You don't think Hilary's sister is guilty either, do you?'

Dale sighed. 'No. No, I don't.' He sat for a few moments, staring pensively off into space. Then he turned and looked at me. 'OK, you win. But I don't feel good about waiting until practically the last minute to tell Doris Sharp. She's a bundle of nerves as it is, without the pressure of less than two days to get ready. It doesn't seem fair.'

What's being done to Arleen isn't fair either, I wanted to scream at him, but I kept my cool. 'How about this,' I suggested. 'Call Doris Sharp and tell her that there is a chance – an outside one – that the contest will be pushed up and she might be called to participate. That way she'll be on alert. Suggest she practice her pizza, just in case.'

'OK,' Dale said at last. 'That seems fair enough. This stays between us, though. The board wouldn't be too happy if they got wind of what you intend to do.'

'Don't worry. Mum's the word.' I got up, walked around the desk, leaned over and gave Dale a kiss on the cheek. 'Thank you.'

Dale's cheeks reddened, and the corners of his lips tipped up. The look he gave me was long and searching. 'Do you really think you can clear Arleen? Solve Driscoll's murder like you did Jenny Lee's?'

'I'm sure as heck going to try,' I said, and then I walked out without a backward glance.

The first thing I did when I got back to my office was call Hilary. My BFF answered on the first ring. Everything was fine – or as fine as things could be. Arleen was depressed, but that was understandable. Right now she was downtown with their mother, talking to the attorney. 'I still can't believe Mac's aunt got Tad Bronson to defend Arleen,' Hilary said. 'I'd like to say she's as good as cleared, but . . . I don't want to jinx anything.'

'I was surprised when Dale told me too,' I confessed. 'Bronson isn't cheap, and I'm sure Arleen's bail was high.'

'Two hundred fifty thousand. Mom put up every penny from the investments Dad left her. As for the attorney, we lucked out there. Mac's aunt got him to defend Arleen pro bono.'

Pro bono? I was impressed. Either Mac's aunt had more clout than I'd thought, or she had something on the attorney. Knowing what a pistol Mac's aunt could be, either scenario was entirely possible.

'Tiff? You're still going to investigate, right? You're still going to try and prove Arleen didn't do it.'

'I'm not going to just try, *I am* going to prove it,' I said, with far more confidence than I felt. 'Don't worry, we'll have Arleen's name cleared in no time.'

Once I finished reassuring Hilary, it was time to reassure myself. True, I wasn't a professional detective, but I'd read plenty of crime novels and watched the shows on TV. I liked putting pieces of puzzles together. Plus, Bartell had said that I had good instincts. It was time I followed them. I looked up Peter Hagen's number and dialed it. I got voicemail. I left a message, saying there was something I'd like to discuss with him, and then I figured it was time to move on.

A Slice of Heaven was located in the heart of downtown Branson. It had been Giovanni Ferrante's flagship pizza parlor, the one that had launched his career and been the inspiration for at least two dozen other restaurants throughout the South. While I'd reviewed his other Italian restaurant, Bellissimo, when I first started working for *Southern Style*, I'd never set foot in his original pizza parlor – until now.

The aromas of garlic, spice and sauce hit me the moment I stepped through the double glass doors. A wide counter extended the length of the main room on the right, behind which were two large pizza ovens, a microwave and a stove. To the left were several soda machines, and a glass case where several delicious-looking pizzas, strombolis and calzones were on display. The wide marble counter had stools in front of it, and was wide enough for patrons to enjoy a slice and a soda. On the opposite side of the room were several booths, and the walls were covered with framed photographs of locales in Italy.

The wide back room boasted twenty tables covered with white and red checked tablecloths. Right now, it was just eleven, so the pizzeria was deserted, except for a white-haired man in a white apron behind the main counter. As I watched, he took a hunk of dough, slapped it on the counter, and then molded it into a round shape. He reached for a pan of sauce, covered the dough with it, and then sprinkled it generously with mozzarella cheese. He put the pie into the oven and reached for another hunk of dough. I coughed lightly, and his head snapped around. He frowned when he saw me.

'I'm sorry, miss.' His voice held a trace of an Italian accent. 'Margery must have left the door unlocked when she came in. We're not open for business right now, so no pizzas are ready yet.'

'That's all right,' I said. 'I'm not here for pizza. I was wondering if Giovanni Ferrante was here today?'

The man's features morphed into a deep frown. 'Who wants to know?'

'Tiffany Austin.'

He shot me a quizzical look. 'Tiffany Austin? Bon Appetempting's Tiffany Austin?' At my nod, his face creased in a smile. 'Well, well, I follow it regularly. Pleased to meet you.' He wiped his hands on his apron and extended one to me. We shook, and then he raised a finger. 'Just one moment.' The man disappeared through a door off to one side, and about five minutes later he returned, followed by Ferrante. 'Tiffany!' Chef John boomed. He came forward and took both my hands in his. '*Buongiorno!* What brings you here today?'

I smiled at him. 'It occurred to me that I've never been in your flagship pizzeria, Chef John. I decided it was time I rectified that situation.'

'*Bene! Molto bene!* You must have an early lunch with me. A brunch! I shall have Pietro prepare something special.'

'That would be nice,' I said.

Ferrante motioned for me to follow him into the dining area. There was a table for two off in one corner. He motioned for me to sit, and then he vanished into the back room, returning a few moments later with a large bottle of red wine and two glasses.

'I have taken the liberty of ordering our entrées,' he said as he set the wine and glasses down. He looked me up and down and grinned. 'I forgot to ask – will you be reviewing your meal today, or are you here strictly as a customer?'

'Just a customer.'

'Good. I have told Pietro to prepare our appetizer: bruschetta, with a traditional topping of diced tomatoes, fresh basil, garlic and olive oil served with toasted bread. That will be followed by the house salad: Romaine lettuce and artichokes tossed in a lemon vinaigrette with Parmesan cheese sprinkled on top. And for the entrée, oven-roasted chicken breast with mushroom marsala sauce served over wild rice – unless you would prefer the pan-seared flounder in a delicate wine and garlic sauce over linguini?'

I could feel my mouth start to water. 'Chicken will be fine. It all sounds delicious.' I patted my waistline. 'There's a good chance I won't eat dinner, after this brunch.'

'Ah, but you must save room for dessert. Tiramisu. My pastry chef makes it deceptively light.'

'Deceptively being the operative word.'

Chef John poured the wine, a robust Merlot, into the glasses. He raised his. 'To good food – and good company.'

I took a sip of the wine, which was indeed delicious, and set my glass down. 'I suppose Dale contacted you about the change in plans for the contest?'

Chef John took a large sip of his wine. 'Yes. I have to tell you, Tiffany, I find it hard to believe that Ms Hanson could have killed Driscoll. Not that the man didn't deserve killing but . . . that girl didn't seem the type.'

'I couldn't agree more,' I said. 'But the board of *Southern Style* feels that the longer the contest is delayed, the higher the risk of detrimental publicity.'

Chef John let out a long sigh. 'Ah, yes, and publicity is the name of the game, unfortunately.' He lowered his voice to a whisper and added, 'Just between us, both Anastasia and I gave Ms Hanson very high marks, higher even than that Kurt Howell. We were both certain she would win.'

'Yes, it is a shame. I for one do not believe Arleen killed anyone. I think someone else was responsible.'

Chef John poured some more wine into his glass. 'The news reports said that the DA had an ironclad case.'

'Built on circumstantial evidence.' I ran my finger around the rim of my glass. 'I heard that you had some dealings with Driscoll yourself.'

Chef John's head jerked up. 'Dealings?' His features morphed into a deep frown. 'If you are referring to the bad blood between Driscoll and myself, I assure you, it was really nothing worth killing over. I just did not like the way he characterized me in his so-called fiction work.' He offered me a thin smile. 'Vain, no?'

'Perhaps, but I was thinking more along the lines of Driscoll being Leon Santangelo's silent partner in his pizza dough business. I heard that you were considering buying him out.'

He frowned. 'Where did you hear that?'

I took a sip of wine before I answered. 'Are you denying it?'

Chef John hesitated, then shook his head. 'No, there is no sense in denying the truth. Driscoll approached me a few weeks ago. He said that he needed cash, and he wanted to know if I would be interested in buying out his percentage of Santangelo Pizza Dough. The offer he made was very generous, and I told him I'd think about it.'

'I see.' I took another sip of wine. 'But since you mentioned his novel, I've heard a rumor that Driscoll was in the process of writing another one.'

'Ah, yes.' Chef John's lips twisted in a wry smile. 'He was. At least I think he was.'

'What do you mean?'

'Well . . .' Chef John reached up to scratch at his forehead. 'When Driscoll approached me, I told him that I'd consider his offer so long as he refrained from mentioning me in any future works of fiction he planned to write. He laughed and said he'd just finished another novel, but was considering a major rewrite.'

'Really? Did he say anything else about it?'

Chef John chuckled. 'He said I was definitely not in it. Other than that, he did not elaborate any further. He was too concentrated on trying to convince me to buy him out.'

'So locking down this deal with you was the reason he came to Branson?'

Chef John shrugged. 'Truthfully, I am not sure why he came to Branson, or even why he agreed to judge that contest. I was not pleased to see him there, because he'd been pressuring me for an answer and I'd been putting him off. He managed to corner me at the contest, though, and I had no choice but to tell him what I'd decided.'

'You decided against buying out his interest?'

Chef John nodded. 'Yes. Believe me, investing in Santangelo's business would have saved me a great deal of money, but . . . I just could not bring myself to do business with the man. I just didn't trust him.'

'When did you tell him about your decision?'

'Right before we started the tasting. He wasn't happy, but he didn't fly off the handle. Actually his exact words were, "I expected as much" . . .' Chef John paused. 'I remember his assistant, that young girl, came up to him and he barked at her to get out of his sight. So rude! That other contestant, the truck driver, went over to her and put his arms around her. It looked as if he were trying to calm her down.' Chef John shook his head. 'Driscoll's tantrum didn't seem to faze the girl that much. I had the impression it wasn't the first time he'd spoken to her like that. Actually, it seemed to bother the trucker more. He seemed more upset than the girl – I heard him mutter something very uncomplimentary under his breath.' Ferrante swiped at his forehead. 'He gave Driscoll quite the dagger-look, too. I remembered thinking how odd it was for him to get so upset over a girl he didn't know.'

'That is odd,' I agreed. I filed it away to ask Howell when I saw him next. 'Did Driscoll mention anything about the book to you at the tasting?'

'He did not, and I did not ask.' Chef John leaned back in his seat. 'Enough talk about Driscoll. It will ruin my appetite – and here comes our first course.'

An hour later I was back in my car after a delicious lunch with Chef John. I'd managed to scarf down every morsel on my plate, but I'd had to take a raincheck on the tiramisu – the waistband of my skirt was tight enough already. I'd also crossed Chef John off my suspect list – he'd shown me a selfie of him and Anastasia sampling pizza on his phone, taken right around the time Driscoll would have been murdered. I imagined Bartell had no doubt done the same.

I turned the key in the ignition and then whipped out my phone to check my messages. I had one from Dale, reminding me about my deadline, and one from Twyla, asking if everything was all right. None from Peter Hagen, or Beth March. I pulled out of the parking spot slowly and headed in the direction of the Haverford Inn. Since Beth had never answered my note, it was time for another in-person visit. Either she hadn't gotten the message, or she was avoiding me, and I was determined to find out which one it was.

I arrived at the Haverford Inn and parked in one of the spaces reserved for visitors. As I pushed through the front door, I noticed a large sign over by the elevators: OUT OF ORDER. Great. I made a quick turn and headed straight for the stairs. It was a five-floor climb up to the Presidential Suite, and I took the stairs slowly, using the time to focus on the questions I wanted to ask Beth. I reached the top floor and, just as I was about to open the door, it flew open. I stared, open-mouthed, at the person on the other side, someone I'd never expect to run into here.

Kurt Howell.

EIGHTEEN

We stared at each other for a few seconds, and then we both said in unison, 'What are you doing here?'

Kurt gave a self-conscious laugh. 'Caught,' he said, raising both hands. 'I just thought I'd stop by and offer Driscoll's assistant my condolences. See if there was anything she needed.'

'That was nice of you,' I said. 'I thought I'd do the same.' I paused and then added, 'I heard how nice you were to her when Driscoll went off on her during the contest. You really championed her cause.'

Howell waved his hand. 'I hate to see women abused like that. Especially by a blowhard like Driscoll. I guess I shouldn't speak ill of the dead, but in some cases, it's justified. The man was a real cad.'

I tilted my head to one side. 'For someone who said they didn't know Driscoll, you seem to have his personality down pat.'

'I don't – didn't – know him, but sometimes it doesn't take much to tell what someone's like, just from casual observation. I watched his segments on *Good Morning Branson*. It was easy to peg him as a pompous sort just by watching how he interacted with his guests. He was especially critical toward the female chefs who appeared on his show.'

'I have to confess, I never watched his show, so I'll just take your word for it.'

He paused and then said, 'I heard the police have a suspect in Driscoll's death.'

I wasn't about to discuss any details with him, so I just shrugged. 'I heard that as well. They're very cagey with details, right now, though.'

'Sure, sure. I just thought, on account of the contest and all, and since you found the body . . .'

'That I might know something? Sorry, I don't know details

about the investigation. What I can tell you is that the contest will continue. You should be hearing from Dale Swenson about the particulars very soon.'

His face brightened. 'Oh, good. I was wondering about that.' His gaze traveled to the gold watch on his wrist. 'Is it that late already? Sorry, I have to get going. It was nice seeing you.'

He gave me a quick wave and bounded down the stairs. I went into the hallway and walked swiftly toward the suite. I rapped on the door, and waited. A few seconds later I heard footsteps, and then the sound of a latch being thrown. The door swung open. 'I thought I told you not to bother . . . oh!' The look on Beth's face was a combination of mingled consternation and surprise. 'Tiffany. Hello.' She held up her hand, and I saw an iPhone clutched in it. 'I was just about to call you.'

'I'm sorry to just drop in, but I was in the neighborhood.' I tried to inject a note of concern into my tone. 'I hope I haven't come at a bad time?'

Beth worried at her lower lip. 'There are no good times, anymore,' she said in a morose tone. 'Now's as good as any, I suppose.' She hesitated, then swung the door all the way open. 'Please come in,' she added, in a tone that sounded more resigned than hospitable.

I stepped over the threshold. The Haverford Inn might have a worn-down appearance, but you would never know it by the Presidential Suite. The carpeting was a thick pile, rust-colored, a perfect foil to the dark cherrywood sofa, chair and coffee table in the main part of the suite. A marble fireplace was at one end of the room, and the pale peach walls were covered with tasteful oil paintings depicting the four seasons. The atmosphere of the room was actually pretty inviting. I wondered what the other two rooms were like.

'Your note said you had something to discuss?'

I started and looked over my shoulder to find Beth right behind me, her hands on her hips. She must have realized how she sounded, because she passed a hand over her eyes. 'I'm sorry,' she murmured. 'I didn't mean to come off sounding so rude, it's just . . . I think I'm still in shock. I'll feel better when this whole nightmare is over, Mr Driscoll's killer brought to justice, and Detective Bartell says that I can go home.' She smiled thinly.

'I'm going to have to start looking for a new job, and I don't mind telling you I'm dreading it.'

'Yes, I can imagine,' I murmured. 'I just had a few questions, if you wouldn't mind. I promise I won't take long.'

'OK. Please, have a seat.'

She waved me toward the sofa, then settled herself in the chair across from me. I folded my hands in my lap. 'I'll come right to the point. I've heard Mr Driscoll had another reason for being here in Branson, besides this contest.'

Her brow puckered. 'No, I don't think so,' she said. 'He'd planned a motor trip, but Branson wasn't in his itinerary until he got Mr Santangelo's call.'

'I see. So he planned this trip himself? You had nothing to do with it?'

Beth shook her head emphatically. 'No. Mr Driscoll liked to take charge of things like that. Whenever we travelled, he'd make all the arrangements.' Her hand came up and her fingers twined in the thin gold chain around her neck. 'I know it's a bit unusual, admins usually take care of such details, but that's what made working for Mr Driscoll so interesting. He was definitely not your average employer.' A ghost of a smile played across the girl's face. 'I was privy to much of his business, but there were certain aspects he liked to keep to himself. He could be rather . . . unpredictable at times.'

I wasn't about to argue that point. 'I assume he planned on continuing with his trip after the contest ended?'

'Oh, yes. He made it very clear that once the contest was over, I was to return to Atlanta and he'd continue on. He anticipated being gone for about a week.'

'And you've no idea where he was headed?'

She shook her head regretfully. 'None. I got the sense it was personal, and he rarely discussed his personal life with me.'

'I heard a rumor that Driscoll planned to open another restaurant.'

'Yes, he wanted to,' she said slowly. 'He was having a bit of trouble getting all his ducks in a row, I think. I heard him on the phone a few times with a realtor, discussing different locales, but I don't believe anything was ever finalized.'

'With a realtor? Do you happen to know who?'

I fully expected Beth to say Colleen Collins, so I was startled when she replied, 'I think his name is Claude Follet. He's with the Smith-Blackthorne Realty group in Gainesville.'

My face fell. 'Gainesville? Are you sure that's where he was looking? Not here in Branson?' Gainesville was known far and wide as the 'Poultry Capital of the World'. It attracted mainly fishermen and boaters. Not exactly the spot I'd pick to open an exclusive restaurant.

Beth shook her head. 'I'm positive. I know he didn't want to open another one in Branson.'

'I see. What about an interior decorator? Do you know if he'd been in touch with anyone?'

Beth's lips compressed into a thin line. 'I don't believe so. He hadn't settled on a venue yet, so the prospect of consulting a decorator would have been premature. Very premature.'

From her tone, I figured that was all I'd get out of her on that particular subject, so it was time to switch gears. Summoning up a disarming smile, I asked, 'I also understand he was working on a new book?'

Her eyes lit up a bit. 'Oh, yes. The cookbook. He was very excited about that. It was to be a collaborative effort. He'd make arrangements with various chefs who'd appeared on his show to provide original recipes, and he even had a few of his own that he was throwing in.' She let out a soft giggle. 'I sampled one of them. It was for a chess pie. I was a bit leery at first, but it really was delicious.'

'I'd heard about the cookbook,' I ventured, 'but I'm talking about his other book – the novel.'

Beth shot me a puzzled look. 'I'm sorry. I'm confused. You said *novel*?'

'Yes. He'd previously published one under the name B. J. Driscoll. It was called *Full Disclosure*.'

She frowned, but avoided meeting my gaze. 'Never heard of it.'

I cocked my head at her. 'Really? You were his assistant, and yet you were never aware that your employer had written a novel?'

Beth bristled. 'As I've said, Mr Driscoll could be an extremely private person. If he didn't think I needed to know something, well, he didn't tell me. And I confess, I'm not much of a reader.'

'Well, this new one was to be a sequel, of sorts. The advance buzz has everyone in a tizzy. It seems Driscoll revealed quite a few skeletons in quite a few people's closets in his first book, and there's speculation that there was more to come in this new novel.'

Beth sighed. 'That part, about rattling the skeletons, doesn't really surprise me. Mr Driscoll was good at that. But I assure you, I knew nothing about it, nor was I privy to any of his notes.' She paused. 'That could explain a few things, though.'

'Such as?'

She leaned forward. 'There was a reporter nosing around who upset Mr Driscoll very much. He avoided her like the plague. I think her name was Charlene something.'

'Could it have been Charlotte Horn?'

'That's the name!' Beth snapped her fingers in the air. 'I remember, at the contest, she tried to approach Mr Driscoll several times, but he managed to avoid her. It got so bad, though, that at one point I confronted her, told her to leave him alone.'

'I believe they worked on the same paper, years ago.'

'Yes, that's what Mr Driscoll told me. He didn't hold her in very high regard. He said she was a real barracuda, would do anything for a story.' Her lips clamped into a thin line. 'I'll bet she made all this up about Mr Driscoll writing another book.'

'Why would she do that?'

Beth looked at me like I had three heads. 'Why, for a story of course. Reporters are like that. They will make up stuff, and the more sensational the better. To be quite frank, I wouldn't trust her. She was very demanding that day, bordering on uncouth. I'd be happy never to lay eyes on her again.'

'It sounds as if she made quite an impression on you.'

'Yes, and not a favorable one.' Beth paused, took a deep breath. 'I'm sorry. I didn't mean to go off like that. It's just . . .' She started to choke up and turned her head away.

I laid my hand on her arm. 'I'm sorry, Beth. I know Driscoll's death has upset you.' I got an audible sniff in reply. Then I said softly, 'I couldn't help but notice that you started to call Driscoll by his first name several times.'

She looked up at me, her eyes moist. 'Yes, I confess I did call him Bartholomew sometimes.' Her cheeks reddened slightly. 'I know the persona he projected, and don't get me wrong, he had a temper but . . . he was good to me. I looked up to him, like . . . like an older brother.'

I looked her straight in the eyes. 'Then you weren't in love with him?'

There could be no mistaking the look of genuine shock that crossed her face. 'You thought we were lovers? Oh, gosh, no. I could never think of him in that way. *Never.*'

She sounded so emphatic that I found myself believing her. As for the book, it was possible Driscoll might have kept it from her. If their relationship was a brother/sister one, he might have thought he was protecting her. 'OK, then. But if you should happen to run across anything pertaining to another book when you're cleaning out his files, I'd appreciate it if you'd let me know.'

'I will, but I don't anticipate finding anything.' She sighed. 'There's so much to do, I don't know where to begin. Mr Driscoll's lawyer will take care of the will, but I have to handle some issues regarding his morning show contract – and the cookbook, of course.' She paused, reached into the pocket of her jacket and whipped out her cell. She looked at the screen and frowned. 'Excuse me one moment. I have to take this.'

Beth moved into another room and I sat back down on the sofa. I reached into my purse for a mint, but it slipped from my grasp and fell between the seat cushions. I dipped my hand down to grab it, and as I did so my fingers came into contact with something rough. I pulled it out and saw that it was a slip of paper – a closer inspection showed that it was a duplicate copy of a check, drawn on the private account of Bartholomew Driscoll. The check was made out to a Harmony Steele in the amount of fifty thousand dollars. In the bottom left-hand corner was written, *First Installment.*

I heard footsteps and swiftly jammed the copy into the pocket of my jacket, seconds before Beth came back into the room. She tossed me an apologetic smile. 'I'm sorry to cut this short,' she said, 'but there are some pressing matters I must attend to.'

I rose. 'Of course. I understand what a difficult time this is for you.'

As we walked to the door I remarked casually, 'That was nice of Kurt Howell to check in on you.'

She stopped and stared at me. 'Who?'

'Kurt Howell. The male contestant in the pizza contest. I saw him at the elevator earlier. He said he'd been to see you.'

Beth's eyes darted away for a brief instant, and then focused back on me again. 'Oh yes. *Him.*' Her nose wrinkled, as if she'd smelled bad fish. 'He wanted to stop by to offer his condolences, and to see how I was holding up and if there was anything I might need.'

'I heard that he stuck up for you when Driscoll snapped at you. That was very nice of him. After all, he didn't have to.'

'It's true, he did, but . . .' She leaned forward and said in a low tone, 'I have to confess, I didn't care much for him. He impressed me as an opportunist. Someone who knows which side of the bread has the butter. I'm sure that line about offering his condolences was just that – a line. I got the sense he was trying to find out details about the contest – who the new judge is, when the contest is going to be resumed. I don't know anything, of course, so I couldn't tell him anything. I don't think he was very satisfied.' She shrugged and added, 'I doubt I'll hear from him again.'

I stepped into the hall and Beth wasted no time in closing the door. I walked slowly toward the stairs. I believed her when she said there was nothing romantic between her and Driscoll. My antennae had gone up, however, when I'd quizzed her about Driscoll's second novel. I had the sense she did know something about it, but why was she lying? Maybe out of a sense of loyalty to her dead employer? Or was there something more to it?

My hand closed around the check in my pocket. Who was this Harmony Steele? Could she be the 'mystery woman' that Charlotte was looking for, and why had Driscoll written her a check for such a large amount? The note at the bottom, first installment, triggered a possibility in my mind: blackmail. Could this Harmony Steele have something on Driscoll, maybe something concerning that suspicious death? Blackmail payments could also explain Driscoll's need for ready cash. I bit my lip.

Here I had some good clues to discuss with Charlotte Horn, and I didn't have any idea how to reach her!

My phone pinged with an incoming text. My heart leapt when I saw it was from Charlotte Horn, short and to the point:

Major Development! Meet me at gazebo in the park 11 p.m. tonite!! A few seconds later, I got another text:

Come alone!!!!

NINETEEN

I texted Charlotte back that I would be there *alone* (minus exclamation points), and that I had some interesting developments myself to discuss with her. I left the inn and went straight to my car. I put in another call to Peter Hagen, and once again I got his voicemail. I left yet another message asking him to call me, then looked at my watch. I had plenty of time to kill before my meeting with Charlotte, so I decided to pay a quick visit to Hilary and Arleen. No sooner had I parked in front of their house than the front door flew open. Hilary, in purple sweats and sweatshirt, bounded down the steps to meet me halfway. She threw her arms around me in a giant bear hug. When she finally released me, I said with a laugh, 'Wow! What was that for?'

'For being the amazing friend you are,' she said. 'So have you got any news? Have you solved the murder yet?'

'I wish,' I said. I linked my arm through hers. 'How's your mom holding up?'

Hilary rolled her eyes. 'She's been a complete wreck. She's so afraid Ar is going to prison, and she'll lose all her money, maybe the house too. Aunt Agnes said she could come and stay with her for awhile, and I finally convinced her to go.'

'That's a good idea.' I knew Hilary's aunt Agnes. She was a librarian who lived in Duke, two towns over. The women were sisters and, like Hilary and Arleen, were as alike as night and day. Whereas Mrs Hanson was highly excitable, Agnes Mason was always cool, calm and collected. 'If anyone can calm your mother down, it's her. Not that she doesn't have reason to be upset, but it's the last thing Arleen needs right now.'

'You can say that again,' Hilary agreed. 'She's on the couch, in sulky mode. I keep trying to get her to snap out of it, but nothing works.'

'Think she'll talk to me? I'd like to pick her brain about what happened, see if she can remember anything else.'

Hilary made a sweeping motion with her hand. 'Be my guest.'

I followed Hilary inside the house and into the living room. Arleen sat, curled up on the couch. I paused, because I'd never seen Hilary's sister ever look anything but pulled together. The Arleen sprawled on the sofa was clad in a well-worn pair of sweats with holes in the knees. Her hair was sticking out at all angles, and her face was bare of makeup. She had a woebegone look on her face. An old movie, *What Ever Happened to Baby Jane?* was playing on the TV, and Arleen was staring at the screen as if her life depended on Joan Crawford not lifting the cover off that silver platter.

'Arleen,' Hilary said. 'Tiff's here.'

Arleen didn't look over, just kept staring at the television. 'Swell.'

Hilary huffed at a stray strand of hair. 'I told her if she keeps her eyes glued to that movie, sooner or later she's gonna end up looking like Bette Davis.'

When that remark produced no reaction, I walked over and stood in front of her, blocking her view of Joan Crawford twirling madly around in her wheelchair. 'Arleen, I was wondering if I might speak with you.'

Arleen sighed. 'Sure, why not. Better here than the visitors' room at Statesville Prison, I guess.'

Hilary stamped her foot. 'Will you stop talking like that? You're not going to prison, Ar. You didn't murder anyone.'

'No, I didn't, but apparently the evidence indicates otherwise. Hang 'em Hartford can't wait to get me in her clutches. Thank God Georgia doesn't have the death penalty.' She groaned. 'I should have told Detective Bartell about the apron when I had the chance.'

I sat down on the sofa next to Arleen and looked her right in the eye. 'Tell me the truth, Arleen. You'd met Driscoll before this contest, hadn't you?'

Arleen hung her head. 'Yes,' she said softly.

Hilary sank down on the couch on the other side of her sister. 'Ar, why did you lie to us about it?'

'I was so ashamed,' she said, her voice a mere whisper. 'Driscoll did back out of the judging, but it was on the second day. He was there for the first round of competition. There was a part where you have to sit in a room with each judge individually, and they ask you a series of questions. Well, when I sat with Driscoll, he wasn't interested in the questions. He was interested in putting his arm around me. He tried to kiss me,' she cried. Her expression resembled that of someone who'd just bitten into a sour lemon. 'Ew!' She banged the side of her head with her palm. 'I can't get it out of my mind ever since this all happened. I keep seeing him standing there, telling me how beautiful I was, and how he could make sure I got far in the contest, maybe even win it. All I had to do was – well, you know.'

'Play ball?' I asked. Arleen nodded miserably. 'What did you do?' I said softly.

'What do you think? I hightailed it out of that room as fast as I could.'

'Why didn't you report him?'

'Why do you think?' she said bitterly. 'Who would believe me? It would have been my word against his. I don't know if he tried to pull the same stuff on any of the other girls. I was too ashamed to say anything. I thought the fact he was doing that was an indication that he didn't think I had a chance in the contest.'

'But you did go far, and without his so-called help,' I reminded her. 'You were runner-up, right?'

'Right.' Her expression brightened a bit. 'Honest, I'd put all that out of my mind until Sunday when you said that he was going to be a judge. Then it all came tumbling back.'

'And Bartell knew all this when he brought you in for questioning?' I asked.

Arleen nodded. 'It was one of the first things he brought up. I thought about denying it, but then I figured what was the point? So I admitted it was true.' She sighed. 'My lawyer said that I should have kept my mouth shut, but to be honest, I was tired of doing that.' She looked at me miserably. 'I should have followed your advice about the apron, I know. Oh, I'm such a dork!' Arleen dropped her face into her hands. 'And now I'm gonna go to prison.' She shot us a sideways glance. 'Not only could my mother lose this house, but I look terrible in orange!'

I slid my arm around Arleen's shoulders. 'Your mother isn't going to lose the house, and you are *not* going to prison,' I said.

'Not if I have anything to say about it. And just for the record, I don't think Bartell thinks you're guilty either.'

Arleen lifted her head to look at me. 'Well, you could have fooled me,' she mumbled. 'I'll tell you who did seem sympathetic, though – the guy who came to arrest me. Hoffman, I think his name is? He was actually pretty sweet about it all. He let me get changed, and he never even put the handcuffs on me.'

'I suppose he chatted with you about the murder?'

She nodded. 'We got to talking. He said that he'd heard some pretty bad things about Driscoll. I told him that it was no loss that Driscoll was dead, even though I wasn't the one to do it. I said that he was an evil man, and the world was better off without him.'

I looked at Hilary. 'Ever hear of good cop, bad cop?'

Hilary folded her arms across her chest. 'Yep. So you think Hoffman was playing good cop?'

'It's possible. He might have wanted to gauge Arleen's reaction to Driscoll's murder, see if there was enough anger there to commit murder.'

Arleen paled. 'Oh no? You really think so? Then I played right into their hands.'

Hilary looked at me. 'Think Bartell put him up to it?'

I shook my head. 'I doubt it. Bartell's not too thrilled with him. He's the captain's nephew. My guess is he did that all on his own, maybe trying to prove himself.'

Arleen threw her head back against the sofa. 'I guess my lawyer's right. I have to learn to keep my big trap shut.'

'Well, you're not speaking to anyone else, not if I have anything to say about it,' Hilary declared. 'Reporters were lurking around outside earlier, hoping for a statement. I told 'em to back off, and see Tad Bronson if they wanted any kind of a statement.'

'Well, I'm sure Tad can handle the press. No doubt he's used to this sort of thing.'

'But doesn't not making a statement make me look guilty?' asked Arleen.

'The circumstantial evidence is doing a good job of that already,' grumbled Hilary.

'Well, I don't want to get your hopes up, but I did get a text from that reporter Charlotte Horn,' I said. 'She wants me to meet her later tonight. According to her text there's been a "major development".'

'Is that good? What sort of major development?' Hilary wanted to know.

I shrugged. 'I'm not sure. The last time I saw her she said she was tracking down a lead on Driscoll's mystery woman. I asked her for details, but she said it was too dangerous. Then she vanished on me, James Bond style.'

'That woman was a little weird,' Arleen said. 'I remember seeing her backstage. She was talking with lots of people. That chubby guy who looks like Santa Claus but was ogling all the girls . . .'

'You mean Leon Santangelo?'

'Yep. She spoke with him for a few minutes – probably fending off an advance. And she had quite a conversation with Colleen Collins.'

My ears pricked up. 'She did?'

'Yes, and Colleen didn't seem too happy to be talking to her. She tried to get away from her a few times, but that reporter was like a dog with a bone.' She paused. 'I also saw her with that other girl, you know, the one who followed Driscoll around like a lost puppy.'

'You mean Beth March?'

'Is that her name? Then yes, her. Only that time it looked to me like Beth was getting the upper hand in the conversation. It seemed pretty intense, and finally the reporter just turned and walked away.'

'When I spoke to Beth earlier, she said she'd confronted Charlotte, told her to leave Driscoll alone,' I said. 'So that checks out. Apparently she didn't lie about that.'

Hilary raised an eyebrow. 'You caught her in a lie?'

'Not outright. I asked her about Driscoll's second novel. She denied knowing anything about it, but I had the feeling she does.'

'Maybe what's in that book is really explosive,' suggested Hilary, 'and she's trying to protect someone from a scandal.'

'Like who?' cut in Arleen. 'The only one she would know would be Driscoll, and he's dead.'

'Well, maybe she wants to protect his memory or something,' Hilary retorted.

'I still think Driscoll was being blackmailed over something, and I'm betting it's got something to do with this mystery woman,' I said. I pulled out the copy of the check and handed it to Hilary. 'I found that sticking out from under the sofa in Driscoll's suite.'

Hilary let out a low whistle. 'Wow! So if this Harmony Steele rates this much money, she's got something really good on Driscoll. I wonder what it could be?'

'Charlotte intimated this big story on Driscoll had something to do with a mysterious death,' I mused. 'I tried researching suspicious deaths on the Internet, but I didn't get too far. I could expand the net, but it will take time, and that's a commodity we don't have.'

Hilary tapped at the paper with her forefinger. 'Blackmail makes sense. I mean, those books of his were million sellers. He had to get a fortune in royalties each year. I bet he had the first dollar he ever earned stashed away somewhere.'

'I'm not so sure. He lived a lavish lifestyle. That car of his wasn't cheap. Between paying off this Harmony Steele and trying to set up another restaurant, I can see where he'd have cashflow problems,' I said.

'Well, there's a little time before the trial,' Arleen said. 'Hartford's pushing for next week, but Tad's trying to stall for at least two.'

I hesitated then looked at Arleen. 'There's something else I need to tell you. The board of *Southern Style* wants the contest to continue – this weekend.'

Arleen let out a moan. 'Oh no! That means I have to give up my spot!'

Hilary threw her sister a look. 'That's what you're worried about? Not being convicted of murder?'

Arleen tossed her head. 'I'm trying to stay positive. Isn't that what you've been telling me?'

'Yes, but positive on staying out of jail, not winning a contest.'

I clapped my hands. 'Don't fight, girls,' I said. 'I told Dale to hold off notifying the next runner-up for forty-eight hours. I'm hoping that after meeting with Charlotte later, we can finally solve this thing so Arleen can participate in the contest.'

For the first time that afternoon, Arleen's face split in a small smile. 'And so I don't have to wear orange,' she added.

I stayed a while longer and, by the time I left, Arleen's spirits had lifted, albeit not all that much. It was just six o'clock when I pulled into my driveway. I could see Cooper and Lily at the picture window, anxiously awaiting my return. They greeted me effusively, and I apologized to them for being so late. I went promptly to the fridge and spooned out their favorite dinner dishes, and as they happily hunkered over their bowls, I pulled my laptop over and typed in 'Harmony Steele'. I got lots of hits for 'Harmony' and 'Steele' but nothing for the two names together. Then I called up my white pages app and did a general search for Harmony Steele. I got two hundred hits. I put in Georgia, and it narrowed down to seventy.

I figured in order to be the 'mystery woman', our Harmony would have to be in her mid-to-late forties – that should narrow down the list considerably. It did – to five. I whipped out my cell phone and started calling. Three weren't home. I debated leaving a message then decided against it. Better to call back. The fourth Harmony was a retired schoolteacher, who'd never even heard of Bartholomew Driscoll. The last one had just moved to Georgia from California to be near her daughter and grandchildren. She had heard of Driscoll, loved to watch his morning segments, and I spent fifteen minutes listening to her go on about celebrities who had been taken from us all too soon. Fortunately a 'call waiting' beep on her end cut into her diatribe on how she'd mourned for months after Elvis passed. I hung up with a sigh. This part of my investigation was a dead end – at least for the moment.

I pulled out my whiteboard and studied it. I still considered Peter Hagen a viable suspect. That argument had been too intense, and the bad blood between them was palpable. I still wasn't sure about Colleen Collins, either. She'd found him his first restaurant and had a major crush that obviously hadn't been returned. I picked up my black marker and added another name – Dolores Carlson. I still had the feeling that she'd been more connected to Driscoll than she'd let on, and then there was the fact he'd wanted her to do the interior for his new restaurant.

Could something have gone down between them bad enough to commit murder over?

I studied the remaining names. I didn't want to erase Charlotte's – not yet, anyway. I lingered over Beth's name. I had a sense there was more there than met the eye, but just what it was escaped me. I decided to keep her on the list. Bartell said Santangelo also had an alibi for the time of death, so I erased his name as well. I still wanted to talk to him, though. If they'd been close, maybe he could shed some light on the mystery woman.

I looked at the clock on the wall. It was a few minutes before eight. I could take Cooper for a walk, and then have a late supper before meeting Charlotte at eleven. With any luck, maybe whatever she had to tell me would break the case wide open and Arleen would be able to participate in the competition.

Of course, if I had known then how this night was *really* going to end . . . I would have taken my furry family and run for the hills.

TWENTY

Roy's Brew Barn was nestled in the center of town, a stone's throw from City Hall and the high school. The first thing I noticed was that the neon sign above the entrance had finally been fixed. No more 'Ry's Bw Brn', which had made the bar's title seem like an exercise in speedwriting. Now the bright yellow lights proudly spelled out 'Roy's Brew Barn'. I also noticed that the outside had gotten a makeover in the form of a fresh coat of paint and a hedge trimming. The only familiar thing left was the badly scarred wooden door. I hoped they hadn't changed the menu, because in spite of the tavern's less than stellar appearance, the food was always outstanding.

The interior was much the same as it had been the last time I'd been here. Two girls in tight denim jeans and even tighter sweaters were plugging quarters into the jukebox that sat in the far corner, and a few seconds later a Billy Joel tune blasted into life. There was a large crowd gathered around the U-shaped bar that took up most of the room, laughing and chatting away as they scarfed down beers and chips loaded with salsa. I frowned as I noted that all the tables in the eating area were filled, and the cluster of people off to my left indicated there would be a wait for a table. I considered leaving, but I'd been craving one of Roy's famous empanadas all day. I'd just started to move toward the bar area when I caught sight of a familiar face seated alone in a booth in the far corner of the room. I hesitated only briefly before wending my way over. I stopped beside the booth, and turned on my most dazzling smile.

'Hello, Colleen.'

Colleen Collins looked up from her gin and tonic with a start. She paled visibly at seeing me. 'Oh, hello Tiffany.'

'This is a great place, isn't it?' I said in a cheery tone. I made a show of looking around the crowded tavern. 'I was dying for an empanada, but it looks like a looong wait . . .' I gestured toward the sea of bodies standing to the left of the bar. 'You were lucky to get a table.'

'Yes, I suppose so.'

I rubbed at my stomach, which let out a low growl. 'I love their empanada sampler. Have you tried it? I reviewed it for the blog a few weeks ago.' I smacked my lips. 'Just talking about it is making me ravenous. I haven't eaten since lunch.'

Colleen nibbled at her lower lip. She looked as if she were waging an inner battle. Finally she sighed. 'It does look like a long wait. Would you like to sit here? I'm almost done.'

'Well, if you insist.'

I scooted on to the bench opposite Colleen. A waitress appeared almost immediately. 'What'll ya have, sweetie?' she asked.

'A club soda with a twist, please, and an empanada sampler.'

'You got it.'

Once the waitress had departed, I looked at Colleen. 'You'll be getting a call from Dale Swenson, most likely tomorrow,' I said. 'The contest is being resumed this Sunday.'

Colleen's eyes widened. 'So soon?'

'The board of *Southern Style* is afraid to wait much longer. They're afraid the adverse publicity will turn people off.'

Colleen fidgeted with the cocktail napkin in front of her. 'I can understand that.' She looked at me. 'To be honest, Tiffany, I'm not even sure I want to continue. It seemed like fun at first, but . . . I didn't realize how much pressure it would be. And after all that has happened . . .'

'I know. I guess Driscoll's death must have hit you pretty hard, considering how you felt about him.'

She glanced up sharply. 'Excuse me?'

'Well, you had a relationship with him. After all, you found him the venue for Ambrosia. I saw it on your website.'

'Oh . . . that.' She waved her hand. 'It seems like a thousand years ago.'

I leaned forward. 'You were in love with him, weren't you?'

Her fingers wrapped around her glass and her head dipped down. 'Love is such a strong word. I was . . . infatuated with him. Driscoll could be charming, and he had a way of making a woman feel like a million dollars.' She barked out a hollow laugh. 'I know that seems hard to believe, but it's true. The man could be a charmer. He could also be a heartless cad. I was unfortunate enough to see both sides of him.'

'I imagine the cad side was a bit hard to take.'

She looked at me. 'I didn't kill him, if that's what you're thinking. I've been over this with Detective Bartell already. I have an alibi for the time of death. I was out in the audience, talking with my aunt.'

'Dolores Carlson?'

She looked surprised. 'No, my Aunt Phyllis. Aunt Dolores couldn't make it that day.'

'You know that the knife that killed Driscoll was a Gyuto – the same make as yours.'

Her eyebrow quirked upward. 'Yes, and if you know that, then you must also know the murder weapon wasn't my knife. Mine was mixed in with Kurt Howell's cutlery. I actually picked everything up from the police earlier.'

'Mixed in with his? How did that happen?'

'Who knows? Maybe Arleen did it when she grabbed the murder weapon. Maybe she meant to grab my knife instead of hers and got them mixed up.'

The waitress returned, set my drink in front of me, and then withdrew. I took a long sip of my soda and set the glass down. 'You don't like Arleen, do you?'

Colleen smiled thinly. 'I think the feeling was mutual.'

'Arleen thought you were trying to sabotage her pie. Were you?'

Colleen's eyes narrowed. 'I've already said no.'

'You were jealous. You saw Driscoll coming on to her earlier.'

'Oh, all right.' Colleen tossed her wadded napkin across the table at me. 'I did pull the plug on her oven, all right? I was jealous. But I didn't kill Driscoll over it.'

'You told Bartell that Arleen threatened Driscoll.'

'Well, she did. You were there, you heard her.'

'And you know very well she didn't mean it in that context.'

Colleen sighed. 'Maybe not, but trust me, my statement didn't mean all that much in the face of whatever else they've got. Melissa Hartford is on every newscast, crowing about a slam-dunk conviction.'

The waitress returned with my sampler. I pushed it off to the side. 'You spoke with Charlotte Horn at the contest, right?'

'That reporter. Yeah. So?'

'She quizzed you about your relationship with Driscoll, right?' Colleen looked puzzled. 'No.'

Now it was my turn to look puzzled. 'No?'

'No. If you must know, she wanted to know about the Grays.'

'Who?'

'The Grays. They were our neighbors in Valdosta. I really don't know why she asked me – I was only a teenager, I barely remembered them. I told her to ask my Aunt Dolores, she used to be friends with Sarah Gray. That was who she seemed interested in.' Colleen glanced at her watch. 'I have to go. I've got a late showing of a property.'

Colleen slid up and out of the booth before I could utter a word of protest. She tossed a twenty down on the table and hurried out of the bar. I picked up my drink, took another sip. I pulled the empanadas back in front of me, but my appetite for the moment seemed nonexistent. Who the heck was Sarah Gray, and why had Charlotte been asking about her? Unless . . .

'Penny for your thoughts.'

I looked up to meet Philip Bartell's intense gaze. I tried to make my tone light. 'Fancy meeting you here.'

'Yes, for a change we're not at a crime scene.' He gestured toward the spot Colleen had just vacated. 'Want some company?'

I shrugged. 'Suit yourself.'

As Bartell moved to sit down, his hand brushed my side, and an electric shock coursed through me at his touch. The waitress appeared almost immediately. She offered Bartell a wide smile and leaned over, displaying a good amount of cleavage.

'Good evening, sir. What would you like to drink?'

He pointed to my club soda. 'I'm on duty, so I'll have what she's having.'

The waitress hurried off, and Bartell looked at my empanadas. 'Are you going to eat all those?'

I pushed the plate toward him. 'I was when I first came in, but I've since lost my appetite.'

Bartell selected one of the empanadas, took a large bite, then picked up a napkin and wiped his lips. 'Just as good as I remembered. So.' He set the empanada down and pinned me with his gaze. 'Care to tell me what you were doing talking to Colleen Collins?'

I took a sip of my soda. 'It was crowded when I came in, and I was hungry. I saw Colleen and asked if I might sit with her.'

Bartell's gaze didn't waver. 'That's all?'

I fidgeted a bit in my seat. 'Well . . . no. I had a few things I wanted to clear up.'

'I see. Such as?'

'Well, for one thing she admitted she lied about not sabotaging Arleen's entry. She admitted pulling the plug on her oven. If she lied about that, who knows what else she might be lying about?'

Bartell took another bite of empanada, chewed and swallowed before he answered. 'To be honest, I rather liked her for the murder too, but she does have an alibi. The aunt confirmed they were together around the TOD, plus there are photographs of them – taken by *Southern Style*'s own photographer, to be exact – that confirm it as well.'

'I know,' I sighed.

The waitress returned with Bartell's drink. 'Would you like anything else?' she asked.

He smiled at her. 'I'm good for now, thanks.'

The waitress withdrew with a disappointed look. Bartell leaned forward, reached out and grasped my hand. 'I'm glad I ran into you tonight,' he said. 'I want to be sure there are no hard feelings between us.'

'You mean because you arrested Arleen? I know you were only doing your job,' I said. 'I'm sure Hang 'em – excuse me, Melissa – Hartford most likely put a lot of pressure on you to make an arrest.'

'And Pierce, not to mention the mayor.' Bartell picked up his mug, took a long sip, set the mug back down. He picked up a spoon, scissored it between his fingers. 'As I told you before, the evidence – granted it's circumstantial – against Arleen is pretty tight. Of course, the fact she withheld valuable information didn't help her case either.'

'I told her to come clean with you.'

'Advice she didn't take.' He paused. 'For what it's worth, I don't have her pegged as a cold-blooded killer.'

'But Hartford does, right?'

He shrugged. 'Melissa seems to feel the case against her is airtight.'

'But you disagree?'

'I said I don't have her pegged as a killer. I have no hard evidence to substantiate that belief. Without hard evidence to the contrary, the DA wants me to close this and move on to other things. My hands are tied.'

I looked at him. 'Well, mine aren't.'

Bartell let out a groan. 'Look, Tiffany. I know how much you want to play Nancy Drew and clear your friend, but please . . . stay out of it. Let us handle things.'

'You just said your hands were tied. Pierce won't want you wasting your time on a case he feels is solved. And that's a shame, because if you ask me, there are plenty of other, better suspects.'

Bartell clucked his tongue. 'Why do I get the feeling you've been conducting your own investigation? OK,' he leaned back in his seat. 'Out with it. What have you found out?'

'To be honest, I'm on the fence about the brother, Peter Hagen. The argument I overheard was too intense, and Hagen did threaten him.'

'The problem with Hagen is, there's no evidence that links him directly to the murder,' Bartell pointed out.

'You mean like a sliver of apron or fingerprints on a knife?' I said with a curl of my lip.

'Touché,' Bartell said softly. 'What else?'

'When I spoke with Colleen earlier, she said that Charlotte was quizzing her about some old neighbors of theirs back in Valdosta, the Grays. Now, it's possible this Sarah Gray that Charlotte seemed so interested in could be Driscoll's mystery woman, but I think I might have a better candidate.' I pulled out the copy of the check and laid it in front of Bartell. 'I found this tucked under the sofa cushion in Driscoll's suite.'

Bartell picked up the check, and his brows drew together. He looked up sharply. 'What were you doing in Driscoll's suite?'

'Attempting to grill his assistant about a novel he supposedly wrote.'

Bartell shook his head. 'Wait, you're losing me. What novel?'

I explained about the first novel, and what I'd read in the article that hinted at a second. 'Minnie Mae seemed to think that if there was one, it would be even more scandalous than the first. And from all accounts, the first was pretty bad. He turned on his own brother, for goodness' sake.'

Bartell drummed his fingers on top of the check. 'So what's the connection between this Harmony Steele and the novel?'

'Well, if she's the mystery woman, maybe she was black-mailing Driscoll. Maybe she wanted to do some revealing of her own, on the so-called suspicious death that Charlotte hinted he was involved with.'

'If that scenario is true, it wouldn't have made sense for her to kill Driscoll. She was the one getting the money. It would have made more sense for Driscoll to kill her to stop the payments.'

'That's true,' I cried. 'But even if this Harmony isn't the mystery woman, there's some connection, I know it.'

'Sounds like a long shot to me.'

'Maybe, but I have to exhaust every possibility, since my suspect list is getting shorter.' I tossed him a thin smile. 'It's too bad you couldn't have waited a few more days to arrest Arleen. Then at least the contest would have been over and she could have participated, maybe won.'

'Sorry, but once that toxicology report came back, I had no choice. That Natrol was the most damning piece of evidence against Arleen.'

'Because it made it look like she laced his bottle to make him an easy target?'

He started to answer, stopped as his cell buzzed. He took out his phone, glanced at the screen, groaned. 'Bad news?' I asked.

'Depends on how you look at it. It's Hoffman.'

'How is your protégé doing?'

'Don't call him that . . . please,' Bartell said with a groan.

'Oh, come on. He can't be that bad.'

'Truthfully? He's got a lot to learn, and it's like training a small puppy . . . but, I hate to admit it, the kid's got some promise. With the right training, why he could be pretty good someday.'

'Arleen liked him. Said he acted like a gentleman when he arrested her.'

'See, that's what I mean. He shouldn't be acting like a gentleman when he's arresting a suspect. The kid's got a lot to learn.'

I chuckled. 'I'm sure you'll do an excellent job of teaching him. You need a good assistant.'

He smiled. 'Well, it would free me up for other things. Activities I've sorely neglected.' He paused. 'People I've sorely neglected.'

The look he shot me sent a tingle up my spine. I blushed and stammered, 'Would I know any of those people?'

'I think you might.' He put his finger under my chin and lifted it so that he could look into my eyes. 'Now, is that everything? You're not holding anything back from me, are you?'

I hesitated. I knew that I was probably being more than a bit foolish following Charlotte's instructions, but I felt at this point I had to go through with it. I tossed Bartell a look of mock innocence and laid my hand across my heart. '*Moi?* Keep something from you?'

'It's not like you haven't done it before.' Bartell gave me a searching look. 'I know you, Nancy Drew. I know just how strong that curious streak of yours is, and how far you'll go to satisfy it. Doing something foolhardy isn't out of the realm of possibility.'

'Well, thanks a lot.' I tossed my napkin down on the table. 'If you're not going to believe me . . .'

He held up both hands. 'OK, OK. I stand corrected. Look, it's like I told you before. I just don't want you getting hurt. If you latch on to something that could be potentially dangerous, I want you to tell me right away. Let me handle it.'

'I know, I know. Because otherwise you can't take me to dinner at the Chez Marcel, right?'

'You don't want to miss out on that lobster Newburgh, trust me,' Bartell said with a smile. 'Now, do I have your word that you won't do something stupid?'

Before I could think up a good answer, Bartell's phone buzzed again. He looked at the screen and sighed. 'I really have to go. Hoffman just texted me again. Pierce wants to see us now.' He paused. 'I might as well tell you, since it'll be all over the news later. Hartford won her bid to rush Arleen's case to trial. It starts Monday.'

My heart sank. 'That soon?'

Bartell's lips thinned. 'That's how certain she is of conviction.' He gave me a long, searching look. 'I'll be in touch,' he said. 'And remember what I told you. You run across anything pertinent, anything at all, you call me. Got it?'

'I do.'

Bartell left. I glanced at my watch, then signaled the waitress and ordered a double espresso. I had less than an hour before my scheduled meeting with Charlotte, and I needed to be wide awake and alert. Hopefully, her 'major development' would result in good news for Arleen.

The gazebo was located in Chauncey Park, on a little hill that overlooked the river, surrounded on both sides by dense shrubbery. It was definitely a secluded area, but it was also very beautiful in the daytime, particularly in the fall with all the leaves changing colors. In the dark, though, it could appear downright spooky. I slid my car into a spot in the rear parking section which was only a short walk from the appointed meeting place. There wasn't another car in the parking lot, and the only sound was the wind whistling through the trees. I leaned back and rested my head against the headrest, checking my watch every few minutes. No other car pulled into the lot. When my luminous dial finally read eleven on the dot, I exited my car, locked it, and made my way slowly toward the gazebo.

'Charlotte,' I called in a stage whisper. 'Charlotte, are you here? It's Tiffany.'

Silence.

I hesitated. It was possible that Charlotte could have walked here. There were a few hotels in the area. I glanced at the stairway leading up to the gazebo. Maybe Charlotte was waiting up there for me. I started for the stairs at a fast clip, which slowed considerably as I almost tripped on a loose paving stone. I righted myself before I fell and climbed the stairs slowly, pausing every few steps to take a quick look around. Midway up, I saw something pink on the side of one of the steps. I paused to pick it up. It was a small notebook. A glimmer of recognition nipped at me as I flipped it open to the first page. A chill flickered down my spine as I saw what was written there:

Property of Charlotte Horn.

I hesitated, then slid the notebook into my purse and kept on going. As I reached the top step, I stumbled again as my foot came in contact with something slick. My hand instinctively reached out to grasp the railing; I looked down and saw a splotch of red.

No. It couldn't be. Blood?

My hand slid off the railing and my foot slipped again, sending me forward. Instinctively I put out my hands to break my fall and a gasp left my throat as, instead of the wood I expected to touch, I felt something else instead. Something soft and barely warm.

I pushed myself upward and stared down at what I'd fallen over. It was Charlotte Horn, and she was most certainly dead.

TWENTY-ONE

C harlotte was half-sitting, slumped sideways against the railing at the top of the stairs. Her eyes were closed and I could see what appeared to be blood on the collar of her pink silk blouse. I leaned over for a closer look. The back of Charlotte's skull was red with blood. It looked as if she'd been struck from behind. I glanced around, but saw nothing in the vicinity that could have rendered such a blow. Perhaps the assailant had taken it with him or her. I placed two fingers against the base of her throat, and my stomach clenched as I realized something else.

The body was still warm. Rigor hadn't yet set in. She couldn't be dead too long. The thought that the killer might be somewhere close by struck me – hard – and I glanced around cautiously. Was he or she still out there, watching? I pulled out my cell and punched in 9-1-1. A few seconds later the operator came on the line. 'Your location, please.'

'I'm calling from the gazebo just outside of Chauncey Park,' I said. 'I want to report a murder.'

Twenty minutes later, the park was ablaze with lights. My 911 call had brought a quick response. A squad car with two officers and park security had all arrived in record time. Fortunately, the officers who responded to this call weren't the same ones who'd been at the high school. I'd just given my statement to the apple-cheeked police officer (who, with his shock of red hair, could have been a dead ringer for Richie Cunningham) when a sleek dark sedan pulled up next to my convertible. Bartell fairly leapt out of the car on the passenger side, and I could tell from the expression on his face that he was definitely not happy to see me standing there. He hurried over to me and laid both his hands on my shoulders.

'I knew you were keeping something from me,' were the first words out of his mouth.

I ducked my head to avoid looking into those penetrating eyes. 'Calm down,' I said. 'It's not as bad as it looks.'

His eyebrow twitched. 'This is the second body you've found this week. How much worse can it get?' He nodded at the apple-cheeked officer. 'Thanks, Daley. I've got it from here.'

He took my arm and led me over to the far corner of the gazebo. He whipped out his notebook. 'OK, talk. I'm assuming you know who the corpse is?'

'Yes, it's the reporter I told you about, Charlotte Horn. I'd seen her earlier in the evening. She said that she was following a lead on Driscoll's mystery woman.' I saw the look in Bartell's eyes and added quickly, 'I thought about telling you, but if this were a dead end, I didn't want to waste your time,' I said. 'Anyway, she didn't tell me very much, only that she'd be in touch.'

'So you didn't hear from her after that?'

I flexed my fingers into a fist. 'No, I got a text from her after I visited with Beth March. She said there'd been a major development, and she asked me to meet her here at eleven. She told me to come alone.'

Bartell's lips thinned. 'And that didn't set off a warning bell in your head, that you should have confided in me?'

'Is that your oh-so-subtle way of telling me "I told you so"?' I snapped. 'Yes, it did set off a warning bell, but I never expected . . . to find her . . . like this.' I made a futile gesture with my hand.

Bartell let out a long sigh. 'You are your own worst enemy, you know that? What if the murderer was still here when you came? You could have been killed.'

'That thought crossed my mind,' I said. 'The coroner can confirm, but I don't think Charlotte was dead for very long before I arrived.'

'You didn't touch anything, I hope?'

I shook my head. 'I couldn't help it. When I came up the steps I almost fell over the body. My hand touched the top of her head. I touched the collar of her blouse, too, when I felt for a pulse.' I paused and then added, 'The back of her head is covered in blood. She was attacked from behind and struck with . . . something hard enough to crack her skull, but I don't see any sort of weapon lying around here.'

Bartell gave me a hard look. 'I see. And is that your professional observation? You're now adding medical examiner to your résumé?'

I flushed. 'No, I'm just making an educated guess based on an observation. Isn't that what detectives do?'

'Let me remind you that you are not a detective, Tiffany. You're a food blogger who just happens to keep turning up dead bodies.'

I resisted the urge to stick my tongue out at him. Instead I said, 'I've been thinking about the murder weapon. You know, it's possible the killer used something he or she found in the park.'

'You have a theory?'

'When I came here, I stumbled over a loose stone at the bottom of the steps. It's possible the killer saw the stone was loose and decided to use it as a weapon. Not a bad idea, actually. The assailant would be able to replace the stone, no one would be the wiser, and he or she walks away with no incriminating evidence.'

'And I suppose you can show me where this loose stone is?'

Together we walked down the steps. I found the stone with no problem. Bartell dropped to his knees, pulled out his cell phone. He shone a bright light directly on the stone, then looked at me. 'You're right. There's blood here.' He handed me his phone. 'Hold this.'

Bartell whipped out a pair of latex gloves from his jacket pocket, snapped them on. He lifted the stone from its slot, turned it over. I shone the light on it. Bartell examined the stone, his lips pulled into a tight line. Finally he looked over at me. 'I can see brain matter and hair here, too,' he said. He shouted across to the techs. 'I need an evidence bag, pronto.'

A tech came over, placed the stone inside an evidence bag, sealed and tagged it. Bartell took his phone back and said, 'Sample will make the final determination, but I do believe we have our murder weapon. He should be along any minute.' He glanced at his watch, then at me. 'You can go, for now. But I'll need you—'

'To be available for more questioning and to give a formal statement,' I finished the sentence for him. 'Don't worry. I know the drill.'

Cooper and Lily greeted me sleepily when I returned home. I shrugged out of my jacket and walked over to the refrigerator.

I looked down at my two furry babies. 'Well, I didn't eat any of those delicious empanadas, so now I'm hungry. How about you guys?'

Lily let out a loud meow and Cooper gave a sharp yip. I laughed. 'You two are always hungry.'

I spooned out food for the kids: sardines for Lily, chicken for Cooper, then pulled eggs and a hunk of cheddar cheese out and laid them on the counter. I also pulled out some red potatoes, garlic, and green onion. I got my skillet out of the cupboard and switched on the stove. I poured olive oil into the skillet and sliced the potatoes while the oil heated. Then I put the potatoes in the skillet, added the green onions and garlic, and let it cook while I beat the eggs and milk together. Once that was done, I poured the eggs and milk over the vegetables and sprinkled generously with cheddar cheese. I covered it and let it cook for five minutes before taking it off the stove and transferring the completed frittata to a plate.

Cooper glanced at me hopefully as I sat down at the table. I wagged my finger at him. 'Oh, no. You've had your dinner. This is my midnight snack.'

Cooper returned to his own food bowl, and a quick glance at my kitchen clock assured me that this was indeed a post-midnight snack – it was almost one in the morning. I popped some frittata into my mouth, decided it needed a bit more salt. As I got up to retrieve the salt shaker from the cupboard, I brushed against my purse. It tumbled to the floor, contents spilling out all over. I bent to retrieve them, and my eye fell on the little pink notebook. I snatched it up and walked back to my seat.

'Almost forgot about you,' I murmured. I turned the book over in my hand. A pang of guilt arrowed through me. This was the second time I'd kept possible evidence from Bartell. Although, to be technical, I'd found this on the stairs, not at the scene of the crime. It was splitting hairs, but . . . oh, well. I'd call Bartell tomorrow and offer to drop the notebook off. After I'd had a look at it, of course. I opened it and eagerly started to flip through the pages. Charlotte's handwriting was cramped and hard to read. There were a few pages where my name was mentioned. I skipped over those.

The next few pages were just random notes, observations on

Peter Hagen and Leon Santangelo's actions at the cook-off, nothing I didn't already know. The next to last page had something curious. Two initials were printed there: SG. There was a phone number too, with an area code I didn't recognize. I flipped to the last page and saw a business card tucked inside the back cover flap: *Colleen Collins, Ventnor Realty. 770-555-6938*

I fingered the business card. Was Colleen Collins the person who was giving Charlotte her 'major development'? She'd said she had an appointment for a late showing, but she could easily have lied. I looked at the initials again. SG. Hm. Colleen had said that Charlotte was inquiring about her old neighbors, the Grays, and a Sarah Gray in particular. Could SG mean Sarah? I looked at the phone number printed beneath the initials: 334-555-7894. I whipped out my smartphone, called up my phone search app. A few minutes later I had my answer. The number belonged to the Serendipity Home in Auburn, Alabama.

I frowned. All this had to mean something, but what? I recalled Peter Hagen mentioning that their mother lived in a rest home. Could it be this one? I looked at the kitchen clock again. It was after one in the morning, way too late to call anyone tonight, but the clock was ticking in more ways than one. According to my deal with Dale, I had less than two days left to prove Arleen's innocence before we had to notify Doris Sharp that she'd be cooking in the final round Saturday. I stifled a yawn and headed toward my bedroom. Might as well try and get some sleep. My window of opportunity was getting slimmer by the moment, and tomorrow was shaping up to be a very, very, busy day.

TWENTY-TWO

I spent a restless night tossing and turning and was wide awake before my alarm went off at five thirty. I got up, showered, dressed and went downstairs, a hungry Lily and Cooper at my heels. I set their food out and then called Dale to leave a message that I'd be working from home today. It wasn't a complete lie: I'd finished my Saturday column before going to bed last night, and I planned to hit the 'send' button to forward it to the copy editor before I left.

I'd looked up Peter Hagen's address before I'd gone to bed, and just as soon as I'd taken Cooper for his morning walk, I set out for Hagen's house in Augusta. It was a little over an hour's drive, and I'd dressed comfortably in white pants and a sleeveless teal top. It was a typical humid, sticky day, but I enjoyed the feel of the wind whipping through my hair, so I drove the distance with the top on my convertible down, listening to Billy Joel warble about the 'Piano Man' and his 'Uptown Girl' on my CD player.

I arrived on Peter Hagen's tree-lined street shortly before nine. I hadn't called ahead, because, as Hilary puts it, there's nothing quite like the element of surprise – and Hagen hadn't responded to my other messages anyway. I breathed a sigh of relief when I saw the black Maxima in the driveway. Hagen was home; now I had to hope he'd be amenable to a visitor. I parked off to the side, walked up the short walkway on to the covered porch and rang the bell. A few minutes later the man himself appeared in the doorway. He looked at me, a puzzled expression on his face. 'Can I help you?' he asked.

'I hope so.' I held out my hand. 'I'm Tiffany Austin. I don't know if you remember me, but we met at the pizza cook-off last weekend. I called and left you a few messages.'

'Of course.' Recognition flashed in his blue eyes. 'I am so sorry. It's finals week, and I'm afraid I wasn't as diligent about returning calls and e-mails as I usually am.' His gaze swept me up and down. 'Was there something you needed from me?'

'I wanted to apologize. I should have told you that day that your brother was dead, but the police were pretty emphatic about not broadcasting that information.'

Hagen waved his hand. 'No need for you to apologize,' he said. 'It was a bit of a shock, but to be truthful I wasn't all that surprised. My brother wasn't a nice person. It's safe to say he had more enemies than friends.'

'That's what I wanted to talk to you about, if you don't mind,' I said.

Peter Hagen actually looked amused. 'My brother's enemies? How much time do you have? We could be here quite a while.'

'Actually I wanted to speak about one specific person. The love of your brother's life, to be exact.'

The corners of Hagen's lips drooped. 'Ah, let me guess. You've read *Full Disclosure*?'

'No, but I've heard about it. I've also heard about his sequel.'

Hagen swung the door wide. 'I think it's best if we talk about this inside.'

I stepped inside. The lighting in the hallway was dim, but not dim enough that I couldn't recognize the expensive Isfahan Oriental rug on the floor. There was a small wooden table off to one side, overflowing with paperweights of all shapes and sizes. Hagen caught me looking and smiled. 'My hobby,' he said. 'I've collected them for years.' He went over and picked up a round one covered with multicolored dots. 'This is an antique Clichy, patterned millefiori on a lace filigree background,' he said proudly. 'I got it for a steal – two hundred. It's worth easily three times that.'

Hagen put the paperweight back and I followed him down the narrow hallway into the living room. It was sparsely decorated, but what was there was in excellent taste: a leather sofa and loveseat, an antique coffee table, a Steinway piano off to one side in front of built-in bookcases that overflowed with leather-bound volumes. A large mahogany bar took up one corner of the room.

'I'd offer you a drink, but it's a bit early, even for me,' he said with a smile. 'I could offer you a cup of coffee.'

'I'm fine, thanks.'

'OK, then. Let's get down to business.' Hagen waved me

toward the sofa, then seated himself on the loveseat across from me. 'What exactly is it you want to know?'

'I'll be honest with you, Mr Hagen. I've heard that the reason your brother came to Branson had to do with a woman.'

Hagen let out a snort. 'Well, that's not a surprise. Bart fancied himself quite the ladies' man, and he had a string of dalliances to prove it. Some of them have threatened to kill him before, but this is the first time anything ever escalated into actual violence.'

I leaned forward. 'I also heard a rumor that your brother might be involved in a suspicious death that occurred twenty-two years ago.'

Hagen's eyes appeared to mist over for a moment. Then he said in a quiet tone, 'You must mean Sarah. Sarah Gray.' Hagen let out a long sigh. 'She was the love of my life for quite a while.'

'Until your brother's book came out?'

Hagen's gaze hardened. 'My brother wrote that very early on in his career, before he became known for his restaurant reviews. He was in love with Sarah, as was I at the time. He decided to help things along by doing a big reveal. Well, it worked.'

'So you really were involved with a co-worker?'

'Yes, and not just any co-worker. She was a tenured professor, and my boss.' He sighed. 'It was a horrible mistake on both our parts. The affair didn't last long, but Bart managed to overhear a conversation between us, and he put the whole thing in his book. He'd always had a crush on Sarah, and he knew she wouldn't stand for any type of infidelity. He was right. Sarah confronted me, and I admitted my indiscretion. She broke up with me, and naturally Bart was there to pick up the pieces. I did jump for joy, though, when she left him.'

'She left him? He didn't break up with her?'

Hagen shook his head. 'No. They were together for a little over a year. It was a volatile relationship. Bart was just starting to get recognized, and he was neglectful of Sarah. He was also jealous as heck of any man she even so much as glanced at.' His hand came up to rub at his temple. 'I remember seeing her in the grocery store one day. They'd had a terrific fight because he found out she'd been seeing Leon Santangelo. It was nothing romantic – she'd just needed someone to talk to.'

'I take it that was after he separated from his wife?'

Hagen nodded. 'Yes. The funny thing was, Sarah and Dolores were fast friends too. Anyway, Bart flew off the handle, confronted Leon. The two of them didn't speak for months. Eventually, Sarah felt she couldn't take it anymore, and she just up and left.' He paused. 'She did leave a note. It was very brief, said something like, she saw what he was like and she couldn't live with it. Told him not to try and find her.'

'That does sound drastic.'

'Yes, and Sarah's parents were frantic. They blamed Bart for their baby girl leaving them. They both hired PIs to try and locate her, but Bart's found her first. She'd moved out of state, Alabama I believe. Bart took off after her. The way I heard the story, she tried to get away from him and ran her car off a cliff.'

'Oh my goodness,' I gasped. 'So I suppose Sarah's was this suspicious death?'

He nodded. 'There were several different accounts. Someone actually sent the police an anonymous note saying that Bart ran Sarah's car off the road. He denied it, of course. Eventually it was ruled an accident.'

'Did you believe that?'

'Oddly, yes. You had to see him when he returned. He was terribly upset. He actually seemed . . . almost human.' Hagen let out a soft grunt. 'That kinder, gentler Bart didn't last long, though.' He looked at me. 'Do you mind if I ask you why you are interested in all this?'

'Not at all. I know the girl they've arrested for Driscoll's murder. She's my best friend's sister, and I think it's all a terrible mistake.'

'Not according to your DA.' Hagen pointed to a newspaper on the coffee table. 'She's calling it an open-and-shut case.'

'I'll admit the circumstantial evidence is overwhelming, but . . . as I said, I know the girl. She's no killer.'

Hagen leaned back in his chair. 'Killers fool people all the time, Ms Austin. Remember Ted Bundy? He had everyone fooled.'

I took a deep breath. 'Mr Hagen, do you know anything about a second book your brother was supposed to be writing? And I'm not talking about the cookbook.'

Hagen's eyes widened. 'You know about that, huh?'

'I heard it was a tell-all book, even worse than his previous. I think that maybe someone your brother mentioned in this book is the real killer, and they framed Arleen to take the fall.'

Hagen stroked at his chin. 'Well, mind you, that could be anyone. Bart had a number of deals going on that produced a lot of bad blood, and women – well, there were a ton of scorned ones out there.'

'Is the name Harmony Steele familiar to you?'

He started. 'Harmony Steele? I don't know anyone by that name, but . . . I do know Sarah had a little calico kitten she named Harmony. She was crazy about that cat.' He rose. 'I'm sorry to cut this short, but I'm on a deadline. As much as I'd like to stay and chat, I have to get back to grading those papers.'

He walked me to the door, where I paused. 'One last thing, Mr Hagen. You mentioned that your mother is in a nursing home. Would it be the Serendipity Home?'

Hagen shook his head. 'Oh, no. Mother is in the Westwood Convalescent Center. I've never heard of the Serendipity Home.'

I got back to Branson a little before eleven and decided to grab some takeout from Po'Boys. As I entered the restaurant, I spied Leon Santangelo sitting at a corner table. I hesitated only briefly before wending my way over and stopping right next to his table. 'Good morning, Mr Santangelo.'

He glanced up, his mouth full of roast beef po'boy. He hastily chewed and swallowed. 'Well, well, if it isn't Branson's premier food blogger. To what do I owe this honor?'

'I was wondering if you could answer a few questions for me?'

Santangelo picked up his napkin, dabbed at his lips. He motioned for me to have a seat. 'Before you begin your inter-rogation, I should mention that I've been cleared as a suspect by the police. I have an alibi.'

'Yes, I know. I wanted to ask you about Sarah Gray.'

Santangelo's head jerked up. I saw surprise in his eyes. 'Sarah? What about her?'

'She was the love of Bart Driscoll's life, correct? I understand you also went out with her.'

He dabbed at his lips with his napkin. 'No, I was a friend to her when she needed one. Driscoll was treating her badly, and she just wanted someone to talk to. Usually she called Dolores for things like that, but my ex was out of town at the time.'

'So she was friends with both of you.'

'Yes, but she was much closer to Dolores. The two of them were like sisters. Bart thought I was making a move on Sarah, though, and boy did he let me have it. Read me the riot act.'

'You said they were like sisters? How about after Sarah left town? Did she still keep in contact with Dolores?'

Santangelo picked up his sandwich. 'You'd have to ask her that. I mentioned something to Dolores at the time and all she would tell me was that Sarah had an excellent reason for leaving, and not wanting Driscoll to find her.' He took a bite of his sandwich, chewed and swallowed. 'In the beginning, he blamed himself for her death. After a while, though, the blame shifted to Sarah herself. If she'd listened to him . . . if she'd been more co-operative . . . if she hadn't left him, she'd be alive today.' He shook his head. 'Bart was a pretty unforgiving guy. To this day, I'm not sure if he still loved her or hated her. Although, you know what they say. There's a fine line between love and hate.' He waved his sandwich in the air. 'And now, if there's nothing else, I'd like to finish my lunch. There's nothing I hate worse than cold roast beef.'

I pulled back into my driveway a little after one, locked the car and went inside, my takeout sandwich firmly clutched in my hand. My furry kids were asleep in their respective beds, but I saw Cooper's nose twitch as I laid the bag with my sandwich on the counter. I shed my jacket and went to the cupboard for a plate. As I set the sandwich on the plate, I reflected on what I'd learned today. In spite of Hagen's remark about coincidences, I had to admit I was more in favor of the Philip Bartell theory on them: there was no such thing as coincidence, especially when murder was involved. My conversation with Santangelo had been interesting as well. It reinforced my belief that Dolores Carlson knew more than she let on about the mysterious Sarah, and that was most likely why Charlotte had been interested in her.

It all meant something; I just had to figure out what.

I pulled out my cell phone, which I'd shut off during the trip, and saw that I had two missed calls and one message, all from the same New York number. I clicked on the 'retrieve message' button and a second later heard, 'This is Natalie Forbes. I'm an editor at Appleseed Press. I'm calling in response to your e-mail about Bartholomew Driscoll's novel. Can you give me a call at your convenience?'

I wasted no time in calling the number back. Miss Forbes's phone was answered by her assistant Jenn, who told me that Ms Forbes was out to lunch, but she'd see that she returned my call. I didn't have to wait long. About twenty minutes later, Natalie Forbes called back. She wasted no time with pleasantries, but got right to the point.

'Yes, we did have Mr Driscoll's book lined up for next fall . . . and it's a shame what happened to him, because that book was going to be hot, hot, hotter than hot.'

'Really?' I tried to keep the mounting excitement out of my voice. Not only had I gotten an editor to speak with me, I'd gotten *the* editor. 'So you've seen the manuscript?'

'Not exactly.' Natalie's voice dropped an octave. 'Mr Driscoll's agent sent us an outline and we made an offer to him based on that. Then a few weeks ago, Mr Driscoll called me himself. He said that he'd fired his agent, and he'd been rethinking the novel and wanted to make some changes. He sent me a revised outline.' She blew out a breath. 'I wasn't sure what to expect, but I was pleasantly surprised.'

'What sort of changes did he make?'

'He changed the dynamics between the main male and female characters. Instead of it being a bitter love affair, it now read more like a modern *Romeo and Juliet*. Frankly, I thought this version might even sell better. Unfortunately, he never sent me either version. I spoke with his assistant – a Beth something. She claimed to know nothing about it.'

'Can I ask what happens in a case like this? I imagine you paid Mr Driscoll an advance. Is there any way to recoup your loss?'

'Fortunately we hadn't paid the advance yet, since Mr Driscoll never signed an official contract. But if the manuscript does turn up, we fully intend to publish it.'

'Do you think that's a possibility?'

'I'm hoping. And Mr Driscoll's agent is very hopeful he can put his hands on it.'

'Wait – I thought you said Mr Driscoll had fired his agent?'

'Apparently he hired another one right before his death. He seemed very confident he could lay his hands on the manuscript. He promised to get back to me by the end of next week.'

'I see. I don't suppose you have the name of this agent?' I asked. 'It occurred to me that perhaps he could give me some insights on Mr Driscoll for my, ah, article.'

'That's a good idea. I'm sorry I don't recall the name offhand – I think it was Chris something – but I'll have my assistant e-mail it to you.' She laughed. 'I don't even know if it's a male or a female. All my contact was by e-mail.'

'That would very helpful, thanks.'

'No problem. Give me your e-mail address. I'll have my assistant get it out to you by close of business today. Oh, and if you still plan on doing your article, let me know when it's published. I'd love to read it.'

'Sure. Oh, one last thing. Do you recall the names of the main characters? I might add it to my article, if that's OK with you.'

'Can't see it would do any harm. The man was Bart Dickson, a noted chef. The woman was Sara Greyson, a nurse at a conva-lescent home.'

I hung up, feeling elated. I was headed in the right direction, although I still wasn't entirely sure where that was. I did a swift recap in my mind: Peter Hagen had said the love of Driscoll's life was Sarah Gray, who was most likely the SG in Charlotte's notebook and who was also most likely the Sara in Driscoll's novel. Real-life Sarah had died under suspicious circumstances, and the name Harmony had been significant to her. Lastly, the number in Charlotte's notebook was for the Serendipity Home and, according to Driscoll's editor, the main character in the novel had worked at a home. Coincidence? I thought not. Now I knew what my next step would be: I had to contact the Serendipity Home and see what I could find out.

Loud barking summoned me to the kitchen. Cooper was dancing around in front of the back door, teeth bared. 'Coop! What's wrong?'

I knelt down beside the spaniel, and immediately saw what

had excited him. Someone had slipped an envelope under the door. I picked it up and turned it over. My name was printed in block letters across the face. I slit it open with the edge of my nail, and a single sheet of paper fell out. I gasped as I read the crudely printed message:

DON'T LET WHAT HAPPENED TO CHARLOTTE
HAPPEN TO YOU.
MIND YOUR OWN BUSINESS.

TWENTY-THREE

I let the note fall to the floor and flung open my back door. I stepped out and looked around. There was no one in sight. I looked around the back area. The ground near the patio was damp, because I'd had the sprinklers on earlier. I took a few steps and paused as I saw footprints in the soft ground. They appeared large – maybe a size ten or eleven. I'd normally think a man, but I knew women had large feet too. I knew that Beth March appeared to have a small foot, but Colleen Collins's had looked pretty big. I was a size nine and I was willing to bet Colleen was a size larger, maybe more.

I snapped a few pictures with my camera and then went back inside. Cooper was still pacing back and forth in front of his doggie bed. Lily sat upright in hers, watching Cooper, and I had the impression she was wondering what all the fuss was about. I bent over and gave Cooper a scratch behind his ears. 'You did good, Coop,' I told the spaniel. 'Now we have to tell Detective Bartell.'

I dialed Bartell's number and got his voicemail. I left a message. 'Call me as soon as you get this,' I said. 'Someone left me a threatening note.' I hung up and looked at the furry kids. 'OK, now we wait and see what Bartell has to say.'

Coop gave a short yip, turned around twice, then went over to his doggie bed. Lily yawned, stretched, and started to wash her face. Clearly they thought their work was done.

Well, mine was just beginning. Time was running out to clear Arleen and get her reinstated in the cook-off. I couldn't afford to waste a moment.

I went over to the kitchen table and booted up my laptop. I unwrapped my soft-shell crab and Louisiana sausage po'boy and, in between savory bites, looked up the Serendipity Home. I found a few with that name, but the one I honed in on was located in Auburn, Alabama – a two-hour drive from here. According to its mission statement, the home opened its doors to the infirm, the elderly, as well as teenagers and battered women – maybe an ideal place for a woman like Sarah Gray to gravitate towards. I'd just finished entering the address into my smartphone when I heard a loud knock at my back door. I walked over and peered out through the side curtain at the all too familiar figure who paced back and forth on my back porch. I opened the door and stood, a hand on one hip. 'I assume you got my message?'

Bartell pushed his way inside. 'Where's the note?' he demanded.

I picked it up off the kitchen island where I'd put it and handed it to him. He read it, his frown deepening. At last he looked at me. 'I can try and get fingerprints off this, but I bet it'll be a dead end.'

'I wouldn't take that bet,' I agreed. 'There might be something else you can use, though.' I took him outside and showed him the footprint. 'Of course, it's possible whoever did this could have worn a larger shoe, you know, to throw you off his trail.'

'We'll check it out anyway. I'll have Hoffman come down and make a plaster cast.' He looked into my eyes. 'Care to bring me up to speed on your sleuthing? Because you're obviously touching a nerve with someone.'

'I have a lot of clues, but nothing that makes any sense . . . yet,' I admitted. 'We can discuss them over a cup of coffee, if you want.'

'Sounds good. I skipped my usual cup and haven't had time to get any today.' He paused and then added, 'I have some news for you, too.'

We went inside, and I walked over to my Keurig. 'I have to go to the market. I only have Newman's Special Blend. Is that OK?'

'Fine.'

Bartell eased one hip against my kitchen island, and I saw the dark circles under his eyes, the stubble on his chin. He rubbed at his chin self-consciously. 'I know. I look a fright. I only got an hour's sleep, if that.'

Bartell watched as I slipped a coffee pod into my Keurig. I got a mug down from the cupboard, and pressed the start button on the Keurig. The coffee brewed in under a minute, and I put the mug in front of Bartell, along with a container of milk and some Sweet N Low packets. 'You said you have some news for me?'

'I do.' Bartell put a splash of milk in his coffee, added the sweetener, stirred and set the spoon down on the island. He took a long sip of the coffee, then set the mug down too. He wiped at his lips with the back of his hand. 'I needed that,' he said, and then his eyes met mine. 'I got the coroner's report and the lab report on the stone back late last night – or should I say, early this morning. I had them put a rush on it. Charlotte died of a subdural hemotoma resulting from a severe blow to the head. You were right – that stone was the murder weapon. It tested positive for Charlotte's blood.'

'Great,' I said. 'You didn't learn anything else? There was no DNA from the killer on the stone?'

He shook his head. 'Nothing we could use.' He picked up the cup again, eyed me over the rim. 'You think Charlotte's death and Driscoll's are connected, don't you?'

I looked at him in surprise. 'Why, yes. Don't you?'

'They don't necessarily have to be.'

'Oh, come on, Bartell!' I cut him a double eye roll. 'Charlotte Horn is following Driscoll, trying to tie him to some suspicious death that happened twenty-two years ago. Driscoll gets murdered, but Charlotte is still investigating. She tells me she's hot on the trail of Driscoll's mystery woman, asks me to meet her at that gazebo at eleven, and then she turns up dead too. How can they not be related?'

'Pierce is suggesting robbery. Charlotte's purse was missing, and there was no jewelry on the body. Plus, the stone as the murder weapon could suggest the murder was a spur-of-the-moment thing.'

'To be honest, I don't remember Charlotte wearing any jewelry.' I huffed in frustration. 'I know why he's saying that. He's thinking if he subscribes to the theory the crimes are related, it will weaken the case against Arleen. Did anyone check if she had an alibi for last night?'

'Hoffman went out there. Arleen was home – he woke her up, actually. She'd gone to bed around ten. Hilary and Mac were in the living room, and from where they were sitting, they'd have seen Arleen if she'd gone out.'

'Well, at least she won't be charged with Charlotte's murder too,' I said. 'That's a plus.'

Bartell drained his mug and walked over to put it in the sink. When he'd finished, he reached out and spun me around to face him. He placed both hands on my shoulders and looked me up and down. 'OK, now your turn.'

I filled him in on my conversations with Hagen and Santangelo, and then brought out Charlotte's notebook. As he started to roll his eyes, I held up my hand. 'Before you chastise me about withholding evidence, let me just say I didn't find it at the crime scene. I found it on the stairs *below* the crime scene.'

Bartell thrust his jaw forward. 'That's splitting hairs, Tiffany.'

I handed him the book and ignored his comment. 'There's a definite tie-in between that home and Sarah Gray and Driscoll, and I think I have a way to get the missing information.'

He flipped through the book. A hint of a smile pulled at the corners of his mouth. 'I'm guessing it wouldn't do much good to try and talk you out of whatever it is you're planning.'

'Try and understand, Bartell. Hilary asked me to try and clear Arleen's name. Hilary's my very best friend. She has faith in me – not to say she doesn't have faith in the Branson PD,' I added quickly.

He held up his hand. 'I understand.'

I cocked my head and studied him. 'You really do? You're not upset?'

'Upset? No. Concerned? Yes.'

I smiled and took a step toward him.

'Just don't do anything stupid, Tiffany, please.' He held out his arms, and I walked into them. He pressed me close against his chest. 'I know being a snoop is part of who you are, and I don't want to change you. But at the same time, I don't want you walking headlong into danger. Please, please, promise me that you'll keep me apprised of whatever you find out.'

I snuggled against him. 'I will,' I mumbled into his chest. 'I promise.'

He tucked his thumb under my chin and raised my head so he could look into my eyes. 'OK, so how about you tell me about this plan of yours.'

Uh-oh. I should have seen that coming. 'I haven't worked out all the details yet,' I said quickly. 'But don't worry, it's nothing dangerous.'

'Uh-huh.'

'No really. Trust me, after my last encounter with Eric I have no desire to put myself in that sort of position again.'

'I'm sure you don't. But you might not have a choice. Danger just seems to follow you.'

I reached up and patted his cheek. 'You're sweet to worry about me, but I'm a big girl. I'll be fine, honest.'

He closed his eyes, let out a sigh. 'Stubborn – there should be a picture of you next to that word in the dictionary.'

I batted my eyelashes at him. 'Oh, Detective Bartell,' I said, in my best Scarlett O'Hara imitation. I fanned myself with my hand. 'You flatter me so.'

'Very funny.' He took both my hands in his. 'How about if I assign Hoffman to keep an eye on you?'

'Are you that desperate to get him out of your hair?'

The corners of his lips twitched. 'In a word – yes.'

'Thanks for the offer, but I don't think Pierce would go for that.'

Bartell sighed. 'You're probably right. Excuse me a minute.' He reached into his pocket, pulled out his iPhone, glanced at the screen, then at me. 'I've got to go. I realize I can't talk you out of whatever scheme you're cooking up. Just promise me—'

I made a crossing motion over my heart. 'I won't do anything stupid, I promise.'

He leaned over and gave me a peck on the cheek. 'I guess that'll have to do . . . for now. You've got my number. In case of anything, don't hesitate to call.'

I shut the door behind Bartell and leaned against it. Cooper and Lily trotted over to me. Both shot me accusing looks.

'OK, OK. So I do have all the details worked out. I just didn't say anything because, well, what I have in mind might not be considered legal, exactly. Knowing Bartell, he'd never have gone for my idea.

'But I didn't lie . . . my plan is definitely not stupid. It could be considered slightly illegal, but it's definitely not stupid.'

Cooper gave a sharp yip and Lily a loud meow. Apparently my furry kids didn't agree with me. Well, I'd show them!

I went upstairs, peeled out of my clothes and dressed carefully in a navy-blue sheath and knotted a navy and white patterned scarf around my neck. I abandoned my usual clear gloss and swipe of mascara in lieu of full makeup: foundation, blush, concealer, highlighter, kohl eyeliner and the reddest lipstick I had. The result was the face in the mirror staring back at me looked older, and, dare I say it, sophisticated. Just the look I was striving for. Cooper and Lily looked startled when I walked back into the kitchen. They both approached me cautiously and sniffed at my ankles. 'Yes, it's me,' I told them. 'If I'm going to impersonate a rich debutante, I need to look the part.'

My plan was simple: I was fairly certain if I went to the Serendipity Home and point-blank asked for information on Sarah Gray, I'd be shot down faster than a turkey at Thanksgiving. I'd have more luck posing as a potential donor. Money always had a way of loosening lips. I'd done some Internet surfing and decided I'd pose as Victoria Peterson, the daughter of Ira and Gloria Peterson, who owned Peterson's Mills. They were worth several million dollars, give or take a thou. What made Victoria an optimum choice was the fact that she herself had been adopted from a foundling home.

The traffic was thankfully light, and in just under two hours I pulled up in front of the Serendipity Home. I'd looked it up on the website. The mansion had originally belonged to Madeline DuPres, a wealthy dowager who'd had intensive home care the last few years of her life. When she'd passed away twenty-five years ago (at the ripe old age of ninety-three), she'd left her entire estate, including her rambling, forty-room Victorian mansion, to the healthcare group who'd cared for her so diligently. They'd used the inheritance to form the Serendipity Home, which catered to older people needing care, as well as abandoned children and expectant mothers without families or proper healthcare. The foundation operated entirely on the investments left them by Ms DuPres, as well as generous endowments from patrons.

I gave my name to the apple-cheeked receptionist and mentioned I was there to talk about a possible sizeable donation, taking care to emphasize the word *sizeable*. The receptionist made a quick phone call, and then ushered me down a long hallway and into an office that rivaled the size of the main conference room back at *Southern Style*. The woman seated behind the massive cherrywood desk rose and extended her hand. I judged her to be somewhere in her middle to late fifties. She wore a tailored blue suit with a white collared shirt. Her iron-gray hair was done into a soft chignon at the nape of her neck. Her jewelry consisted of a plain gold band on the third finger of her left hand, a pair of small gold button earrings and nothing else. Her grip, as she took my hand, was firm and strong.

'Please have a seat, Mrs Peterson. I'm Alicia Albert, the director here. Emily tells me you're here to make a donation?'

'Yes, Mrs Albert.' I sank into the butter-soft leather chair and crossed my legs at the ankles. 'My family is considering making a donation here,' I said in a soft voice. 'It's between you and another charity. My father wanted me to gather some information first before he made a final decision.'

Mrs Albert leaned forward, and I could almost see the dollar signs in her eyes. 'Of course, anything at all. What did your father need to know?'

'Well, he always checks into a company's employees when he considers doing business with them. He says it mitigates risk.'

Mrs Albert nodded. 'That's very true. He has no worries in that respect. We do extensive background checks on all of our employees.'

'I see. And is this information kept in a secure location?'

'Absolutely. I used to keep everything in here, but we've grown so over the years that space started to get a bit tight, so we're in the process of transferring all the files to a locked room in our basement. Only I and my assistant will have access.'

'That's wonderful. How far back do these records go, exactly?'

'Inception. The older records are still here, in my private office.' Her gaze flicked briefly to an oak filing cabinet in the far corner. 'All perfectly safe from prying eyes, trust me.' She leaned forward. 'I've an idea why your father is concerned. He wants to make sure our records are guarded against identity theft, right?'

I smiled. 'Very good, Mrs Albert,' I said. 'Now I have a list of some other things Daddy needs to see in order to make his final decision.' I reached into my tote bag, whipped out a sheet of paper and passed it across to her.

Mrs Albert's eyes scanned the typed page. At last she looked at me. 'Getting all these financials will take a good bit of time. Can I have my secretary e-mail them to you?'

'Oh, I don't mind waiting,' I said sweetly. 'Daddy does so want to take care of this today, and he already has the other charity's information. The sooner I can get all this to him, the sooner he can make his decision.' I leaned forward and said in a confidential tone, 'I really shouldn't say this, but just between us – the other charity balked quite a bit at gathering the information. If I were to report back to him how co-operative you were . . . well, let's just say your chances would be excellent.'

That was the right thing to say, because Mrs Albert's face lit up like a Christmas tree. She pushed back her chair. 'I'll get right on this, as long as you don't mind waiting, but it could take an hour, maybe two?'

I leaned back in the chair and stretched out my legs. 'I've got all the time in the world.'

'OK, then. I'll send Dalia in with some refreshments for you in a bit.'

'Take your time.' I made a show of removing my tablet from my tote. 'I can take care of some other important things while I wait. Now what did I do with my hairdresser's number?'

Mrs Albert departed, list in hand. The minute the door closed, I put the tablet on the desk and started for the filing cabinet in the corner. I pulled at each drawer. Locked tighter than a drum. That figured. I went back to the desk and opened every drawer. Nothing. 'OK,' I said. 'Plan B.'

I got a nail file out of my bag and set to work. Fifteen minutes later, I held my breath as I opened the drawer marked, 'A–J'. I breathed easier when I saw the drawer was full of manila folders. Apparently they hadn't gotten around to transferring these yet. I thumbed quickly through them. There was no file marked 'Gray' at all. I felt a bit dejected, but I wasn't giving up. Maybe it had been misfiled. I jerked open the drawer marked R–Z and started to paw through the files. I was halfway through the pile when I saw one labeled SARAH STEELE. Printed below Sarah's name was another: HARMONY STEELE. I grabbed the file and shut the drawer.

There was a copy machine right outside Mrs Albert's office.

I opened the door and looked up and down the hall. No one was around, so I slipped out and headed straight for the machine. Just as I approached it, Sarah's file slipped from my grasp. I did a quick maneuver to catch it before it hit the ground, but not in time to stop some photographs from sliding out. I snatched them up and looked at them. The first one showed a lovely girl, blonde and blue-eyed, displaying a trim figure in black slacks and a V-necked blouse. I turned the photo over. Printed in black marker were the words: *Sarah Steele, first day here.* The date was January, twenty-two years ago. The second photograph was simply marked Sarah and the date was July, also twenty-two years ago. It showed Sarah leaning against a wall. I couldn't see her face very well because her head was bent, looking downward. Her hands were across her stomach, which protruded over the waistband of her jeans. Either Sarah had gained a lot of weight, or . . .

'Oh my gosh,' I cried as the full import of the photo hit me. 'That's why she left him! Sarah Gray was *pregnant*!'

TWENTY-FOUR

For a minute I just stood there, staring at the photo. I'd thought that Sarah might have changed her name to Harmony and sought employment at the home. Now I saw that I'd been half right. Leon Santangelo's words came back to me: 'Sarah had an excellent reason for leaving, and not wanting Driscoll to find her.' Having a baby seemed an excellent reason to me. I did some quick calculations. She looked almost ready to deliver in the second photo. I estimated she must have been about eight weeks along when she'd left Valdosta, which would have made her due date sometime in August.

I heard voices coming from somewhere down the hall, and I realized I wasn't going to have time to copy the files. I went back into Mrs Albert's office and shoved them down in the bottom of my tote. I slung it casually over my arm and opened the door a crack, peered out. Mrs Albert stood about four feet away from the door. Beside her was a portly, balding man, dressed in a navy-blue suit that looked expensive.

'I don't know why her father wants these figures,' Mrs Albert was saying to the man. 'But if a sizable donation depends on it, what's the harm?'

The man coughed and looked at Mrs Albert over the top of his wire-rimmed glasses. 'It's most irregular,' he said. 'I've never heard of such a thing.'

Mrs Albert waved her hand. 'Oh, you know how these rich people can get, Mr Jarvis. Now, are you going to get me what I need or not?' She tapped her foot impatiently. 'I'd hate to go to the board and tell them we missed out on a sizeable donation because of you.'

Mr Jarvis let out a long sigh. 'All right. I can see there's no arguing with you, Emily. But some of those records they're requesting are in that file cabinet in your office.'

Oh no! I held my breath. I'd come so close . . . was I about to get caught?

'No, they're not,' Mrs Albert said, her tone somewhat testy. 'Adele had them all moved to the basement last week, remember? There are only a few very old employee files left in my office. To be honest, we were considering shredding them.'

'Oh, that's right. Very well, then, come along. If you can show me where they are, it shouldn't take long.'

I waited until the sound of footsteps had died away, and then I sagged against the door. 'Close one,' I murmured. Well, at least one thing was in my favor. If they were considering shredding the files, they wouldn't be so quick to notice two were missing. I opened the door and peered cautiously out. The hallway was deserted. I slipped into the hallway, pulled the office door shut, and walked rapidly back to the reception area, where I saw a different girl seated at the desk. I walked over to her and smiled.

'Could you tell Mrs Albert that I had to leave? It's – ah – a family emergency just came up.'

'Sure thing.'

I turned and walked swiftly toward the door. Behind me, I heard the girl shout, 'Excuse me, miss? I didn't get your name?'

I kept on walking.

I got into my car and peeled out of the parking lot in record time. Because I just couldn't go the two-hour drive without knowing, I pulled over at the first rest stop on the highway and parked in a secluded corner. I took the file into the backseat and tucked in for some reading. And it was interesting reading indeed!

Sarah Steele née Gray had indeed been pregnant when she arrived at the Serendipity Home in January twenty-two years ago. Seven months later, she'd given birth to a baby girl that she named Harmony Elizabeth. The copy of the birth certificate in Harmony's file listed the child's father as 'unknown'. Sarah continued to work at the home right up until she took ill two years ago.

One more thing was evident, at least to me: Sarah Gray hadn't died in an auto accident. She'd faked her own death so that Driscoll wouldn't find out she was pregnant. She had hated him that much – or feared him, maybe.

I closed the file and drummed my fingers on top of it. I had an idea noodling around in the back of my head as to the real killer, one that would clear Arleen completely, but before I could approach Bartell with it, I needed more proof, and I had an idea where I could get it.

It was shortly before seven when I parked my car in front of Dolores Carlson's home. I hurried up the short walkway to the porch and rang the bell. Lucky for me, Dolores was home. Her eyes widened when she saw me standing there. 'Ms Austin? I'm sorry? Did we have an appointment?'

'No, Ms Carlson, we don't. But I do need a few minutes of your time.'

Her brows drew together. 'I'm sorry, Ms Austin, but I'm in the middle of a consultation . . .'

'I'll wait. This is important. It concerns your old friend Sarah Gray.' I paused. 'And her daughter.'

Dolores's face paled beneath her rosy blusher. She swung the door wide. 'Come on in.'

I followed her down the short hallway. She motioned me toward the living room. 'Have a seat,' she directed. 'I'll just be a few minutes.'

I went into the living room and seated myself on the sofa. I pulled out the files on Sarah and Harmony and spread them out on the coffee table. A few minutes later, Dolores swept back into the room. Her eyes bugged when she saw what was on her coffee table. She pointed to the files. 'Where did you get those?'

'I paid a little visit to the Serendipity Home. I'm sure you know it. That's where your friend Sarah worked, right up until her death . . . last year.'

For a long moment Dolores didn't say anything. Then she put both hands on her hips. 'You really are quite the detective, aren't you?' she said.

'I'm trying to clear an innocent woman,' I said. 'You knew all these years that Sarah was alive, didn't you?'

Dolores sank into the Queen Anne chair. All the fight seemed to drain out of her. 'Yes,' she said at last. 'I knew.'

'Sarah left Valdosta because she was pregnant, didn't shc?'

Dolores nodded. 'She was frantic when she found out. She and Bart had been having problems – lots of them. He was consumed with jump-starting his career. After he'd written that

damned book, he finally started to get noticed as a food critic.
He was beginning to get offers from the big-time magazines and
papers for reviews, and he was gone a lot. He ignored Sarah
most of the time, and he was jealous as hell if she so much as
glanced another man's way. It was laughable, really, considering
his own reputation with the ladies. Sarah finally decided she
didn't want a relationship like that, but every time she tried to
talk to Bart, he put her off.' Her lips twisted into a wry smile.
'She turned to Leon for comfort a few times when I had to go
out of town, and Bart found out. He called her terrible names.
Told her that if he ever caught her cheating on him, he'd make
sure she ended up with nothing. She tried to tell him there was
nothing romantic between them, but he still kept on about it. I
think deep down he did believe her, but he felt the need to punish
her. That's how cruel Bart could get.

'When she found out she was pregnant, she was positive he'd
accuse her of cheating on him. She figured he'd peg Leon as
the father. She didn't want a scene like that, so she took off.
She heard the Serendipity Home opened their doors to unwed
mothers, so she went there. They took her in, and after she gave
birth they employed her as a cleaning woman, since no nursing
positions were available. Harmony was only a few weeks old
when that PI Bart hired found her. She was desperate – she
didn't want Bart to find out about Harmony. So she called me,
asked for my help.'

'So whose idea was it to fake her death? Hers or yours?'

'Both of us, actually. It seemed a good idea at the time. If
Bart witnessed it, then he'd call off his PI and she'd be left in
peace. So we orchestrated a meeting. Sarah argued with him,
then jumped in that broken-down wreck she called a car and
took off. Bart, of course, followed. Sarah was always a speed
demon. She got to the curve before Bart, and I was waiting in
my car. She got into mine, and when we saw Bart's car coming,
I released the brake and we let Sarah's car tumble over the
guardrail.'

'Rather cruel, even for Driscoll,' I remarked. 'I'm puzzled,
though. How did Bart not see you?'

'There was a large clump of shrubbery nearby. I'd parked
behind it. We drove off while he was looking at the ruins.

'In hindsight I suppose what we'd done was cruel but trust me, he deserved it. Sarah did have some second thoughts afterward, but they vanished quickly once she heard how Bart seemed to rebound so quickly from her death.' Her lips twisted into a grimace. 'I sent an anonymous letter to the police, claiming that Bart had intentionally run her car off the road. A mean thing to do, I know, but he was such a cad! Anyway, nothing came of the charges, and Bart and Sarah went on to live their own lives.'

'So did you stay in touch with her over the years?'

Dolores nodded. 'I did. Sarah and I were always the best of friends. Her living in another state didn't change that.' Her lips twisted into a wry smile. 'Even though I'd never had children, she would often call me for advice. Like last year, right before she passed. She called me because she was worried about some boy Harmony was seeing. She thought he was a bad influence. All he thought about was money, like Bart.'

'And Driscoll never knew he had a daughter?'

'Not as far as I know. But, Bart had ways of finding out things, so who knows? If he knew, he never made an effort to contact her.' Dolores paused. 'I do know that Sarah told me she was going to tell Harmony the truth about her father, before she died. She'd always told her that her dad had died overseas, but I guess toward the end she started feeling guilty about leaving her daughter alone in the world. I guess she figured Bart was better than no father at all.' She shook her head. 'I tried to talk her out of it, but Sarah could be even more stubborn than Bart, when she set her mind to it.'

'Where is Harmony now?'

'I have no idea. Last I knew, she'd graduated a local business school in Alabama. Toward the end, all Sarah wanted to talk about was that loser boyfriend of Harmony's. Keith something. Huett, I think. She said all he was interested in was money, making a quick buck by any means possible. She was so afraid she'd end up married and miserable.'

'Charlotte Horn found out the connection between you and Sarah, didn't she?'

'She didn't come out and say it, but she suspected. She quizzed my niece, and then called me. I avoided her questions. I never admitted that Sarah faked her death, or that I was in contact with her, but . . . I suspect Leon might have had a hand in that.'

'Leon knew Sarah was alive?'

She nodded. 'He found a letter she'd written to me. He promised he wouldn't say anything, and in return I gave him back the deed to our summer home in the Carolinas.' She shook her head. 'I'm sure he never admitted anything outright, but he most likely intimated it to that reporter. He was angry with Bart for pressuring him about buying out his interest in the business.'

'Yes, it did seem like Driscoll had a need for quick cash. Do you know why?'

'Leon said that his financial advisor had made some bad investments for him, and then absconded with a good deal of his money. He wanted to open another restaurant, so he needed quick cash. As it was, he had to change the venue to somewhere less expensive.'

'So you don't think Driscoll was being blackmailed?'

Her eyes widened. 'Blackmailed? By who?'

'Harmony, perhaps?'

Dolores's lips puckered slightly. 'Well . . . it could be possible, I suppose. But I doubt it. Sarah took great pains to raise that girl right.'

'What about the boyfriend? Could he have talked her into it?'

'Now that I'd believe. Sarah really didn't trust him.'

I rose. 'Thank you for clearing all this up, Ms Carlson. Just one last thing. Did Sarah send you any photos of her daughter?'

'Yes, she did. She sent me one when Harmony graduated business school.' Dolores rose, crossed over to the desk in the far corner of the room. She opened a drawer, took out a large photo album, and brought it over and laid it on the coffee table. 'It's in here somewhere . . . ah, yes. This is it.'

Dolores slid the photo out from under the plastic sleeve and handed it to me. I looked at the slender girl with the long blonde hair and the wide, cornflower-blue eyes, wearing a blue cap and gown and smiling at the camera, and a picture arose in my mind's eye of another photo I'd seen recently.

I'd met Harmony Steele – only I knew her as Beth March.

I tapped the photo. 'Would you mind if I kept this for a few days? I promise to return it.'

She shrugged. 'Help yourself. Are we done here? Because I do have another appointment.'

I slid the photo into my tote. 'Yes, we are. And thank you very much for your co-operation, Ms Carlson.'

Back outside, I got in my car and turned in the direction of the Haverford Inn. I had a pretty good idea what must have happened. Sarah had told Harmony the truth about her father before she died. Harmony had been curious about the man, so she'd decided to find out for herself. She dyed her hair, took on the name 'Beth March' and got a job as Driscoll's admin. During the course of employment, maybe egged on by the boyfriend, or maybe not, she must have decided she was entitled to some of dear old dad's cash to make up for all the years of neglect. She decided to blackmail him, but in order to keep her identity secret, she had to do it either via mail or the phone, or possibly the boyfriend was acting as a go-between. In any event, Driscoll changed his mind. That must have been the phone call I overheard that day. He might have threatened to expose her scheme to the police, and she panicked. It would have been easy for her to drug his water and slip Arleen's knife off the counter. Driscoll would never have expected his loyal assistant to be behind the blackmail, let alone pull a knife on him.

If my theory was right, Arleen was as good as cleared. Unfortunately, that was all it was: a theory, and with some weak spots at that. So before I could take any of this to Bartell, I needed absolute proof, and I could think of only one way to get it. I pulled into the parking lot of the Haverford Inn and shut off the car. I pocketed the keys, pulled out my cell phone, and hit the speed dial for Bartell. My call went straight to his voicemail.

'Listen, Bartell, I'm at the Haverford Inn. I just found out that Harmony Steele is Driscoll's daughter. She's been posing as Beth March. Come straight here when you get this. I might be about to do that something stupid we talked about.'

I pushed through the door into the lobby. There was a different clerk on duty, a large, heavy-set woman with a sour face who looked even more formidable than the other clerk. I decided not to enquire and just take my chances. I sauntered over to the elevators, got in, and hit the button for the top floor. As the carriage began its ascent, I debated my options. If the girl was a killer, confronting her with my theory wouldn't be the smartest way to go. I'd have to be subtle – definitely not my strong suit. The problem was solved for me as the elevator doors slid open and I saw a maid's cart positioned outside the suite door. Obviously Beth was out – here was my chance! I quickened my pace down the hall. The maid was just exiting as I approached.

'Oh, thank goodness,' I greeted her effusively. 'I forgot my key.' I reached into my pocket, pulled out a twenty-dollar bill, and pressed it into the startled girl's hand. 'Thank you so much,' I gushed.

'You're velcome,' the girl said. She had a heavy accent, and I figured she probably didn't know much English. She knew Andrew Jackson though. She slid the twenty into her pocket, gave me a big smile, and pushed her cart toward the elevator as I closed the door behind me.

I had to be quick, because I had no idea when Beth might return. I walked down the short hall and pushed open the first door. I saw at once that this had to have been Driscoll's room. The closet door was open, and I saw several expensive-looking suits hanging there. I took a quick look around and was just about to leave for Beth's bedroom when I caught a glimpse of something brown jutting out from underneath the bed. I leaned down and pulled out a leather briefcase. The initials BJD were emblazoned on it in gold.

I tried to open it. It was locked. I bit my lip and sat down on the edge of the bed. Oh, well, it wasn't like I hadn't done this before – today, in fact. I got my nail file out of my tote bag and started working on the lock. A few minutes later, I heard it click back. I was getting really good at this! I held my breath and opened the briefcase, then let out a gigantic sigh, because it was empty! I frowned. That didn't make sense. If it were empty, why hide it under the bed?

I started to feel around inside, and my nail caught on a piece of lining. I gave a sharp tug, and the lining ripped. I shoved my hand into the opening. I felt something hard and pulled out a flash drive. I dipped my hand in again, and pulled out another. Versions one and two, no doubt, of Driscoll's 'hot, hot, hot' novel – the novel Beth had claimed didn't exist.

I shoved the flash drives into my jacket pocket, closed the briefcase and shoved it back under the bed. Then I tiptoed across the hall and into Beth's bedroom. The first thing I noticed was the suitcase, half-full, lying open on the bed. I frowned. As far as I knew, Bartell hadn't said she could leave town. Was she planning a quick getaway? I walked over and peered into the suitcase. A small toiletry case lay on top. I picked it up, opened it, and shook the contents out on to the quilt. A prescription bottle caught my eye, and I snatched it up. The label had Elizabeth March's name on it, and the prescription was for Natrol. I opened the bottle and shook out the contents. There were supposed to be sixty pills, but only half were there. I looked at the date – one week ago. No way could she have taken thirty pills in that amount of time. Which could only mean one thing.

I replaced the pills in the bottle and shoved it into my jacket pocket along with the flash drives. This should be good enough to show Bartell, I reasoned. I retraced my steps back into the main suite, and was just about to put my hand on the door handle when I heard a soft click. The door swung open, and I found myself staring into a pair of cornflower-blue eyes, minus the dark-rimmed glasses. Beth regarded me with a puzzled expression. 'Tiffany? What are you doing here? How did you get in?'

'Cut the act, Beth,' I said. 'Or would you prefer I call you Harmony?'

Beth's face paled. 'You know? H-how did you find out?'

'That doesn't matter,' I said briskly. 'What matters is, I've called Detective Bartell and he'll be here any minute to arrest you for the murder of your father, Bartholomew Driscoll.'

'What?' Beth stared at me, then shook her head. 'You're crazy. Yes, I am Harmony Beth Steele, but I most certainly didn't kill Bart Driscoll.'

I eyed her. 'You deny that you were blackmailing him?'

The look of shock on her face was genuine. 'Blackmailing him? Why on earth would I do that?'

'You didn't threaten to reveal to Charlotte Horn that you were his illegitimate daughter – Harmony Elizabeth March?'

'Goodness no! Why would I tell her anything? She was looking for something to ruin him. I hadn't even told him the truth yet.'

I frowned. 'He never gave you a check for fifty thousand dollars?'

Her jaw dropped. 'No.'

I scratched at my head. 'I found a copy of a check made out to you for that amount the last time I was here. It was hidden in the seat cushion. If he didn't give it to you, when who?'

Beth shook her head. 'I have no idea what you're talking about. Mr Driscoll never gave me any money other than my salary. And to be perfectly honest, I didn't want anything from him.'

'He made a check out to you . . .' I stopped speaking as something Dolores said clicked in my brain. '*Sarah was concerned over the boy Harmony'd been seeing, Keith Huett. All he was interested in was money. She was afraid he'd be a bad influence . . .*'

I was remembering something else too, something I'd heard casually in passing, but now took on a greater significance. Just like that, all the pieces fell into place. My hand shot out and grabbed her wrist. 'Beth, we've got to get out of here . . . now.'

'What are you talking about, Tiffany? Why?'

'I'll explain later, but we've got to hurry.'

I gave her a push toward the door. At that moment, the knob turned, and the door swung inward. Kurt Howell stood on the threshold. In his right hand he held a small caliber automatic pistol. He looked at the two of us and smiled.

'Looks like I got here just in time,' he said.

TWENTY-FIVE

For a moment we all just stood there, and then Beth found her voice. 'Keith, what on earth are you doing? Put that gun away.'

I tightened my grip on Beth's arm. 'He's not going to put it away, Beth. What he's going to do is kill us, just like he killed Charlotte Horn, and your father.'

Beth swung around to face me, her eyes wide. 'What? That's crazy.'

I looked over the top of Beth's head at the man I knew as Kurt Howell. 'But it's not so crazy, is it Kurt? Or should I call you Keith? You didn't think it was crazy when you decided to blackmail Driscoll in Harmony's name. He didn't take it too well, did he?'

'Sit down, the two of you, and shut up,' Keith growled. He waved the gun at us, and we both backed up into the suite. Keith motioned for us to sit down on the loveseat, and we did. I thrust my hand in between the cushion and looked up at him.

'The last time I was here, I found a carbon copy of a check made out to Harmony Steele for fifty thousand dollars,' I said. 'It was hidden right under this cushion. You never got the original, though, did you?'

Beth shook her head. 'I'm confused. What are you talking about? Original of what?'

I turned to her. 'I'm talking about the fact that your boyfriend here – Kurt Howell slash Keith Huett – was blackmailing your father over you, isn't that right?'

Keith's lips curved in a snarl. 'You're a lot smarter than you look, you know that? Yeah, it's true. I called Driscoll and told him that I had information about his long-lost daughter and if he wanted to know what I knew, he was going to have to come across with some serious cash.'

Beth whirled on him. 'You did *what*?' she cried.

Keith looked at her reproachfully. 'I had to. You didn't want to go along with our original plan anymore.'

'Just what was this original plan?' I asked.

Keith looked at me. 'Before Beth's mother died, she told her the truth about her dad. I knew who Driscoll was – I'd entered a cooking competition a few years ago where he was the judge. I knew firsthand what a horrible person he was, but I also knew he was loaded. I mean, look at the car he drove. Beth had just graduated from business school with honors, and I knew Driscoll was looking for an assistant. He'd mentioned it on that show of his a few times. I told her that she should dye her hair, change her name, and apply for the job. I figured she'd get it with her qualifications. Then she could work for him, see what he was like, decide what she wanted to do.'

'I wasn't sure if telling Mr Driscoll I was his daughter was the right thing to do or not,' Beth cut in. 'I'd heard quite a few negative things about him, most from my own mother. But on her deathbed, she confessed how much she'd loved him. She told me I'd been born out of that love, and whatever sort of cad Bart had been, he deserved to know the truth.'

'But you didn't think so?'

She shrugged. 'I didn't know the man, but from what I'd heard I didn't like him much. Keith convinced me to go through with this plan. It was a good way to get to know him, he said.'

I looked at Keith. 'You also thought if the two of them got along, Driscoll might be willing to part with some money for his daughter, right?'

'That was the original plan . . . until Beth got a gander at the old boy's revised book.'

I turned to her. 'So you *did* know about it!'

She nodded. 'Yes. Mr Driscoll left the flash drive out one night, and I was curious. I'd seen bits and snatches of the first version, and the chapters he wrote about Sara Greyson – my mother, Sarah Gray – well, I could just feel the venom he felt for her oozing off those pages. The second version was entirely different. I can't explain it really. It was just softer, gentler . . . as if he'd somehow managed to recapture his original feelings for her. He almost caught me reading it too. I had to act very nonchalant.'

'That was the beginning of the end,' said Keith. He pointed an accusing finger at Beth. 'After she read that, she told me that

Driscoll'd changed, he wasn't the same man. She felt bad about deceiving him, and she had second thoughts about hitting him up for money. She'd decided that she'd like to keep on working for him, keep the relationship just the way it was.'

'And that's when you decided to take matters into your own hands,' I said. 'You called Driscoll and told him you had information about his daughter.'

'That's right. At first he balked, but then he wanted proof. So I e-mailed him her birth certificate. He said that didn't prove anything, the father was listed as unknown. I told him that I bet that reporter, Charlotte Horn, would feel differently. I said unless he came across with some serious cash, I was going to send what I had to her.'

'And he refused?'

'No. Just the opposite. He said he'd pay me. He said he was strapped for cash, and right now fifty thousand was all he could come up with. I told him it would do for a first installment. He was supposed to give it to me the day of the contest. We'd made plans to meet outside of Branson in the late afternoon. But when I called him that night to finalize our meeting, he said he'd changed his mind. If he truly had a daughter, he wanted the world to know it, and he didn't care what anyone thought. He said he'd torn up the check he wrote to me and I should get the hell out of town, and break things off with his daughter, or it would be the last thing I ever did.' Keith's tongue swiped at his lower lip. 'I was so mad, I didn't know what to do. And then Fate stepped in. Driscoll was judging the cooking contest I'd entered. I knew I couldn't pass up that opportunity to rid the world of that phony blowhard.'

'So you decided to make Arleen the patsy, because you saw her splash him with water backstage. You stole her knife and drugged his water with Beth's Natrol.'

'Smart girl,' he sneered. 'Yeah, that's how it went down. I put some of Beth's Natrol in a few of the bottles. He was slurping down that water all morning. When Arleen hot-footed it out of that kitchen, I slipped in and confronted him. He turned his back on me, just for a moment, and I plunged the knife in. He was so light-headed he didn't realize what was happening. The old boy never saw it coming.'

Harmony's face went white. 'Oh my God. You really did it. You killed my father!'

'And Charlotte Horn,' I said calmly. 'What about her?'

'That nosy witch just wouldn't let it go. Santangelo had tipped her off about Harmony Beth Steele, but she didn't know she was his assistant, Beth March.'

'So if she didn't know that, why did you kill her?'

'Because she'd figured out that I was posing as Driscoll's new literary agent. Beth said that Driscoll had fired his agent when he tried to press him on keeping the original version.' He moistened his lips, swallowed, and then said in a high, girlish voice, 'I called the editor, told her I was Driscoll's new agent, and I was confident I could get the book to her.'

I stared at him. 'That voice! That's the one I heard talking to Driscoll.'

'When I was younger my voice was very high. I got teased a lot. It eventually deepened, but I can still imitate a woman pretty good.' He waved the hand holding the gun in the air. 'Once I found the manuscript, I planned to bring it right down to the publishing house and wait for the advance check. Beth had mentioned that they were paying Driscoll seven figures for the book. I figured that first check would be more than enough for me to change my looks and identity and start a new life somewhere before anyone ever figured out what happened.'

'But Charlotte Horn did figure it out,' I said. 'How?'

His face darkened. 'Yep. The editor, Natalie, called me on the burner phone number I'd given her, all excited about a reporter – Horn – wanting to do a story on Driscoll's new book. Natalie gave my description and phony contact info to her, too. When I saw her at the contest, I tried to keep out of her way, but she managed to catch a glimpse of me, and later on I found out she'd gotten hold of my bio, so she was aware of my Alabama roots. I kept a close eye on her after that. Then a friend of mine who works at the Reeltown City Hall texted me that a reporter had been asking about me, so I figured it would only be a matter of time before she made the connection between me and Driscoll.'

'So you followed her to the gazebo that night,' I said. 'And you killed her.'

'It didn't start out that way,' Keith protested. 'I figured maybe I could bribe her, offer a percentage of my take, but she wasn't having any of it. I'd grabbed that loose stone from the walkway just in case I needed it – turns out I did. She turned her back, and I clobbered her.' He paused. 'I had no idea she'd gotten in touch with you to meet her there. I got away just in time.' He paused and jabbed his finger at me. 'Had you arrived a few minutes earlier – well, I don't have to draw you a picture, do I?'

Beth fell back against the sofa cushion. 'Oh my God, Keith. What's happened to you?'

'Nothing happened to me. *You* changed,' Keith lashed out, his tone accusatory. He looked at Beth and shook his head. 'It's too bad, Harmony Beth. We could have been happy together, running our little restaurant in Alabama like we originally planned. But I guess now I'm gonna be a solo act, on a nice, warm tropical island.'

I eyed him. 'And just how do you propose to open this restaurant, Keith? Your little scheme to get money out of Driscoll fizzled.'

'There's still the manuscript,' he said confidently. 'With Charlotte Horn and you two out of the way, there'll be no one to identify me as a bogus agent. I'll claim to represent the estate and sell the manuscript for big bucks. By the time the publishers find out the truth, me and all that money will be off on an island somewhere.'

My hand closed over the flash drives in my pocket. 'One slight problem,' I reminded him. 'You have to find it first.'

'It's in here somewhere,' he said. 'Driscoll hid it pretty darn good, but I am going to ransack every inch of this suite until I find it. First, though, I've got to take care of you two.'

He raised the gun and pointed it at me. I held up my hand. 'Wait,' I said. 'What if I told you that I have the manuscript. Both manuscripts.'

Keith's eyes narrowed. 'I'd say you were lying.'

'I'm not,' I said. 'They're on flash drives. They were hidden in Driscoll's briefcase.'

The eyes narrowed down to mere slits. 'I already searched that briefcase. They weren't there.'

'They were hidden inside the lining. A corner ripped off and I found them inside.'

He held out his hand. 'Give them to me.'

'I don't have them. I put them in a safe place, though. If you let Beth go, I'll show you where they are.'

'Nice try, but I can't do that. I can't let either you or Beth free.'

'Then believe me, you'll never find the manuscripts. You can tear this place apart, but you'll never find them. Only I can lead you to them, and I'll only do that if you set her free.'

'Why should I do that? She'll call the cops to come and arrest me, and save you.'

I wondered how Keith could not see all the flaws in his hare-brained scheme. No publisher in their right mind would turn over a huge check just on the say-so of one person claiming to be the deceased's agent. How could he possibly think he could get away with it, especially if he left two more bodies in his wake?

'You could take me hostage,' I blurted. 'The police wouldn't touch you as long as you had me. Then, once you got your money, you could set me free and go live on your exotic island. No one would ever be able to find you.'

I saw him hesitate and I prayed that his greed would win out over his common sense. 'OK fine,' he said at last. 'She can live. But she's not going anywhere.' He reached out and grabbed Beth's wrist, twisted it cruelly. Then he dragged her over to the hall closet, threw her inside, locked it and pocketed the key. 'By the time anyone finds her, you're right. We'll be long gone. Now . . .' he pointed the gun right at my heart. 'Show me where you hid them. And no funny business, or I swear, I'll shoot you, manuscript or no manuscript.'

I had the feeling he meant it, too. I rose slowly. It took all my will power to keep my knees from buckling under me. I gestured toward the hallway. 'They . . . they're in Driscoll's room.'

'Fine. Lead the way. And remember, no funny stuff.'

I started to move slowly forward. My mind was racing. I had no idea what I was going to do once we were inside that room, other than pray for a miracle. I'd barely taken two steps when a thunderous knock sounded on the suite door, followed by someone shouting: 'Open up! Police!'

Keith swung toward the door. 'What the heck?' he cried.

I pivoted and swung out with my right foot, catching Keith in a very sensitive spot. He let out a howl and doubled over just as the door burst inward and Brandon Hoffman, gun drawn, barreled inside. Hoffman leapt at Keith and hit him on the side, using his weight to drive the other man to the ground. They rolled over once, Keith on top, and for a moment I thought he was going to jam his elbow into Hoffman's throat.

Hoffman, however, had other ideas.

He flipped Keith over with his leg, gaining control of Keith's arm in the process. With one hand he knocked the gun out of Keith's grasp. It skittered across the carpet and landed next to my feet. I picked it up. Keith cried out as Hoffman's knee planted down firmly on his kidneys. Two other officers burst through the door at that moment. They rushed over to relieve Hoffman of his burden.

'Read him his rights,' said Hoffman as they snapped handcuffs on Keith's wrists. They jerked Keith to his feet and pushed him unceremoniously out the door. Hoffman turned to me. 'Are you all right, Ms Austin?'

'Thank goodness you showed up when you did,' I said. 'I was trying to think of a way to overpower him, but I was coming up blank. Your shout was the diversion I needed.' I reached into my pocket and pulled out the flash drives and the bottle of Natrol. 'Those flash drives are Driscoll's manuscripts. That was what he was after. And that Natrol is what he used to drug Driscoll's water before he killed him.'

Hoffman dropped the drives and bottle into a plastic bag. 'We got word that Ms March had recently filled a prescription for Natrol,' he said, 'and then Detective Bartell got your message. He's tied up and couldn't come, so he sent me to fetch you before you did the "something stupid" you mentioned.'

'Keith Huett – or Kurt Howell, whichever name he's going under now – confessed to murdering both Driscoll and Charlotte Horn,' I said. 'He was going to kill both me and Beth . . . oh, my goodness, Beth.'

I hurried over to the closet. 'Beth – are you all right?'

'Yes,' came a muffled voice. 'I hate small spaces, though. Can someone get me out of here?'

'Keith took the key,' I said to Hoffman.

'That's all right.' He shot me a wide, boyish grin. 'I can break the door down.'

TWENTY-SIX

'To borrow a quote from old Willie Shakespeare, "All's well that ends well", no matter what went on in between.'

It was Sunday afternoon, and Hilary and Arleen and I were all gathered on the high school auditorium stage. The pizza bake-off had just ended, and the gleaming silver trophy stood on the table in the center of the stage, waiting for the proud owner to claim it.

Arleen looked at me, her eyes shining. 'Just in case I haven't said it enough, Tiffany. Thank you.'

Hilary reached out, grabbed my hand, gave it a squeeze. 'I echo those sentiments a hundred-fold. It's not many friends who would put themselves in danger at gunpoint to clear a friend's sister of a murder charge.'

'That makes two close calls at gunpoint,' I said. 'Not to mimic Philip Bartell, but I do certainly seem to be a magnet for danger.'

'You're also a pretty good sleuth.'

I turned to see Philip Bartell standing in back of me. I blinked at him. 'Wow! Was that an actual compliment?'

'Yes, it was. You have good instincts, that I'll admit. It's your penchant for getting yourself into dangerous situations that needs some work.'

I saw Hoffman standing behind Bartell and waved him over. 'Well, fortunately this time your protégé was there to save me.' I smiled at Hoffman. 'I honestly don't know what might have happened if you hadn't shown up when you did.'

He gave me a shy smile and made a little bow. 'All in a day's work, ma'am.' His glance travelled to Arleen. 'I'm glad things turned out good for you too,' he said.

Arleen beamed at him. 'So am I. And I, for one, hope they throw the book at Kurt Howell – or should I say Keith Huett?'

'Oh, don't worry. Melissa Hartford is already salivating on obtaining her next conviction. It's pretty much a slam dunk for her, especially with Tiffany here and Beth March as her star witnesses,' remarked Bartell.

'How is Harmony Beth doing?' I asked.

'She's still upset over her father's death, although I don't think Kevin's involvement came as all that much of a shock to her,' Bartell said. 'She mentioned in her statement that her dying mother tried to warn her about him, but she was too stubborn to pay her any mind.'

'I for one cannot believe that girl is Driscoll's daughter,' said Hilary. 'She's so nice.'

'Sarah's influence, most likely,' I said. 'I admit I thought she was the killer at first. When I confronted her, though, she seemed genuinely shocked. Then I remembered Dolores telling me about Sarah being upset over Harmony's money-hungry boyfriend, and what Chef John had said about Kurt Howell comforting Beth when Driscoll was short with her. The final piece of the puzzle fell into place when I remembered Kurt telling me he was originally from Alabama. He'd casually mentioned his hometown wasn't far from Auburn. I realized he had to be the no-good boyfriend; unfortunately, by that time, it was almost too late.' My lips twitched upward. 'Had I known how good he was at impersonating a woman's voice, it might have clicked into place sooner.'

'According to the statement he gave, he got the idea after Sarah told Harmony the truth about her parentage,' said Hoffman. 'Keith was a pretty good amateur cook, and he'd participated in a contest Driscoll had judged. He saw firsthand how conceited the man was, and how much he valued his spotless reputation. He felt that Driscoll would think his fans would see his fathering an illegitimate child as a blemish on that reputation. According to him, shaking him down for money was only what he deserved.'

'Beth's motives were more pure,' I added. 'She was truly curious about this man Sarah said was her natural father. She knew nothing about him, other than what she read in the newspapers and magazines. So, with a little nudge from Keith, she decided she'd find out for herself. She dyed her hair, bought a pair of glasses, and interviewed for the job as Driscoll's assistant. Graduating top of her business class didn't hurt, neither did the letter from Dolores Carlson.'

'Dolores later admitted that she wrote the girl a letter of reference, but it was a general letter, not directed at Driscoll,' Bartell said. 'Anyway, Beth worked for Driscoll for nearly a year, and during that time, they struck up a pretty good relationship. So good, in fact, that she was afraid to reveal her true identity. She was afraid that if Driscoll knew she was his daughter, it would ruin their camaraderie.'

'Which didn't sit well with Keith. He wanted Beth to get her father to cough up some money to make up for neglecting her all those years,' Hoffman added. 'When Keith saw that Beth was reluctant to do that, he hit upon the idea of blackmailing Driscoll with the knowledge that he had a daughter.'

'And that plan backfired on him too, right?' Hilary asked.

Bartell nodded. 'Yep. Driscoll wanted proof, so Keith e-mailed him a copy of the birth certificate. Driscoll balked, because it read "Father unknown" but then Keith e-mailed him a copy of that same picture you found, Tiffany, that clearly showed Sarah was pregnant. Driscoll was stunned, and agreed to pay up. Now this is where the story gets interesting . . .

'Apparently, after he saw that photo, Driscoll confided in Leon Santangelo. Santangelo broke his promise to his ex-wife and told Driscoll that Sarah had faked her own death and bore a child – his child. After that, just like the Grinch, Driscoll underwent a massive change of heart. Instead of deepening his bitterness, the news that he was a father seemed to soften him.'

'Like the Grinch on Christmas,' said Hilary. 'His too small heart grew.'

'Exactly. He decided he'd use whatever resources he could obtain to track down his daughter on his own – hence his need for more cash. Between hiring detectives and opening another restaurant, his depleted capital was stretched to breaking point. He told Keith that he didn't intend to pay him anything at all. Keith threatened him with going to Charlotte Horn with the info again, but this time Driscoll didn't back down.'

'Right,' I cut in. 'Keith said that Driscoll told him he was going to report him to the police. Keith saw red, and decided Driscoll had to die. He swiped Beth's prescription and drugged all the bottles of water. Then he confronted him in the kitchen after Arleen left and killed him. He'd heard Driscoll arguing with

Arleen and decided she'd make the perfect patsy, especially after he found her apron. He'd already pilfered her knife. He made sure to talk in a high-pitched voice, just in case anyone might be listening. They'd think Driscoll was arguing with a woman.'

Arleen shook her head. 'That cad. And he did all this over money? And a book?'

'What about the part where Keith posed as Driscoll's agent?' Hilary asked.

'Beth told Keith that Driscoll had fired his agent because he'd argued with him over changing the book,' said Hoffman. 'Keith figured he could pose as Driscoll's new agent, get the advance check, and get out of the country.'

'Keith didn't count on Driscoll guarding both copies of his manuscript, though. He put the flash drives in the lining of his briefcase and then sewed it up. If I hadn't snagged my nail on it, they'd still be hidden there,' I said.

'Maybe not. I think Keith had every intention of ripping everything in that suite apart until he found them,' said Bartell. 'He was convinced the publisher would just turn over all that money to him. Beth didn't know what he was planning, and who knows? If she'd tried to stop him, maybe he'd have killed her too.'

'So what happens to Bartell's book now?' asked Hilary.

'Well, Beth has agreed to send Driscoll's revised manuscript to the publisher,' I said. 'Driscoll's lawyer told her that the day before he was killed, he went to his office and changed his will so that any progeny of his would inherit his estate, after showing proper proof, of course. As his only living heir, she'll collect the advance as well as all the royalties – and she's planning to donate a good chunk of them to the Serendipity Home, in her mother's name.'

'She was especially touched when she saw the new dedication page that Driscoll wrote,' Bartell added. 'He mentioned that the thought of what he might have missed in life – marriage and parenthood – had caused him to take a good hard look at his own life. Putting his feelings – his true feelings – down on paper was the only way he knew of to apologize to the one person besides himself that he'd truly loved.'

'Wow,' I said. 'He really did have an epiphany – about that, at least.'

'You're right,' Hilary sighed. 'All's well that ends well . . . or at least, almost.'

We all turned as Doris Sharp walked up. She picked up her trophy and turned to us, her pretty face wreathed in smiles.

'Land o'goshen, I never expected to win this contest,' the pretty African-American cried. 'Both Arnie and I were shocked when we got the call to replace Arleen and Kurt.' She shifted the trophy in her arms. 'That ten-thousand-dollar prize sure will come in handy, though. My house needs a new roof, and my daughter just got married. It's a godsend.'

As a happy Doris trotted off with her trophy, I laid a hand on Arleen's arm. 'You didn't have to withdraw from the contest, you know.'

Arleen shrugged. 'I know, but after everything that happened, my heart just wasn't in it. Besides, Doris really needed the money. I'm glad she got her act together and won.' Her lips twitched in a half-smile. 'The best part was Colleen Collins coming in last.'

I grinned. 'Some people just can't cook under pressure.'

Hilary reached into her jacket pocket, pulled out her phone. 'Oh, it's Mac. Did I tell you he got out of that Paris junket?'

'He did? How'd he do that?'

'The barracuda came on to him, and he turned her down cold.'

I let out a little yelp. 'You mean Bettina Foxworth actually made a pass at Mac?'

'Yep. He told her in no uncertain terms that he had a girlfriend he was very happy with, so she could forget any hanky-panky. Bettina started to get uppity and threatened to get him fired. That was when he gently reminded her about how much influence his aunt has with the board. He told her if she didn't back off, he'd have to have a little chat with his aunt.' Hilary's grin stretched from ear to ear. 'The next day Mac's boss called him in. Seems Bettina had approached him and asked for a different photographer. She told him that she'd thought it over, and Mac was far too valuable to *Southern Style* to be away for such a long period of time. So . . .' Hilary spread her hands, 'we're going out to celebrate his liberation.'

As Hilary walked off, phone glued to her ear. Hoffman looked shyly at Arleen. 'Speaking of celebrations, if you're not busy right now, I'd sure like to take you out for some coffee,' he said. 'Celebrate the happy ending.'

Arleen's face split into a wide smile and she linked her arm through Hoffman's. 'I'd like that,' she said.

They strolled off, leaving Bartell and me alone on the stage. 'Looks like there are two happy couples,' he remarked.

I looked at him. 'I must say, I'm surprised to see you here today. Don't tell me there are no pressing crimes demanding your attention?'

'Not at the moment.' He reached up to scratch behind his ear. 'I must say, though, I was really impressed by Hoffman.'

'He impressed me too, let me tell you. Talk about timing.'

Bartell reached out and pulled me closer to him. 'You do realize that if you'd followed my direction and stayed out of investigating Driscoll's murder, you wouldn't have been put in that position to begin with?'

I snuggled closer to him. 'Well, like you said, I guess I'm just a natural murder magnet.'

Bartell rolled his eyes. 'Lord, I hope not. You, Tiffany Austin, are one handful. You need your own private guardian angel.'

I lifted my lashes slightly. 'Are you volunteering for the job?'

He tilted my head so he could look into my eyes. 'And if I were?'

I laughed. 'I'd say then you'd have your hands full, between me and Hoffman. You must be a glutton for punishment.'

'Maybe I am, at that.' He glanced at his watch. 'So, what do you say I pick you up at your home at six? That should give you enough time to get ready.'

I looked at him. 'Excuse me? Are you asking me out on a date?'

'Well, I do have the evening free, and I do believe I promised you a dinner at the Chez Marcel when this was all over.'

'That's right, you did.' I bounced an eyebrow. 'OK, I'd be delighted to be your date. To be honest, I've been hankering for some good lobster Newburgh ever since you first mentioned that restaurant.'

'Me too.' He gave a low, sexy chuckle. 'They also make an excellent French onion soup. And let's not forget dessert. They have a four-tiered dessert cart, filled with goodies like Black Forest cheesecake, strawberry shortcake, cannoli . . .'

I gave a blissful sigh. 'My mouth is watering. It sounds like the perfect way to end a meal. I can only think of one better.'

'What's that?'

I shot him a mischievous grin. 'Starting the meal off with dessert.'

Philip's eyes smoldered. Then he pulled me into his arms and gave me a kiss that had me quivering from my head to my toes and drove any thoughts of lobster Newburgh and Black Forest cheesecake right out of my mind (and replaced them with lots of others!).

And to make things even more perfect, an hour later I got a text from Frederick Longo:

Board approved you covering Foodie Fest at Branson Civic Center in two weeks. Get your tastebuds ready!

From Tiffany's Blog:
Pizza Recipes

Cheesy Easy-Bake Pizza
Ingredients:
    1 tablespoon dry yeast
    1 teaspoon sugar (or honey, if preferred)
    1½ cup (375 ml) warm water
    2 tablespoons olive oil
    1 teaspoon salt
    2 cups (250 g) all-purpose flour
    2 cups (250 g) whole wheat flour
    1 cup (50 g) sliced onion
    2 bell peppers, cut thin
    16 oz (450 g) mozzarella cheese, grated
    2 cups (450 g) tomato sauce
    Toppings of your choice

Directions:

Prepare crust: In a large bowl, dissolve yeast and sugar or honey in warm water, then add the olive oil and the salt.

In separate bowl, mix flours together. Add them to liquid mixture, stirring first and then kneading to incorporate. Let dough rise 30–40 minutes. While dough is rising, sauté sliced onions in a pan over medium heat with a little olive oil to caramelize their sugars. Cook until transparent but not browned. Reduce heat, add a little water to prevent browning, and let cook another 10–15 minutes until glossy and sweet. Add sliced peppers and cook 5–10 more minutes.

Once dough has risen, preheat oven to 425°F (220°C). Divide

dough in half. On clean, floured surface, roll out two round, 12-inch pizza crusts, using fingers to roll the perimeter into an outer crust edge as thick as you like. Using a spatula, slide crusts on to well-floured pans or baking stones. If using fresh tomatoes, layer cheese evenly over crust, then scatter your favorite toppings on top, finishing with the herbs. If using tomato sauce, spread over crust, top with cheese and then other toppings.

Bake pizzas in preheated oven for 15–20 minutes, until crust is brown and crisp.

Note: You can substitute pre-made pizza dough if you prefer.

Ricotta Pizza
Ingredients:
>   Pizza dough (you can either make your own as per first
>   recipe, or get the pre-made dough at your grocery
>   store
>   Ricotta cheese
>   Mozzarella cheese
>   Parmesan cheese
>   (Quantity depends on how cheesy you want pizza)
>   Fresh basil
>   Salt
>   Pepper
>   Minced garlic

Directions:

Layer the ricotta cheese and mozzarella cheese on the pizza dough. Sprinkle Parmesan over top. Add salt, pepper and minced garlic. Bake in preheated oven until crust is brown and crisp. Garnish with fresh basil and serve.